The
Summer
Before
The
Dark

The Summer Before The Dark

1977
ALFRED A. KNOPF
NEW YORK

Doris Lessing

THIS IS A BORZOI BOOK
PUBLISHED BY ALFRED A. KNOPF, INC.

Copyright © 1973 by Doris Lessing
All rights reserved under International and Pan-American
Copyright Conventions.
Published in the United States by Alfred A. Knopf, Inc., New York,
and distributed by Random House, Inc., New York.

Originally published in Great Britain by
Jonathan Cape Limited, London.

Library of Congress Cataloging in Publication Data

Lessing, Doris May, date
The summer before the dark.

I. Title.
PZ3.L56684Su3   823'.9'14   72–11044
ISBN 0–394–48428–2

Manufactured in the United States of America
Published May 11, 1973
Reprinted Four Times
Sixth Printing, April 1977

The
Summer
Before
The
Dark

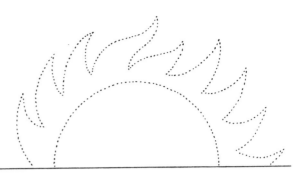

At Home

A woman stood on her back step, arms folded, waiting.

Thinking? She would not have said so. She was trying to catch hold of something, or to lay it bare so that she could look and define; for some time now she had been "trying on" ideas like so many dresses off a rack. She was letting words and phrases as worn as nursery rhymes slide around her tongue: for towards the crucial experiences custom allots certain attitudes, and they are pretty stereotyped. *Ah yes, first love! . . . Growing up is bound to be painful! . . . My first child, you know . . . But I was in love! . . . Marriage is a compromise. . . . I am not as young as I once was.* Of course, the choice of one rather than another of these time-honoured phrases has seldom to do with a personal feeling, but more likely your social setting, or the people you are with on an occasion. You have to deduce a person's real feelings about a thing by a smile she does not know is on her face, by the way bitterness tightens muscles at a mouth's corner, or the way air is allowed to flow from the lungs after: *I wouldn't like to be a child again!* Such power do these phrases have, all issued for use as it might be by a particularly efficient advertising campaign, that it is probable many people go on repeating *Youth is the best time of your life* or *Love is a woman's whole existence* until they actually catch sight of themselves in a mirror while they are saying something of the kind, or are quick enough to catch the reaction on a friend's face.

A woman stood on her back doorstep, arms folded, waiting for a kettle to boil.

There had been power cuts most of the day, because of a strike. Tim, her youngest, and Eileen, her daughter, had driven out into the country early, had gathered fallen wood in Epping Forest and—enjoying every minute of it—had built a fire on the gravel of the path, and fixed over it a tripod made of scrap iron found at the back of the garage. This fire, the cooking on it, the watching of it, the joking about it, had been the family's point of enjoyment all day. The woman, however, had found it all rather irritating. The kettle had taken twenty minutes to reach even the stage of singing: she could not remember having heard a singing kettle for years. Electricity brought water from stillness to turmoil in a moment, and singing was bypassed altogether. . . .

Perhaps she had been insensitive? Perhaps both Tim and Eileen—who were after all grown up, were nineteen and twenty-two—had not enjoyed the day's small contrivings as much as it had seemed; they had been pretending out of social feeling? Their behaviour had been, in fact, the equivalent of one of the old phrases, a convention which people did not know how to lose in favour of the truth—whatever that was?

Just like herself.

The truth was, she was becoming more and more uncomfortably conscious not only that the things she said, and a good many of the things she thought, had been taken down off a rack and put on, but that what she really felt was something else again.

The woman unfolded her arms, took a couple of steps

towards the absurd contraption in the middle of her gravel path, pushed some more twigs under the kettle where it dangled from a bit of bent wire from the tripod, and listened: was the note of the kettle's singing changing at all? She thought it was. If there was going to be a power cut tomorrow, as was threatened, then it would be sensible to get a camper's stove, or something of the sort: this boy-scouting was all very well, but if it rained . . . the strike was likely to go on for some time, they said. This series of power cuts did seem to have come very fast after the last? It did rather look as if crises over power—heat, light, fuel —were bound to become more frequent, and it would be wise to make provision? Perhaps Tim and Eileen were right; a load of wood might be a good idea.

The woman returned to her back step, leaned against the wall, and folded her arms again.

There were the public, or communal, events—wars, strikes, floods, earthquakes; what are felt as Acts of God. There was the feeling abroad, irrational or not, that these events, once high and rare (or had they ever been, was that just false memory?), were moving into the first place of everyone's experience, as if an air that had once been the climate of a distant and cataclysmic star had chosen to engulf our poor planet. The crucial experiences, when you came to think about it, were for more and more people: invasion, war, civil war, epidemic, famine, flood, quake, poisoning of soil, food, and air. For these, the allotted attitudes were even more stereotyped. None go much beyond: *We ought to be doing something about it.* or *Oh woe, alas!* There aren't so many nuances possible for: *My whole family died in the concentration camp,* or *Four of my children have died of famine,* or *My sister and her child were killed by the soldiers.* But it did rather look as if the stereotypes for the public events were more honest than the private ones? *Oh woe, alas!* was about it?

She noted that the kettle was quieter, and reached her arm inside the room behind her, the kitchen, to fetch out a very large china coffee pot that already had the coffee in it. She stood with this in her hand, close to the fire, watching for the steam to start rattling the kettle lid.

It was all nonsense to see things in terms of peaks and crises: the personal events, like the public ones, were long-term affairs, after all. They built up. . . . It is after—at least months, but it is usually years—that a person will say, *My God, my whole life has changed,* talking about a passion of love or hate, a marriage, a testing job of work. *My life has changed because I have changed.*

Steam was now energetically at work on the kettle lid, and pouring out of the spout.

She grasped the handle of the kettle with her oven pad and doused the coffee with hissing and dangerous water. She set the kettle on one side of the fire, but not on the lawn, which would otherwise have a circular yellow patch on it, and pushed some of the half-burned sticks away from the centre of the fire; if it rained, she must remember to get them and the unburned wood under cover. She was no boy scout to know how to start a fire with wet wood.

She took the kettle in one hand, the coffee pot in the other, and left the back garden for the kitchen.

I've been in the crucible, I've been ground fine in the mills. . . . Not without a certain satisfaction were these things said, or felt. Surely that was an extraordinary fact? The sense of achievement was extraordinary? For after all, it was felt as much by people who were among the (comparatively small) numbers of the world's inhabitants who were dedicated to the proposition that a life is no more important than a beetle's, as by those who held the old view, that it matters what we do because we are important in the eyes of a God. Or Gods. But why should anyone care that he, she, has changed, has learned, matured, grown, if he or she, is a beetle? Or even a butterfly? For there is no doubt at all that there does persist the feeling, and it is probably the deepest one we have, that what matters most is that we learn through living. This feeling should be attributed to habit, a hangover from earlier, more primitive times? To the beetle's self-importance? But it was there, there was no doubt of that, "God" having been banished, or pronounced dead, or not. To whom is a beetle expected to present its accounts?

We are what we learn.

It often takes a long and painful time.

Unfortunately, there was no doubt, too, that a lot of time, a lot of pain, went into learning very little. . . .

She was really feeling that? Yes, she was.

Because she was depressed? Was she depressed? Probably. She was something, she was feeling something pretty strongly that she couldn't put her finger on. . . .

The woman put the coffee pot on a tray already laid with cups and saucers and spoons and sugar and strainer, and picked up the tray: before carrying it out of the room she looked back at a table on which dirty dishes from the midday meal were piled. There were dishes there from breakfast, too. Perhaps she could ask Tim to build up the fire again, reboil the kettle, and then call her in when there was enough water to do all the washing up? No, better not, not in the mood he was in; it would be better to do it all herself later.

A woman walked out of a side door over a lawn that needed cutting and was attractively dotted with daisies towards a tree in her garden. This woman was Kate Brown; to be accurate Catherine Brown, or Mrs. Michael Brown. She carefully carried her tray, and she was thinking about the washing up while she continued her private stock-taking, her accounts-making . . . she was wishing that whatever stage of her life she was in now could be got through quickly, for it was seeming to her interminable. If life had to be looked at in terms of high moments, or peaks, then nothing had "happened" to her for a long time; and she could look forward to nothing much but a dwindling away from full household activity into getting old.

Sometimes, if you are lucky, a process, or a stage, does get concentrated. It was going to turn out for Kate that that summer would be such a shortened, heightened, concentrated time.

What was she going to experience? Nothing much more than, simply, she grew old: that successor and repetition of the act of growing up. It happens to everyone, of course . . . *Ah me, time flies!* . . . *Before you know it, life has gone past* . . . *Ripeness is all.* And so on. But in Kate's case it would not at all be a process lasting a decade or two, hardly to be noticed while it went on except in desperate attempts to hold the flood—tinting her hair, keeping her weight down, following the fashions carefully so that she would be smart but not mutton dressed as lamb. Growing old for nearly everybody, unless struck by disaster, the earth sliding away from under one's feet, water flooding a city, bombs destroying one's children and striking one's own heart into an indifference to living—growing old is a matter of years. You are young, and then you are middle-aged, but it is hard to tell the moment of passage from one state to the next. Then you are old, but you hardly know when it happened. Changes have taken place—oh yes, vital ones—in your attitudes to those around you, but you are hardly aware of them, because the ice has ground so slowly down the valley. It is something like that for most people: *I'm afraid I am not as young as I once was.* But Kate Brown was going to get the whole thing over with in a few months. Because while everything seemed so personal, and aimed at her—her patience, her good humour, her time—in fact it would be pressures from the other, the public, sphere pressing on her small life that would give what she experienced its urgency? However that might be, the summer's events were not going to be shaped through any virtues or capacities of her own.

By the time it was all over with, she would certainly not have chosen to have had it differently: yet she could not have chosen it for herself in advance, for she did not have the experience to choose, or the imagination. No, she could not *want* what was going to happen, although she did stand under her tree, the tray in her hands, thinking: It does go on and on! That's what's wrong: there must be something I could be seeing now, something I could be understanding *now*, some course of action I could choose . . .

Choose? When do I ever choose? Have I ever chosen?

A woman, as she might have done any time during the past several hundred years, stood under a tree, holding a crowded tray. She put the tray down on a garden table made of some substance invented in the last decade. The table looked like iron, was so light it could be lifted with two fingers, was balanced so that it did not blow over if a weight was put on one side.

She did not regard that table as a choice; it was chosen for her, like the plastic of the cups, which looked so like china.

She walked back into the middle of the lawn and, before

taking in a breath to call up to the upper windows of the house, was conscious of what would be seen when her husband looked out to say: "Coming!"

A woman in a white dress, white shoes, a pink scarf around her neck, standing on grass.

Now here was an area of choice, conscious, deliberate: her appearance was choice, all exquisite tact, for it was appropriate for this middle-class suburb and her position in it as her husband's wife. And, of course, as the mother of her children.

The dress came off a rail marked *Jolie Madame*, and was becoming and discreet. She wore shoes and stockings. Her hair—and now we reach the place where most energy had gone into choice—was done in large soft waves around a face where a few freckles had been allowed to remain on the bridge of her nose and her upper cheeks. Her husband always said he liked them there. The hair was reddish—not too dramatically so. She was a pretty, healthy, serviceable woman.

She stood on the grass, shaded her eyes, and called up, "Michael, Michael! Coffee!"

An indistinct face from behind panes that dazzled with sunlight shouted, "Coming!"

A woman dressed suitably for a family afternoon walked back across the lawn, but with care so that the grass did not mark her shoes. Her own choice would have been to go barefooted, to discard her stockings, and to wear something like a muu-muu or a sari or a sarong—something of that sort—with her hair straight to her shoulders.

She did not allow her appearance to bloom, because she had observed early in the children's adolescence how much they disliked her giving rein to her own nature. Mary Finchley opposite dressed as she would have done if she had no children and was unmarried: her children hated it, and showed this in a hundred ways.

Although Kate always agreed with Mary when she said, "Why should we scale ourselves down, children shouldn't be allowed to be tyrants"—in fact she always did, always had, scaled herself down. But she could not see that her children were any better than Mary Finchley's for it.

Kate sat under the tree in such a way that her body was in the shade, and her legs were stretched into the sun as if they were stockingless. She was examining her large square house in its large garden. She did this like someone saying goodbye, but that was only because she and her husband had recently been saying that now the children would soon be altogether grown up, it might be time to start thinking of getting themselves something smaller? A flat? They could buy a house in the country and share it with friends—perhaps the Finchleys.

Kate often thought about this, but as of something that was years off.

Meanwhile it was May, the English summer fitful and shallow, and, looking ahead to autumn, there was a hiatus in the life of the family, that organism which pulsed quietly in South London: Blackheath, to be exact. From this suburb every year, increasingly as the children became adults, it was as if that unit, or creature, or organism, exploded outwards, scattering further and further over the globe. It was like a yearly breathing out that began in late spring, with an inhalation in September.

Last year Michael, who was a neurologist of some standing, had gone in July to America for a conference, had taken the opportunity to work for three months in a Boston hospital, had returned only in October. Kate had gone with her husband to the conference, had returned for family reasons, had visited him again in September—her movements always fitting in with those of the children, as of course they had to do. They were coming and going to and from various parts of Europe all summer.

This year Michael was to visit the same hospital in Boston for four months, on exchange with a colleague. The oldest son, Stephen, now twenty-three and in his last year at university, was going on a four months' trip through Morocco and Algeria with friends. Eileen, twenty-two, was accompanying her father, to visit friends made on a camping trip the year before last in Spain. The second son, James, had been invited on an archaeological "dig" in the Sudan, before beginning university that autumn. As for herself, she had decided not to go to the States again. This was partly because she did not want to cramp her daughter's style, which she knew she would. Also, it would be so expensive if three people went. Also, there was the question whether she would be cramping her husband's style . . . to go with this thought there was an appropriate smile, almost a grimace, suitable perhaps for the words: *There has to be give and take in any marriage;* she was quite aware that she was disinclined to examine this area too closely.

For another thing, Tim, although now nineteen, and much encouraged by everyone to be independent, had no plans to travel anywhere. He was, always had been, the "difficult" or problematical one. The house in South London would therefore be kept running for his benefit. She, the mother, would run it. For her, the coming months stretched ahead as they had done for many past summers. She would be a base for members of the family coming home from university, or dropping in for a day or a week on their way somewhere else; she would housekeep for them, their friends, their friends' friends. She would be available, at everyone's disposal.

She was looking forward to it: not only to the many people, but the managing, the being conscious of her efficiency; she looked forward, too, to a summer's expert gardening. When they—she and Michael—did leave this house as a couple retiring from an active scene, it wouldn't be the house that would be missed, but the garden, which was as lovely as an English garden is after twenty or so years of devotion. It looked as if man had not planted it, but as if it had chosen to grow into lawns and clumps of lilies, rose arbours and herb patches. The birds sang in it all the year. The wind blew tenderly in it. There was not a crumb of earth that Kate did not feel she knew personally, had not made—of course with the aid of earthworms and the frost.

She sat taking in breaths of rose, lavender, thyme, and watched her husband come out of the house with their guest.

He was Alan Post, and had nothing to do with medicine, but was a civil servant of the international variety: he worked for one of the bodies associated with the United Nations. He and Dr. Michael Brown had met in the airport lounge at Los Angeles when their aircraft was delayed by fog. They had played chess, drunk whisky, exchanged invitations. A week ago the two men had bumped into each other in Goodge Street, and then lunched together. Michael had invited Alan to a family Sunday lunch.

If there had not been the power cuts, the Browns would have provided the traditional British Sunday meal, not for their own benefit, since they no longer used the old patterns, but for their guest's: the family had often enough joked that when they entertained their many foreign friends, they served traditional dishes like peasants dependent on the tourist trade. But Eileen had cooked the meal today, with Tim's help, before rushing off somewhere. She had made a Turkish cucumber soup—cold; shish kebab over the fire, and an apricot water ice—the refrigerator ran on gas. They had drunk a great deal of sangria, the recipe for which had been acquired by the second son last year in Spain.

Michael and Alan Post sat down and continued the conversation they had enjoyed throughout lunch, and afterwards upstairs in the study. She poured the coffee into the pretty plastic cups she had used in the garden ever since next door's dog had bounced through in pursuit of another dog and had smashed a whole tray full of her best china. Having handed them coffee and chocolate wafers, she set an attentive smile on her face, like a sentinel, behind which she could cultivate her own thoughts. In fact she was thinking of her husband.

Whenever she saw him like this, with a colleague, particularly those from overseas, it was as if he had walked away from her. This was not because he was one of the people whose manner alters depending on whom they are with—not at all, but with Alan Post it seemed that a larger, finer air blew around him, he was expanding, he looked as if he were about to take wing . . . last year, in the States, when she had been with him, she had felt part of the expansion, the enlarging; she had felt as if for all these years of marriage this man had been keeping in reserve some potential that could never find growing room inside the family: they had discussed what she felt, of course. She had half hoped he might say that he had sometimes felt the same about her, but he didn't. Now she thought that this year he would be without his wife, only intermittently with his daughter, for four months: the appropriate smile, dry, ironic, was on her face again. She knew it was there; she had as they say "worked" on that smile, or on the emotions it represented. If this had been the right occasion for it—a younger woman's question for instance (not a woman her own age, she realised, not Mary Finchley)—she might have leaned back in her chair, allowed her eyes to hood themselves in irony, and said: Perhaps we all make too much fuss of this kind of thing when we are young—the little affairs, you know, they are of no importance in a real marriage! Self-congratulation accompanied this smile that was half a grimace, she knew that; also relief, that of a person successfully negotiating a trap, a danger point . . . Sitting under the summery tree, holding up the coffee pot to indicate to the men that there was plenty more in it, smiling, she was hearing herself think: I'm telling myself the most dreadful lies! Awful! Why do I do it? There's something here that I simply will not let myself look at. Sometimes with Mary I get near to it, but never with anyone else. *Now*, look at it all, try and get hold of it, don't go on making up all these attitudes, these stories—stop taking down the same old dresses off the rack . . . She was listening, properly now, to what the men were saying: it seemed that it concerned her in some way, that the conversation had concerned her for some minutes, but she hadn't been listening.

The conference Alan Post had come to London to attend was in difficulties. Or rather, a committee of that conference: the organisation under whose umbrella the conferrings and committee-ings were going on was called Global Food, and its business was what mankind ate. Or did not eat. Due to a series of mischances—flu, a broken hip, the death of a man in Lisbon—when the members of the committee were already sitting around their table waiting to start their deliberations, it was discovered that there were no translators. Now, nothing was easier than to find fluent translators in French, German, Spanish, but it was harder to find people who spoke fluent Portuguese as well as English and who were educated enough for this demanding work. Portuguese it had to be, for this subcommittee was to do with coffee; and Brazil, the world's leading coffee country, used Portuguese. The committee had adjourned so that Portuguese translators could be engaged. Two had been found, two more were needed: Alan Post and Michael were both looking at Kate, waiting for her to say that she would be happy to be a third. Three years before Kate had typed out, as a favour to a friend whose typing was bad, a book for popular consumption on the growing and marketing of coffee. Because of this, she knew a great deal about that commodity. More: she had always been good at languages. Her knowledge of French and Italian was good; her Portuguese was perfect, for on one side she was Portuguese. It had happened that she finished school early, since she was clever, with a gap of three years before she was to go to university—to which, in the end, she did not go, having decided to marry Michael instead. She spent a year in Lourenço Marques with her grandfather, who was a scholar. There she spoke only Portuguese. As the daughter of John Ferreira, an English-naturalized Portuguese who taught Portuguese literature at Oxford, she had never been more than gratefully conscious that her background contained treasures: it was her grandfather who had introduced them to her, so that she became soaked in Portuguese literature, Portuguese poetry, soaked in "the spirit of the language."

What else had she learned during that year in the city on the edge of the Indian Ocean, a year devoted entirely to pleasure? For one thing, her grandfather was old-fashioned, and his attitudes towards women strict. Kate had never dreamed of fighting an old man whom she loved; and besides, why bother?—she was only there for such a short time. But for that time she was never alone with a man, was shielded from unpleasant experience, literary or in life, and tasted a not unpleasant (for a short time) atmosphere compounded of elements so foreign to her that she had had to identify each one separately. She was sheltered and distrusted. She was precious and despised. She was flattered by deference to her every wish—but knew that she, the female thing, occupied a carefully defined minor part of her grandfather's life, as his wife had done, and his daughters. Her image of herself during that period: a girl as fragile as a camellia with a dead-white skin and heavy dark-red hair, wearing a white embroidered linen dress designed to expose and conceal throat and shoulders, sat on a verandah in a swing chair, that she slowly pushed back and forth with a foot which she was conscious of being an object so sexual the young men present couldn't keep their eyes and fantasies away from it. She fanned herself with an embroidered silk fan, using a turn of the wrist taught her by the old nurse, while these young men, all of whom had asked her grandfather's permission to speak to her at all, sat in a half circle in grass armchairs, paying her compliments. The year was 1948. She was a great success in Lourenço Marques, partly because after all she was British, and not all her good intentions could keep her within what her grandfather approved; partly because the combination of short red hair and brown eyes were rare in a country full of señoritas; partly because the strictness of her grandfather was excessive even in this colony, so that on more than one count Kate's behaviour, her position, seemed like a wilful or whimsical play acting, probably undertaken with the intention of being provocative.

When she returned to England, she looked back into a steamy place, full of half-concealed things, one of them being her own wistful longing to be like her own grandmother who—unless this was her grandfather's false memory—might never have left Portugal at all, for all the difference it had made to her way of life. A beautiful woman, so everyone said she had been; a wonderful mother, a cook for the angels, a marvellous, marvellous being, all warmth and kindness, with not a fault in her—yes, well, however all that might have been, the propaganda had its predictable reverse effect, and Kate returned from Portuguese East Africa more than ready to go to university, where she was going to study Romance languages and literature. She actually did get herself up to Oxford, and into residence. Then she met Michael, who after ten years of war and crammed training was just beginning his career. She moved into his lodgings and they started delightfully on what they called The First Phase.

If she had not married, she would probably have become something special in her field? A lecturer perhaps? Women did not seem often to become professors. But these were not frequent thoughts: she had not found children boring. Besides it was not as if her husband cut her off from his interests, from interesting people. She sometimes did translating for him or his colleagues. She had once even translated a Portuguese novel, which earned her little money, but much praise. She met people from all over the world, particularly since the children started growing up, and brought home all their globally scattered friends.

If she had not married—but good God, she would have been mad not to marry, mad to choose Romance languages and literature . . . . . Michael and Alan Post were helping themselves to coffee, and waiting for her. What she was feeling was a kind of panic. Knowing this made it worse. It was stupid and irrational to feel frightened. What of? This was not something she could have confessed to anyone, not even Michael—that when actually faced with a job, quite an ordinary sort of job after all, well within her powers, and obviously only for a short time, she felt like a long-term prisoner who knows she is going to have to face freedom in the morning.

"But I don't see how I can," she said. "Tim is going to be here on and off all summer."

She observed the tightening of her husband's mouth: frequent discussion about Tim had not resolved disagreement. Michael thought his youngest son was overprotected. She, while agreeing that he might have been, could not believe that the way to put things right was to "throw him out and be done with it." How, throw him out? Where to? And why was what the boy doing so bad that he needed such dramatic cure: he sulked, he threatened, he hated, but so had all the children in their different ways. Kate believed that if she favoured Tim, it was because her husband was unfair to him: she was aware that this area was too emotional to be looked at straight; she had attitudes about it, which were known to be hers and which she defended, inside the family and out.

"But the committee won't be going on for longer than —how long did you say?" Michael asked Alan.

By now Alan had understood that there was a problem between husband and wife, and he said, looking at neither, but away over towards the house, where a young boy was emerging and coming towards them, "Not more than a month at most."

"There *is* Tim," said Kate; meaning *Not in front of the children.*

When Tim arrived under the tree, it was clear that he was older than his slight build and light walk made him seem from a distance. He was sulky now. Looking hard at his mother he said, "I'm awfully sorry mother but I've changed my mind. The Fergusons have asked me to go to Norway. They're going climbing. I'll go if you don't mind."

"No, of course not darling," said Kate automatically. "Of course you should go." She was delighted that he was not going to be excluded from the summer's pleasures, as delighted as if she were going to Norway; but the boy had already glanced at his father, who nodded at him. He then smiled formally at the guest, momentarily appearing a completely different person, the responsible man he would become, turned back into a sulky child in his look at his mother as he said, "That's all right then, I'll be off to pack now. I'm going tonight." And he ran off to the house as if escaping.

She shouted after him, "Tim, before you go, see if you can make the kettle boil again, I need the hot water for washing up." But either he didn't hear or didn't want to.

"So when can you start, Kate?" said Alan. "When? Tomorrow? Oh please do?"

Kate said nothing, but she was smiling agreement. She knew she might burst into tears. She felt as if every support had been pulled out from under her. She felt—to use a metaphor she had been using, indeed, developing, in her own thought, and for some time now—as if suddenly a very cold wind had started to blow, straight towards her, from the future.

She said, "Of course I'd like to. Can I do the washing up first?"

They laughed, she laughed. Alan then said, "Well, if somebody else could do the washing up while you telephone?" He gave her a name, a number, and escorted her into the house, using a pleasant formality, like an intimacy that is so easy it is almost impersonal: she recognised this as the air of the life she was about to enter. It was both supporting and relaxing, this manner of his; he stood by her while she telephoned, mouthing at her words she should use—words that would not have come easily to her, because they had the ring of committees. All that finished, he kissed her on both cheeks, and with his arm around her, led her back to the tree on the lawn. He was a good-looking man, of about their age—Michael's and hers—a family man, with a wife and growing or grown children, a man who earned a great deal of money and spent all his life travelling from conference to conference to talk about food with people from dozens of countries. She liked him. She was thinking that after all it would be a release and a relief to breathe that easy impersonal air for a while. She really did like everything about him, including the way he dressed and presented himself: she had not been much liking the way her husband was dressing these days, nor the way he cut his hair. But better not to think about that, for after all it wasn't important.

The reason she felt as if she were falling through the air was because if Tim were not going to be here, there was no point at all in keeping the house open.

Back under the tree, the hot Sunday afternoon proceeded towards evening, while the men were talking about some medical problem in Iran.

The question of the letting of the house had been dealt with in a dozen words.

In the past great discussions had gone on about the letting or the non-letting of the house, everyone having strong opinions about it. They had gone on for days, weeks.

Now she said, "Well, we've never let it before, have we?"

"What of it?" said Michael. "Some visiting family will take it and be glad to, even if we do leave things in the cupboards."

"But what are the children going to use as headquarters if they happen to be in London on their way to somewhere?"

"They can use somebody else's house for once, and about time too."

"But I don't really think . . ."

"I'll ring the agent in the morning," said Dr. Michael Brown, shaming Kate, since he worked from dawn to dusk and would be no less busy than she at her committee.

But the point was, she was feeling dismissed, belittled, because the problem of the house was being considered so unimportant.

And when her committee was over, what would she do? It was being taken for granted she would fit herself in somewhere—how very flexible she was being, just as always, ever since the children were born. Looking back over nearly a quarter of a century, she saw that that had been the characteristic of her life—passivity, adaptability to others. Her first child had been born when she was twenty-two. The last was born well before she was thirty. When she offered these facts to others, many envied her; a large number of people, in many countries, knew the Michael Browns as an enviable family.

The small chill wind was blowing very definitely, if

still softly enough: this was the first time in her life that she was not wanted. She was unnecessary. That this time in her life was approaching she had of course known very well for years. She had even made plans for it; she would study this, travel there, take up this or that type of welfare work. It is not possible, after all, to be a woman with any sort of a mind, and not know that in middle age, in the full flood of one's capacities and energies, one is bound to become that well-documented and much-studied phenomenon, the woman with grown-up children and not enough to do, whose energies must be switched from the said children to less vulnerable targets, for everybody's sake, her own as well as theirs. So there was nothing surprising about what was happening. Perhaps she ought to have expected it sooner?

She had not expected it this summer. Next summer, or the year after that, yes, but not *now*. What she had set herself to face had been all in the future. But it was *now* that it was happening. Only temporarily, of course, for the house would become their family house again in September, would again be the welcoming base for these "children" all now at home less and less often. But there was her husband to consider, a man who much appreciated his home and everything that went with it. When had all the family last been together, with everyone back from university, or various holidays and trips and excursions, at the same time? A very long time ago, when you came to think of it.

But the fact was that she, this kingpin, was to be at a loose end from June to late September. With not so much as a room of her own. A very curious feeling that was, as if a warm covering had been stripped off her, as if she were an animal being flayed.

She and Michael had, of course, discussed this question of her future; talked over her feelings, and his. Discussing everything was the root and prop of their marriage. They believed, always had, that things left unsaid festered, things brought out into the open lost their force. Their relationship had been conducted on this principle from the start.

A great deal of intelligent insight had gone into their view of themselves and this marriage. They had not been wrong about much.

For instance, in their joint bedroom, were two books, side by side, one by Bertrand Russell called *The Conquest of Happiness,* and one by Van der Velde, *Ideal Marriage.* From Kate to Michael—Russell; and from Michael to Kate —Van der Velde. Both inscriptions read: "For The First Phase. With all my love." This commemorated that fact that a phase had ended when their delicious love affair had to end, and they married. They had known that things must change, that the deliciousness must abate, and their long discussions about it all were summed up by these friendly books, From Kate to Michael, From Michael to Kate, *For The First Phase.* Now, picking up these books and opening them on the inscription page, both might have been caught out in a humorous grimace, *had* been caught out by each other, which led to frank and certainly healthy laughter. (Laughter is by definition healthy.) The point was, why the humorous grimace at all? They had been so utterly right, about what had been finishing, and what was beginning—the solid, demanding, satisfactory marriage. There was no room for a humorous grimace. What were they being humorous, ironical, about? And similarly, with certain other long frank open discussions about changes and turning points. Neither would have relinquished these. But Kate had certainly caught herself thinking that perhaps these blueprints of psychological observation, or if you like, manifestos, that accompanied stages or "phases" of the marriage, were perhaps not all they should be?

The discussion, for instance, about the cold wind from the future. Which had taken place three years before: but things had happened since which had not been blueprinted or made into statements of account . . . *For the Ninth— or Nineteenth—Phase.*

What had happened was that Michael's mouth tightened when Tim was mentioned, as now when he said, "I'll ring the agent in the morning." Putting her into perspective, laying her aside. So she felt it. That is what she had been *feeling*, regardless of the dozen or so mental attitudes, garments taken down off a rack, the words she used to describe her situation.

Whatever that situation was, whatever it *really* was, by the end of that summer evening a hundred strands in Kate's life seemed to be pulled together. This was manifested in many telephone numbers scribbled on bits of paper, on addresses of all sorts, and in a conscious effort to win back memories of her grandfather sitting on the verandah of a stone house in a deep garden full of flame trees and lilies. "Catherine! The way to learn a language is to breathe it in. Soak it up! Live it!"

Faced with an interview to judge her ability to translate at speed from English, French, and Italian into Portuguese and back again, she sat up all night, having cleared away the day's disorder of dirty dishes and scraps of food and grease—luckily the power came on again at about ten in the evening—rereading the novel she had herself translated, reliving in her mind walks and talks, meals with her grandfather. By the morning her immersion in the other language was such that if she had jostled someone in the street she would have apologised in Portuguese.

Global Food

But all this, and her anxious choosing of a suitable dress for the interview, her worry over her hair—really very suburban, and she knew it—her inner adjustments of manner away from being Mrs. Michael Brown, all turned out to be unnecessary. As she walked into the office of a Mr. Charlie Cooper, he said, "Mrs. Brown? Thank God you have been able to find the time. You are starting today, aren't you— good."

She had been described by the friend and intermediary, Alan Post, as the formidably highly equipped woman-with-a-family, who had been pressed into abandoning the said family, and into relieving the embarrassment of this great international organisation. From the first she was in a special category, the amateur, made to feel as if she were doing a favour.

It appeared that of the four replacements to the original team of four skilled translators, two had again fallen out for family and health reasons.

"This whole thing is jinxed, it is doomed!" cried Charlie Cooper, "but I am sure our luck will turn with you." And he hurried her along a wide passage that gleamed and shone and was many-windowed, and into a lift that was large and had a picture of a dark-skinned woman smiling agreeably while picking coffee beans off a very green bush, and along another impressive passage, passing a committee on butter, and another on sugar, and into a very large long room, in the middle of which was a gleaming oval table of the size which makes one think at once of the factory there must be somewhere whose whole business it is to create immense tables, long or oval or round, for the use of international conferences.

A committee was in progress. The table had on it glasses of water, pencils, stylos, sheets of scribbled and doodled paper. But the chairs were awry, and empty; the delegates were all downstairs drinking—presumably coffee —and engaged in that most common of contemporary conversations, the one about the total inefficiency and incompetence of any public service or occasion, which conversation will of course get more frequent and more ill-tempered as the numbers of people everywhere multiply and the services, by the law of inertia, fall even further behind demand. Only now did the tactful Charlie Cooper tell Kate that she had been expected that morning at ten, to start her day with the beginning of the first session, and not at twelve, which it now was—but of course, she had not been told, it was not her fault, things were always thus—yes, he could believe it, she had been told to "drop in some time that morning"?—typical!

But could she start now, yes, this very moment, or rather, when the delegates had returned from their enforced coffee break—there was on duty that day, apart from herself, precisely one properly qualified simultaneous translator for the Portuguese language.

Kate had thought this would be a preliminary interview, and had told various interested people that she would be back to arrange food for lunch and attend to the laundry. But if she could go and make a telephone call then . . .

Charlie Cooper's face became agonised—the delegates would be back upstairs in one minute, they had been called back because of her, Kate's arrival. With a great screaming wrench, Kate's years of conditioning for itemised responsibility ripped off her. Charlie Cooper would telephone for her, he would simply announce that Mrs. Brown was otherwise occupied. It was to Eileen that this announcement would be made: suppressing an impulse to send her daughter messages of love and support, Kate allowed herself to be handed over to a young woman who was going to give her instruction into her duties. At each place around the table was machinery for receiving languages not one's own translated into one's own: sound transformed in its passage from speaker to hearer. By Kate, among others. There were switches, each one a door into a foreign tongue. There were headphones. In glass-walled cubicles at either end of the room were more switches, receiving apparatus, headphones. It would be Kate's task to sit in one of these cubicles, to listen to speeches made in English, French, and Italian, and to translate them as she listened into Portuguese, which she would speak aloud into a transmitter connected with the ears of the Portuguese speakers—mostly Brazilian, who did not speak English, or who did, but preferred, nevertheless, their own tongue. She would be like a kind of machine herself: into her ears would flow one language, and from her mouth would flow another.

She would not, of course, be alone all day in her cubicle, even with the shortage of translators. There would be frequent changes and rests and chances for replenishing of vital energies during this extremely taxing task—as Charlie Cooper kept emphasising it was; for he had returned from telephoning her family, an errand he regarded as of so little importance that he did not report on it. She was in the cubicle with him; she had the headphones on;

she was turning switches off and on, with his aid. While he instructed her, he was scribbling a message on a memorandum block saying that the organisation offered sincere and remorseful apologies for the shortage of translators, and implored the delegates' tolerance and patience. With this in his hand he hurried out, to find a typist to copy it. Through the glass of the cubicle Kate—alone now, left to herself—was able to see that the conference room, viewed from this small height, was very pleasant. It had high windows. The walls were covered in a copper-coloured wood that was much grained and whorled and patterned. The floors were deep in dark-blue carpet.

In this room were decided the fates and fortunes of millions of little people, what crops they were going to grow, what they would eat, and wear—and think.

While Charlie Cooper was still laying a sheet of paper —the apology, miraculously multiplied in this brief space of a few minutes—in each place around the table, the delegates came in, laughing and talking. What an extraordinarily attractive lot they were! Such a collection of many-coloured, many-nationed handsome men and women would be what a film producer would try to shoot to make a scene from some idealised picture of united nations. But would the actors have been able to convey such a perfection of casual authority, such assurance? For that was the impression they made. The difference between them and their assistants and secretaries and the attendants of various kinds could be seen by that quality alone. Each man or woman strolled to his or her chair, seated himself, continued to talk and to laugh with a perfection of ease that shouted the one word: *Power*. Every gesture, each look, conveyed conviction of usefulness, the weight of what they represented.

Some of the clothes worn were national costume: there

were half a dozen men and women from somewhere in Africa who made all the others look members of inferior races, so tall and graceful and majestically dressed were they: the folds of their robes, their earrings, the turn of a head—each knew its role. And what authority even the creases in a suit can convey, worn by a man whose decisions are of importance to people hauling sacks of coffee on a hillside thousands of miles away.

The proceedings had begun; and Kate found that her brain, that machine, was doing its work smoothly. A few moments of panic, a feeling that her mind was blank and would be forever, had been dispelled by hearing her own words come out, quite sensibly ordered, and by watching the faces of the people who listened. No one seemed upset by what they heard; everything was as it should be.

And in an incredibly short time—it turned out that it had been two hours—she was relieved by a colleague, was sent off to relax and have a good lunch. She returned to her cubicle with confidence; and by five o'clock that afternoon felt as much a part of this organisation as she did of her family. To which she returned too late for the evening meal, to find that her daughter had cooked it, and that everything was going on quite comfortably.

By the end of that week Kate was initiated into the complexities of that bitter and fragrant herb the world drinks so much of; she could hardly think of anything else. And her house had been tidied and put ready for letting. Then it had been let, until the end of September, and the family had departed to its various destinations without any help from her. All she had said was, in a voice which only a week before would have been anxious, but now was indifferent, "Someone has got to see to it, because I haven't got the time." She had kissed her husband, and her three sons and her daughter goodbye, but had not yet had time to feel any particular emotion.

She was in a room in a flat rented by one of her colleagues; a woman who had translated, but who had been promoted: she now organised conferences. This move from Kate's home into this room, with all the necessities for some months, had taken half an hour, and the act of flinging some clothes into a suitcase.

None of the clothes were any use, anyway. At some point during that week she rushed out to buy the dresses that would admit her, like a passport, to this way of life. Mrs. Michael Brown could not have been called ill-dressed; but it was not Mrs. Michael Brown who was being employed by Global Food.

Before going shopping she had asked Charlie Cooper what she was going to earn. His round, humorous, harassed face—his permanent expression, because of being male nanny to so many committees—became agonised with remorse.

"My dear!" he said. "Accept my apologies! Oh, I don't see how you can—it was really too awful of me! I should have talked about that before anything else. But it's been such a week—really, if you only knew what a godsend you've been!" And he mentioned a sum which she stopped herself exclaiming at. It was in this casual, positively gentlemanly way, as if the world of trade unions, of bitterly contested wages, poverty, the anguish of hunger, did not exist, that the salaries of these international officials, these indispensable fortunates, could be arranged.

She had bought her dresses, half a dozen of them, thinking that at the end of her two weeks with Global Food, she would have a wardrobe fit for an elegant holiday somewhere. But her plans were only for, perhaps, visiting an old friend in Sussex, or an aunt in Scotland. She had not really thought of what she was going to do.

The second week was less pressured. Her work had become something she did as easily as she had run a home—unbelievably, only a few days ago. She did it automatically. In between the sessions in the cubicles, she spent her time in the coffee rooms, watching. She was, after all, an outsider, did not feel that she was entitled to join this privileged throng. She was a migrant; it would all be over in a week. But she sat as if she felt she had a right to it all—her new dresses made this much easier; she drank the superb coffee, she watched. It was like a market. Or like a long, gay, permanently continuing party.

A woman sat in a public room, relaxed but observant, an official in a public organisation, dressed like one, holding herself like one; but letting her life—or the words that represented her thoughts about her life—flow through her mind. Was it that for twenty-five years she had been part of that knot of tension, the family, and had forgotten that ordinary life, life for everyone not in the family, was so agreeable, so undemanding? How well-dressed everyone was. How everybody's skin glowed and shone. And how easy the way a man or a woman would come in here, glance around, find smiles and pleasant looks waiting for them, then wave and sit down by themselves, with a gesture that said: *I need a moment's solitude*—which wish was of course respected. Or casually, almost insolently, look over the room to see which group he or she would join. There seemed never a sign of the tension that you would find after five minutes in any street outside this sheltered place. In any street, or shop, or home the currents flowed and crossed and made new currents. Outside this great public building the conflicts went on. But here? Had these easy well-turned creatures, each burnished and polished by money, ever suffered? Ever wept in the dark? Ever wanted something they could not get? Of course they had, they must have—but there was not a sign of it. Had they ever— but perhaps this was not the right question to ask—had they ever been hungry?

One could not easily believe it. And what problems they had now seemed so extremely small, almost ridiculous, when you remembered the purpose of this building, the reason for its being continuously full of conferring people. For Kate was involved in these problems. Things had already changed; she was no longer "the woman who replaced the translators who had those accidents and who got ill." She was Kate Brown, greeted in corridors by smiles and warm faces; she was stopped increasingly often for advice and information. Where to buy this or that face cream; or that special foodstuff; how to find the restaurant, the hotel, a dress shop, or the right place for British woollen goods or whisky.

In her first week, she had only had time to think, as she flopped exhausted into bed, that she had become a function, she had become, she *was* language for a couple of dozen international civil servants. This week, lying awake later since she was not exhausted, she thought that her first function, that of being a skilled parrot, was being supplanted, and very fast, by one she was used to. How did one do this and do that, find this or that?—they asked *her*, the newcomer! But of course, she was already an old hand, since most people flitted in and out of this building for a few days at a time.

She had become what she was: a nurse, or a nanny, like Charlie Cooper. A mother. Never mind, in a few days she would be free of it all. She would no longer be a parrot with the ability to be sympathetic about minor and unimportant obsessions; she would be free . . . Kate noted that the thought brought with it a small shiver. She noted that she reacted with: *I wish I had gone with Michael to America.* She caught herself thinking, "When I visit Rose I'll be able to help her with the children." Rose was the friend in Sussex whom she might visit.

But she did not want to spend the summer in another family, that was just cowardice. In her room, before going to sleep, she looked at its neatness, its indifference to her, and thought that yes, this was much better than her large family house, than Rose's house, full, crammed, jostling with objects every one of which had associations, histories, belonged to this person or that, mattered, were important. This small box of a room, that had in it a bed, a chair, a chest of drawers, a mirror—yes, this is what she would choose, if she could choose . . . she dreamed. Later, when this night's dream had fallen into place in the pattern, had become the first instalment of the story or the journey that she followed in her sleep, she tried to remember more of it, more of the detail. But while she was sure of its atmosphere, the feel—which mixed anxiety and joy in a way that could never happen in waking life—the details had gone. The dream had become by morning—she had woken in the dark to try and grab the tail of the dream before it slid off and away—like the start of an epic, simple and direct.

She came down a hillside in a landscape that was northern, and unknown to her. Someone said, "Look, what is that strange thing, look, something dark is lying there." She thought, A slug? Surely it can't be, no slug is as large as that. But it was a seal, lying stranded and helpless among dry rocks high on a cold hillside. It was moaning. She picked it up. It was heavy. She asked if it were all right, if she could help it. It moaned, and she knew she had to get it to water. She started to carry the seal in her arms down the hill.

On the day before her two weeks were up, she was invited by Charlie Cooper to meet him over a coffee. She did so, and was asked if she would be free to continue this work for another month. This particular committee was ending, but another was due to start.

"I've been all right, then?" Kate asked. She knew she had, as far as the actual translating went; but she could tell from the warmth of this permanent official's manner that there was more he wanted to say. Charm, from him, one could count on. It was what had earned him this job? But charm had to be put to one side, if one wanted to understand what he really meant, or wanted: "Oh, my dear Mrs. Brown, I should think so. We are absolutely delighted to have found you. What luck for us! And how kind of you to spare us the time." (How delightful, this game, that she was working for them as a favour, instead of for such a very large salary—how unexpected, to find this courtly behaviour, these gentlemanly manners, here, in this newest of modern growths, the international civil services.) "Really, believe me Kate—but we may call each other Kate and Charlie now? Particularly as you are going to be so kind as to go on working for us a little longer—for a long, long time, if I had my way. But perhaps we could discuss that another time? But I must confess it is not your really remarkable skill at your job, really remarkable, since you came straight into it—some people need weeks of training before they can do it at all but you, no—it is more than that. Everyone is saying how marvellously helpful you have been in every way. I mean it. Mrs. Kingsmead, she's the lady from the American delegation, she was saying only this morning she didn't know how she would have managed without all your good advice. I suppose it is because of your large family? Alan Post was telling me about all those attractive young people and how smoothly it all goes along . . . but, well, this is the point. I suppose if a person is good at one thing then she is at another, but if you could stay with us another month, and switch to the organisational side, it would be the luckiest thing. To waste your incredible talents as a translator—it is a crime. But your other capacities are as good. In a way it is all rather awful, asking you to stop doing what you are so good at. Your salary will of course be higher if you accept. A month—if we could just count on a month?"

Of course she would accept. For one thing there was the money: she could not believe it. She had not been able to prevent herself feeling guilty that the rate at which she had been paid for being an exceedingly intelligent and fluent parrot with maternal inclinations had been nearly as high as what her husband, a doctor with so many years of training, and so many more of experience, was earning as a consultant neurologist. (In Britain, not in the States, of course; there he earned much more.) But now it would seem even worse; it was ridiculous. But she simply had to accept the fact that inside this world ordinary rules, values, standards, did not apply. As for leaving her special skills behind—her feelings about this were mixed. What was she actually going to do?

Well, she was doing very much what she did in her home. She started to organise things, to spend much time on the telephone, to see that people and places and things coincided at the right times . . . then, suddenly, there was a hitch. There was a typhoid scare. The usual conflict between the needs of tourism and those of public health confused everything for some days; there was a threat that all unnecessary travel in and out of these islands would be stopped altogether. The epidemic was brought under control, but almost at once there was a strike at the airport. It would be a long strike, the newspapers said. Then it was discovered that due to various oversights, hotel rooms had not been booked far enough in advance for the forty incoming delegates—here was more of the inevitable incompetence everyone delights in deploring. There were flurries of discussion at high levels: telephone calls and telegrams from and to New York, London, Australia, Canada . . . it was being decided that there was no law which said this conference should take place in London. It was to be a general conference, on the endemic theme of how to get food from places which grew too much to places which had too little. There were plenty of attractive and suitable cities—Paris? No, no, in July madness, crammed to the brim . . . the difficulties of getting this conference started were postponing the starting date; it was already nearly halfway through June. One European city after another was thought of and discussed and dismissed: Rome, Barcelona, Zurich. Kate kept thinking, like a housewife, of the telephone bills for all these postponings and suggestings and mind-changes; what was being spent on telephoning alone would be enough to feed thousands for weeks: but she was not being paid to think like a housewife, something less was being asked of her. What was it? She seemed to spend an inordinate amount of time talking about these problems, with Charlie Cooper and other officials. She felt as if she was stuck in something, an organisational marsh; nothing moved, everything delayed and dawdled. She talked. They talked. They were constantly ringing people up in other countries—was this how these great organisations always went on? If so, it was no wonder that . . . Why should they stick to Europe? was being asked. After all, these much-travelled, these almost permanently travelling delegates, who spent their lives conferring at circular or oval tables in light airy rooms with various cities as backdrops beyond long windows—these people could not mind much if they found their sheets of paper, the pencils, stylos, glasses of water, and permanent secretaries in Beirut or Nairobi rather than Rome or London. North Africa? No, it would be much too hot. Perhaps they should go north then—Stockholm? That was a city with the right flavour for calm dispassionate discussion. Oslo? No, Scandinavia was too far north, better to find somewhere central. The Mediterranean, yes; but not the Lebanon or Syria, not an Arab country, or one that was part of that deadlock, Israel and the Arabs. Turkey? Yes, that was better—Istanbul? Of course! But it was hot; it would be every bit as hot as North Africa or Rome. Yes, but it was so attractive, and not used so much for conferences, and it would offer such a feast of sightseeing—archaeological, religious, cultural, social—to delegates exhausted with conferring. How illogical to dismiss so many cities on the grounds of being so full, as well as being so hot, and then say yes, to Istanbul? True. Perhaps it would be better after all to stay in London? But the strike? Well, people could get to France and then come over by boat, couldn't they? Boats and trains had worked perfectly well before the invention of the airplane, hadn't they? Yes, but—you had to admit that the airplane and the international conference went together, they fitted.

The typhoid scare flared up again. Charlie Cooper and Kate Brown took to the telephone to arrange a three weeks' conference under the aegis of Global Food in Istanbul. The delegates, all still in their countries, were informed at unbelievable expense on the telephone that Turkey was to have the honour of welcoming them and not London.

Kate's empty summer was now filled until mid-July; if things delayed even more, perhaps until later. She was feeling that she ought not to have let this happen. She ought to have been thinking, perhaps, about her condition, about the cold wind. She ought to be examining the violent and uncontrollable swings in her emotions about her husband, her children—particularly her husband. For now that she had so much time—she felt as if she was doing nothing, or very little; her days were emptier than they had been for years—she was conscious of her emotional apparatus working away in a vacuum: the objects of her emotions were all elsewhere, they were not present to react with or against her. What was the sense of loving, hating, wanting, resenting, needing, rejecting—and sometimes all in the space of an hour—when she was here, by herself, free; it was like talking to yourself, it was insane . . . it was just as well she was going to be occupied. At least for another month. She went out and bought some more dresses. Then she bought the things to go with them. No, it was not really that these commodities were so different from those she normally wore. It was more, really, of how she would wear them. "The spirit of the thing," as her grandfather would have said.

A woman stood in front of large mirrors in many shops, looking with a cool, not entirely friendly curiosity at a woman in her early forties who was still the same shape she had been all her adult life, give or take an inch or so; who had pretty chestnut hair—tinted of course, because the grey was coming in fast. A cool curiosity, but it easily became an eye-to-eye woman-to-woman collusion that was first cousin to that so very undermining "humorous" grimace, undermining because it seemed to nullify her official or daylight view of herself. Yes, better to avoid the long interchange of eye pressures, which threatened all the time to start off a roar of laughter: yes, she knew it, what was waiting for her was ribald laughter at the whole damned business . . . the kind of laughter that she and Mary Finchley enjoyed (indulged in? used as a prophylactic?) on the occasions when they were together, alone, without husbands, families, guests.

No, she must step back, look at herself as a whole, and confirm that there stood in front of her a pleasant-looking fashionable woman on the verge of middle age. Still on the verge—she had not chosen to enter the state. She could say, as she looked dispassionately at her image, that her *shape*, her attributes, limbs, waist, breasts, mouth, hair, neck, were not different from the equipment with which she had attracted a dozen young men nearly a quarter of a century ago, with which she had married her husband. No different; perhaps even better; since so much chemistry and medication and dieting and attention to hair, teeth, and eyes had gone into this artifact—what would she look like now if, for instance, she had been born into a slum in Brazil?

What was different was—nothing tangible. It was a question again of an atmosphere, something she carried invisibly with her. The reason why, as a young woman, this same assortment of appurtenances, teeth, eyes, hips, and so on, had attracted, whereas now they did not, or not more than any woman of her age (of the minority who have not set themselves outside the business of attraction from a pretty early age, and for a variety of reasons, poverty being the first of them), was this delicate business of "the spirit." Surely the wrong word; but what was the right one

—state? condition? presence? She did not walk inside, like the fine almost unseeable envelope of a candle flame, that emanation of attractiveness: *I am available, come and sniff and taste.* In her case it was because she was, and had been for so long, a wife and a mother who had not been interested—or not often, and then not for long—in attracting men other than her husband.

All this had of course been discussed fully and frankly between husband and wife. It would have had to be. For this area of marriage, so difficult, risky, and embattled, they had had from the start what amounted to a blueprint. And it had all been kept up to date, not allowed to lapse . . . Kate was nevertheless aware that what was taken for granted between herself and Mary Finchley in the encounters they described as "cow sessions" contradicted the marital blueprints everywhere. Why was she thinking so much about Mary? In fact she had been annoyed by her old friend's reaction to the news of this new job. It had been the jolly laugh which had always seemed to Kate crude, and, "Well thank God for that. And about time too!"

At any rate, it was in order for her now to face herself in so many different mirrors, and to light a flame, to set certain currents running. No, not as she had on the brief occasions of uncontrollable attraction during her marriage (referred to by Mary critically, as *the world well lost for lust*) when she had been directed towards a particular man. Now she was doing something very different. Exactly as a young girl does, suddenly conscious of her powers of generalised attractions, so now with Kate: an internal thermostat was differently set, saying not: You over there, yes you, come and get me! but: Ah, how infinitely desirable you all are; if I wished I could be available, but it is up to you, and really it is much more exciting to be like this, floating in the air of general appreciation and approval; it would be an awful bore to confine myself to one.

This is something no married woman does. (Except Mary!) But look what her family went through because of it—no, she was not to be envied, not copied; she probably ought not even to be listened to, let alone enjoyed for roaring sessions of laughter and old wives' talk. Never mind about Mary. No *really* married woman sets the thermostat for Tom, Dick, and Harry. (In discussions on this theme with Michael both were pretty definite on what being *really* married meant.) Not if she wishes to stay married. (Or doesn't mind being like Mary, whose life for the fifteen years Kate had known her had been like a French farce—toned down, of course, for the mild airs of South London.) For what Kate did know, did indeed know, was that not every marriage was a real marriage, and that such marriages were getting rarer and rarer. She was lucky in hers. If you wished to use words like "luck" instead of giving yourself credit for being, and continuing to be (despite Mary) the sort of woman who is really married to a real husband. Being a partner in this sort of marriage means that one cannot adjust the thermostat in any way but one. Except of course for those brief and unimportant occasions that Mary so derided, because she said they provided the maximum amount of misery with the minimum of pleasure . . . if she was not able to think seriously about her marriage without Mary Finchley coming in at every moment, then she had better stop thinking altogether.

Before calling the rearrangement of herself complete, she went to a very expensive hairdresser, who allowed his hands to rest sympathetically on her two shoulders, while he looked over her head into the mirror at her image, just as she was doing. They looked at raw material for his art;

and then he enquired if her hair had always been that shade of red? Of course he was right; but she had been afraid that the very dark red that had been hers by right was too startling for a woman of her age. He said to that, Nonsense; and sent her out with very dark red hair cut so that it felt like a weight of heavy silk swinging against her cheeks as she turned her head. As she remembered very well it had once done always.

It was disturbing, this evocation of her young self. She found herself overemotional. She wished her Michael were there to enjoy her; then, as violently, was pleased he was far away in Boston. What were these swings of emotion, what caused them? In the course of a single hour, her thoughts about Michael were contradictory enough for a madwoman. Why? Surely the truth couldn't be that she was always like this, and was only just beginning to see it? Well, at least she could be sure that she was glad her children could not see her—oh no, no young person likes to see dear mother all glossy and gleaming and silky.

But they were by now scattered over the world, in Norway and the Sudan, in Morocco and New England; just like the delegates she had so recently been looking after, like the delegates who were at that very moment in so many different countries packing suitcases and saying goodbye to wives and children and, in a few cases, husbands.

There were three days left before she had to fly off to Turkey—if the air strike ended in time, for if not she would have to go by train. Three days. There was nothing to do until the conference began. The guilt that she did nothing while being paid so much made her hint to Charlie Cooper that perhaps she ought to be given other work for that time—she could help the translators for instance. For the first time she saw Charlie Cooper irritated. He repeated his many remarks about her value—yet what was she doing? She drank a good deal of coffee with him in his office; she talked to him, she sat twice a day with him and the man who was head of their department, discussing arrangements. This was work? Good God, if she could have the reorganising of this department—more, this building, with its swarms and swarms of highly paid—she must stop this, and besides, it was nothing to do with her. Probably her criticisms were because she lacked the experience to— *Nonsense, it was all nonsense; this whole damned outfit, with its committees, its conferences, its eternal talk, talk, talk, was a great con trick; it was a mechanism to earn a few hundred men and women incredible sums of money.*

It was not the slightest use thinking on these lines; if she was being paid to sit in coffee rooms thinking, then she would sit in coffee rooms thinking. After all, how many years had it been since she had had time to think—nearly twenty-five years. In fact, the last time she had been enabled to sit relaxed, prettily on show, smiling, was that year when she had visited her grandfather. Then, too, in her shockingly seductive white dress, one foot put loose to one side, like a bird's broken wing, while the other, pushing her rhythmically in her swing chair, sent waves of sexual attraction in every direction—then too she had thought, considered, had allowed the words that represented the ideas she had of her life flow through her mind while she looked at them . . . Had she then been subject to this seesaw of feeling? If so, she could not remember it. Perhaps the white dress, which she had never even been able to put on without feeling sly, dishonest, overexcited, had visibly represented one side of a balance, and what she had been thinking another? Thought was not the right word? What she had watched move through her mind had been pretty violent, yes, she could remember, she had been critical, a seethe of impatience behind that slow sweet smile for which she had been, was still so often, commended.

By Charlie Cooper, for one. She had brought with her to this organisation the atmosphere of loving sympathy which was the oil of her function in her home. Had she done this—unconsciously of course—because of the cold wind? She had been frightened to be only a capable translator, arriving at nine thirty, leaving at five, and in between doing exactly what she had been paid for? She had felt that to be not enough? It had been enough for the other translators, four men and a woman. But they were still at it, translating, using their skills, while she, Kate, had been promoted: because she had allowed herself to emanate an atmosphere of sympathetic readiness, which had been "picked up" by the bureaucracy of the organisation? Were they conscious why they had chosen her to be a group mother in Turkey? "A warm personality" is what they said. "Sympathetic." Simpatica.

This large public room filled with tables—but it was not overcrowded, there was plenty of room—was the best of places to sit quietly; how extraordinary that such a busy place could be so private. Much more so than her room in the flat in Burke Street, where her colleague wished to chat when she came in at night, and offered tea and toast in the mornings. Who, in short, was lonely. She, too, found Kate Brown sympathetic.

But here—of course, privacy was already diminishing, for the place was beginning to show patterns, many patterns. Before, coming in hurriedly between sessions of translating, dropping in for a sandwich, needing the coffee, the food, it had all looked random. This was because she had been dazzled by it. But now she was getting used to it, it was hard not to sit there and drift into gratified contemplation of the attractiveness of this new class, the international servants, all young, or youngish, or, if middle-aged, then middle-aged in the modern way with old age an enemy kept well at bay. It was easy to lose any detachment in admiration of the clothes, the cosmetics, the dramatic contrast of so many brown and pink and yellow skins. How harmonious! How consoling it all was: this was certainly how the future would be, assemblies of highly civilised beings all friendly and non-combative, amiably attentive to each other even if, during the actual sessions around the committee tables, they were locked in national combat.

The sexual patterns were, of course, the easiest to see —as always; the casual couplings and friendships that go with international conferences and committees.

The girls that worked in this place were middle-class, or upper-middle-class—"debby girls" as the phrase goes, as the phrase went, in fact. "We have all these debby girls," Charlie Cooper would say. "Absolute loves, they all are, what would we do without them?" They were here not to find husbands—heaven forbid, they would marry their own kind in due course—but to enjoy "interesting work." This meant the company of attractive men—and women, of course—from dozens of different countries and the possibility of being invited to work in one or more of these countries. As Charlie Cooper amiably complained, "Really, I sometimes think that what we are running here is a high-class employment bureau." It meant covetable escorts if not active affairs. As for the delegates who surged through this building in predictable and highly organised tides, these girls offered the possibility of the best kind of dinner and theatre companion, affairs without strings, the choice of secretaries of the most enviable kind to take back home (briefly, before Emma or Jane decided it was time to re-acclimatise) to their offices in New York, or Lagos, or Buenos Aires.

To sit here quietly, as invisible as she could make her-self—it was like the theatre.

A new committee was to begin sitting tomorrow—Synthetic Foodstuffs for the Third World. This was to be an altogether more modest affair than the big thing in Turkey, but the delegates were arriving by every boat from the continent. And behold, by eleven in the morning, all the secretaries and P.R. girls were arranged around the room, by themselves, or in couples, not looking at the doors through which would come their partners in sex or friend-ship for the next month or so. The delegates, of all sizes, colours, shapes, and degrees of good looks, arrived—mostly by themselves. The two teams (it was hard not to see them in sporting teams—*on your marks, get set, go!*) eyed each other. A skilled process this; age, degree of physical fitness, dress sense, probable sexual capacity, all judged in a few glances. Then began the process of intermingling.

"May I sit here? I am Fred Wanaker from New York."

"Miss Hanover? I am Hesukia, Ghana."

By the end of the first day, the couples had already separated off, or it was possible to see how they were going to.

As good as the theatre—better, since she was one of the players.

Even though she didn't want to be, for she was off to Istanbul, where she would be working too hard to have time to think; and she did not now want her attention dis-tracted—she knew now, she was almost certain, that she should have said *no* to Charlie Cooper and all the money

and arranged to stay in London, in a room, quietly, by herself. Absolutely alone.

Meanwhile, though her thermostat was set *low*, she
parried offers. The frequency with which some man, black,
brown, olive-skinned, or pink, offered himself with: "Is
this seat free?" made her switch a sight on herself from
across the room, as these men were seeing her. She saw, as
she had in so many mirrors, a woman with startling dark-
red hair, a very white skin, and the sympathetic eyes of a
loving spaniel. (Dislike of her need to love and give made
her call herself dog, or slave; she was aware that this was a
new thing for her, or she thought it was.) Yet this woman,
to whom so many men made their way, was twenty years
older than some of the girls. This meant that she did not at
first sight (across a room and so much coming and going
of people in between) look her forty-odd years. She was
in that state of eternal youth, to which such a large part
of the time and effort of womanhood is directed (or rather,
as she was thinking more and more often, was becoming
obsessed by, the womanhood of the well-off nations of the
world, who did not look old at thirty). If she observed
carefully, unblinded by personal vanity or prejudice, it
was noticeable that this approaching man, whatever age he
was, hesitated almost imperceptibly as he saw she was not
(which she must look from a distance) a fresh thirty. But,
having hesitated, having given her that skilled, professional
inspection (like a tart's, or a photographer's) with which
we sum each other up in such encounters of the sexual and
professional mart, he always sat down and seemed pleased
enough with what he found: which was an amiable companion for the coffee table. So it seemed that after all her
internal thermostat was obeying her orders.

But she was not here for this sort of pleasure—though

it was certainly pleasurable. She wanted to sit quietly, to relax, to think . . . She must do more than to regulate the flame so that men, having joined her, found her companionable. But what? Surely she did not have to leave off make-up, and wear old woman's clothes, and make herself ugly? (Kate was in one version of that female dilemma exemplified at its most extreme by the young girl who has shortened her skirt to top-thigh level, left all but two buttons of her blouse undone, and spent two hours making herself up: "That *disgusting man*, he keeps staring at me, who does he think he is?" Or the fashionable woman who has plunged her décolletage down to her waist and left her back bare: she gives the man who examines her delights a cold stare. "You are a boor," her eyelashes state.)

Well of course it was ridiculous to expect her, Kate, to turn herself into an old woman just because . . . Soon she discovered that if she wanted to be alone, she should sit badly, in a huddled or discouraged posture, and allow her legs to angle themselves unbecomingly. If she did this men did not see her. She could swear they did not. Sitting neatly, alertly, with her legs sleekly disposed, she made a signal. Sagging and slumped, it was only when all the seats in the coffee room were taken that someone came to sit near her. At which time it was enough to let her face droop to gain her privacy again, and very soon.

It was really extraordinary! There she sat, Kate Brown, just as she had always been, *her* self, *her* mind, *her* awareness, watching the world from behind a façade only very slightly different from the one she had maintained since she was sixteen. It was a matter only of a bad posture, breasts allowed to droop, and a look of "Yes, if you *have* to . . ." and people did not see her. It gave her a dislocated feeling, as if something had slipped out of alignment. For

she was conscious, very conscious, as alert to it as if this
was the most important fact of her life, that the person
who sat there watching, shunned or ignored by men who
otherwise would have been attracted to her, was not in the
slightest degree different from the person who could bring
them all on again towards her by adjusting the picture of
herself—lips, a set of facial muscles, eye movements, angle
of back and shoulders. This is what it must feel to be an
actor, an actress—how very taxing that must be, a sense of
self kept burning behind so many different phantasms.

A long way off she saw Kate Ferreira, in her thin
white embroidered linen dress, standing against the pillar
of a verandah on which were tubs full of white lilies. This
girl was smiling at some young men. She smiled at their
faces, but their eyes were all over her. Through the windows that opened on to the verandah from the living room,
she could see old Maria, her grandfather's housekeeper,
who sat crocheting in a position which would enable her
to watch Kate and the men. That day she had said to her,
"You should not sit with your skirt so high." The skirt had
slipped above her knee. The day before Kate had worn
scarlet shorts for tennis, and Maria had said she looked
lovely. Last winter Kate had observed this scene with her
own daughter: Eileen had been wearing a short skirt all
day, halfway up her thighs. That night she had on a long
dress, to her ankles. As she sat on the floor she noticed a
man look at her ankles: instinctively she pulled the skirt
down over her ankles, and shot the man a resentful glance.

That girl on the verandah, had she been "sympathetic,"
"a warm personality"?

Probably not. Hadn't those qualities been created by
the interminable disciplines of being wife, mother, housekeeper?

When she was in Turkey, if she were to behave as if she were invisible, with not only the thermostat switched to low, but with her "sympathy" switched off too, if she refused to be a tribal mother, what would happen then? Yet the really interesting thing was that she could swear the people who had engaged her had not any idea of why they were engaging her, why they were so very set on having her. This although Charlie Cooper, a man, provided exactly the same quality. So that meant he did not know why he was in his job?

One of the translators whose leaving had caused the crisis that had brought her, Kate, to sit here, was a middle-aged woman who, Charlie said, was "worth her weight in gold." Trying to elicit exactly what her qualities were, Kate could get out of him only that "older women have much more patience than young ones."

At the committee for which Kate had translated there had been a woman delegate, a black woman, from North Africa. She was tall, elegant, witty, chic, cool, distinguished. Her clothes were sometimes the robes of her own country that made her look like a gorgeous bird, and sometimes from Paris: she was different from Kate; both women would have said they had nothing in common. Yet it was noticeable that when she was absent from the committee, things did not go smoothly. Her manner—so indifferent, so sharp, so smilingly unsympathetic and not in any way dedicated to oiling the wheels—had nothing to do with it? She had supplied to that committee the same quality as Kate did for its organisation and peripheral problems.

If she, Kate Brown, were to become a permanent employee of this organisation, what would her real function be? Well of course, for one thing, she would spend inordinate amounts of time talking to Charlie Cooper and drinking coffee with him, and in conference with men talking about how to organise this or that. Working.

If she did stay, then it was likely she would soon inherit Charlie's job, while he, as seemed to be the law, would be promoted upwards. She would fit his job; but he, higher, probably would be uncomfortable, at a loss, feel out of place, but never know why this was so.

What he was good at was to be the supplier of some kind of invisible fluid, or emanation, like a queen termite, whose spirit (or some such word—electricity) filled the nest, making a whole of individuals who could have no other connection.

This is what women did in families—it was Kate's role in life. And she had performed this function, together with the beautiful young woman from Africa, for the committee that was now over. She was going to fill the role again in Turkey. It was a habit she had got into. She was beginning to see that she could accept a job in this organisation, or another like it, for no other reason than that she was unable to switch herself out of the role of provider of invisible manna, consolation, warmth, "sympathy." Not because she needed a job, or wanted to do one. She had been set like a machine by twenty-odd years of being a wife and a mother.

In a corner of a restless noisy room sat a collected figure, female, holding in well-tended but overcompetent hands that day's newspaper, her eyes lowered, her shoulders rather hunched: they were set to withstand the sort of cold a living animal must feel if its skin is ripped off, or the cold a new lamb feels emerging from the wet warmth of a belly, dropping onto frozen ground in a sleety wind.

It would be easy to hold the cold wind off, of course: she could do it indefinitely. It would be easy for years yet. All she had to do was to say to her family—news that they would greet, she knew, with relief—that she had decided to take a job. And then find the right kind of job. Here, probably, why not? What could be more useful than to work for Global Food? Then she would nourish and nurture in herself that person which was all warmth and charm, that personality which had nothing to do with her, nothing with what she really was, the individual who sat and watched and noted from behind the warm brown eyes, the cared-for skin, the heavy curves of her dark-red hair.

But for three weeks, a month, she would be far too busy to think of these things: she would be caring for others. And by this time tomorrow—so she reflected on the eve of her departure to Istanbul—what she was feeling and thinking now, the results of three days' carefully guarded solitude, would seem pretty remote. The best she could do there, very likely, would be to remember that she *had* come to these conclusions, essential ones, and hold on to them. Even if she was not able to remember this for more than a snatched few minutes in every overfull day.

That night the dream came into her sleep again—the continuation of the dream about the seal. Now, because it had appeared twice, it was announcing its importance to her. She had half-forgotten the first instalment; now she must remember it . . . so she was worrying, even while the second part unfolded.

The seal was heavy, and slippery. It was hard to keep it in her arms. She was staggering among the sharp rocks. Where was the water, where was the sea? How could she be sure of going in the right direction? Panic that this was not the right direction made her swerve off to the right along a level place on the hillside, and she went on for a while, but the seal began to make restless movements, and she realised that she had been going in the right direction in the first place. Again she set herself to go north. The poor seal had scars on its sides: it had been humping overland to reach the sea, and had torn itself on rocks and on stony soil. She was worrying that she did not have any ointment for these wounds, some of which were fresh, and bleeding. There were many scars, too, of old wounds. Perhaps some of the low bitter shrubs that grew from the stones had medicinal properties. She carefully laid down the seal, who put its head on her feet, off the stones, and she reached down and sideways and pulled some ends of a shrub. There was no way to pulp this green, so she chewed it, and spat the liquid from her mouth on to the seal's wounds. It seemed to her that these were already healing, but she could not stop to do any more, and she again picked up the seal and struggled on with it.

Kate knew of course that she was about to be flipped from one suave impersonal Organisation into another, in a matter of hours, by means of a suave impersonal Airline. She was, like us all, acquainted by radio, television, films, with the international civil service and their manner of life. But it did not happen like that. On the eve of her departure the strike was definitely called off, and she was sure of her flight; by next morning there was another, of the administrative staff. Kate took the train to Paris where she expected to take a plane to Rome. In Paris she was told the roads to the airport were blocked that day by a demonstration of alien workers, mostly Spanish and Italian—she would be unlikely to get off the ground that day. She took the train to Rome. There it was a question of leaving one circuit of machinery—railways, to link with the other, air travel. There were traffic jams, muddles, all kinds of delay, but she was able at last to make the switch; rather late, however. In Turkey her surroundings were as she had expected: a sleek car took her, by herself, through people who could never expect to sit in such a car, unless their job was to drive or maintain it, and, shielded from her surroundings in every way but through her eyes, she talked French with the chauffeur. The hotel was like, in spirit and style, the building for Global Food. Her room was like the undemanding box she had left. But because she was late, having been so much delayed, she arrived at the same time as the incoming delegates—a thousand small necessary things had not been done, and they were a translator short. She did no more than see her luggage to her room, then presented herself: irritation focussed on her; she was now personifying the spirit of inefficiency about which all over this vast hotel the delegates were complaining—just as she had been complaining yesterday and the day before, in London, Paris, and Rome.

A whole floor had been given to the conference. The large room in which the deliberations would be held was like the one which she had just left, and which she was almost thinking of as "home." It was fleshed in shining wood from ceiling to the floor, which, however, was not thick carpet, but tiles, whose pattern was copied from a mosque. In the middle of this room was a vast table, this time rectangular, set with headphones, switches, and buttons. It was now her task to see that each place was equipped with paper, for doodling and scribbling during fits of boredom when delegates spoke too long, and with pencils, and biros, and water. Or rather, she did not do this herself: she was making sure that the hotel employee whose responsibility it was had not forgotten. His name was Ahmed, a young man, fattish and pale, invincibly agreeable and smiling, her counterpart, her ally, her brother. He spoke French and German and English; was happy she had what he lacked—

Italian and Portuguese; he knew everything about the hotel trade, but had not before assisted at a Conference—or rather, while he knew business conferences, expected this one would be different. They conferred in this language or that. When a boy in braid and buttons came up to Ahmed, Kate heard Turkish in an order being given and taken. She had not heard that language spoken since she had arrived in the country. Sitting and talking with Ahmed, standing and talking, walking and talking, making plans for other people's comfort, she heard Turkish, as it were, out of the corners of her ears—noises offstage, no more. All around her, outside this hotel, was a world where her ears, when they were actually and at last exposed to it, would be suddenly dulled and uncomprehending: the language she did not know was around her like panes of badly cleaned glass, opaque, painful; her ears, as if rebuked, would strain after the exchange of two maids in a corridor—they felt they ought to understand, and if they did not, it was their fault . . . without Ahmed, she would be like a bit of useless machinery.

He had the necessary experience of night life, restaurants, dancing girls, mosques, churches, and suitable short trips out of Istanbul—useful in that order. The city, viewed from hundreds of feet in its air, but in brief glimpses, was all an enticing glitter of roofs and silvery water, and streets which were, like the Turkish language itself, far away, and energetic with a life she felt she ought to be reaching after, understanding . . . a bird flew past at eye level as she stood at a window. It was one she had not seen before. She felt that subtle approaches were being made to her from an unknown world and she watched the bird cross the water fed from the Black Sea to spires and domes on another shore, while Ahmed waited beside her for an answer to a question about eating preferences. By the time the last of the delegates had descended from the skies, entertainments, excursions, cultural delights of all kinds, not to mention the great dishes of a dozen nations, were waiting. And already being enjoyed, for these men and women seemed minimally fatigued, so experienced were they all in this business of crossing continents, arriving delightfully dressed and nonchalant, chattering together in a score of languages. It was clear that this was going to be a good-humored, well-tempered conference. They were liking each other. After all, they always did, these administrators, these so bland antagonists, these tactful interpreters of national interest. For no matter how much they expressed disagreement when sitting around vast tables, and how forcefully they pressed their own country's claims, or even accused each other of double-dealing—*It was Nation X who put the beetle in that season's crop to ruin our trade!—No, it is obvious to the whole world that your crop got the beetle because you weren't growing it properly—You won't allow anybody but your own country to benefit—you always hog everything!—On the contrary, we want to help our unfortunate brothers in the poor countries*—yes, exactly like so many quarrelling children; but no matter how much and how often all this went on, afterwards in the lounges and the bars and the coffee rooms and the restaurants, not to mention the beds, all was understanding and fraternity. Of course; for these people did the same job, spent their lives in exactly the same way—they had everything in common.

That evening Kate joined a sightseeing group of these well-travelled people who, however, had been unfortunate enough not to have seen Istanbul before, and the moment she left the hotel found herself in a city of legend, mystery, and romance, exactly as the guidebooks described it in all the languages she spoke and many she did not. The group was Madame Phiri, a handsome and very French black lady from Sierra Leone, a Mr. Daniel from Brazil, and a Mr. Ferrugia from Italy. They had dinner in a Turkish restaurant, for this was the least that was expected of them, visited two night clubs where they saw belly dancers and sword swallowers, and agreed that very soon these same four would visit a village fifty miles off where there were some interesting antiquities newly discovered. It had been, they all agreed, as they parted in the foyer for the night, a particularly pleasant evening: they spoke like the connoisseurs they were. They then went to bed early—that is, before one in the morning—since the conference would start tomorrow.

Kate did have time before she slept to think of her Michael in—she believed—Chicago, where he was spending a few days with an old colleague who had emigrated to the States. She thought, too, of her four children. She noted that the pang that came with them was at once assuaged: she knew that she was already blooming, expanding, enlarging—she was wanted, needed; she was going to be in demand all day and most of the night.

And now, for the few minutes she had free every day she noted the slow rise of her euphoria—she watched it drily enough. And, since she was too busy to think for long, she could allow thoughts to enter which would have been too painful if there was time for them to invade: how delighted her family had been when she had said that she was busy with her conference in London and would not have time to pack and organise and arrange—and there had been the relief in Tim's voice when she had said, Oh darling, are you all right for Norway? I'm sorry, I am simply too busy to . . .

The fact was, the picture or image of herself as the warm centre of the family, the source of invisible emanations like a queen termite, was two or three years out of date. (Was there something wrong with her memory perhaps? It was seeming more and more as if she had several sets of memory, each contradicting the others.) The truth was that she had been starved for two years, three, more—at any rate, since the children had grown up. The fact that this had taken some time, that it had been a process, that there had never been a moment when she could have said: *now*, they're grown, it's done—was it because of this her memories were turning out to be liars? Of course it had not been the "real" Kate who had been starved. That personage had remained, as always—or at least in her better moments —quietly offstage, in observation that was more often than not humorous. But it had been painful enough, that deprivation; she had sat often alone in her room, raging under a knowledge of intolerable unfairness. Injustice, the pain of it, had been waiting for her all these last years. But she had *not* allowed herself to feel it, or not for long. She had instead carefully tended the image of the marriage (could it be called, perhaps, The Tenth Phase? The Fifteenth Phase?) that was the result of intelligent discussions with her husband. She had not allowed herself to get much closer to what she had been feeling than the humorous grimace. She could not bear to let it all assault her now. Some time she was going to have to! But now, luckily, she was too busy; how very flatteringly busy. Here she was, being smiled upon by chambermaids and waiters, by the hotel manager and the floor managers, by taxi men, and interpreters—and particularly by Ahmed, who adored her. Just as she adored him. Their relationship was that of two eunuchs in a harem. He supported her, understood everything, provided everything: she was unfailingly the one person able to cope with all the problems and needs of these difficult, talented, spoiled, used-to-being-waited-on children, the international administrators, the new elite: she, with her twin Ahmed. While the conference went on, she was in a room nearby, waiting to be of use; and when necessary she was in her little booth, ready at a gesture to switch from French, Italian, English, converting them into Portuguese—all the Portuguese speakers had come to her, congratulating her on her absolute fidelity to the spirit of their language. At coffee and drink breaks, at mealtimes, everywhere, at all hours of the day and night, there she was, the ever-available, ever-good-natured, popular Kate Brown.

During the summer before, on her visit to the States, she had observed her own present condition . . .

All over that continent are repeated variations of a building like a small town, but under a single roof, and these are sometimes miles-long and subdivided into sectors, each self-contained, each of which serves an airline. Some of the large airlines employ girls like the drum majorettes that are used at conventions and carnivals. These girls, dressed fancifully, and in arresting colours, patrol the area alongside the check-in desks of their airline. They are supposed to give information and guidance, and do, in fact, offer these services, but this is not their function. Which is, quite simply, to attach the idea of easily available and guiltless sex to that airline. Not a challenging or difficult or complex or mysterious sexuality—God forbid. The girls are attractive, but not very sexual. They have been chosen for their friendly perky daylight sexiness, and there they are, in ones and twos and threes, walking up and down, smiling, smiling, smiling, and, as you watch them (while the hours pass: if, for instance, your plane is late in leaving) they slowly become inflated, with a warm expanding air. They are intoxicated—but really, literally—with their own attractiveness, and by their public situation, dressed and placed where they will draw so many eyes towards them, and by their own helpfulness. They smile and smile and smile, and soon it looks as if these girls will one by one float off and up, carried by their own expanding gases of goodwill, which are being constantly replenished by so much attention. Yes, off they will float through the airport windows, and bob smiling around the sky like weather balloons among the ascending and descending airplanes. And inside the aircraft are girls in exactly the same condition: the air hostesses, every one of them intoxicated by her position as public benefactor, a love supplier. This isn't true of the big airlines, the international lines, where the girls are working hard supplying attention and love in the form of food to their customers, but all over America the small, brisk aircraft flit, day and night, supplied plentifully by girls with nothing much to do. They offer drinks. They lay before you, with tenderness and intimate smiles, trays of packaged meals. They send loving messages through the intercom: "We love you, we need you, please come again, please love us." And they walk up and down, up and down, smiling, smiling, being admired by men and by women. Their business is to be admired. As they move about displaying themselves, the fever rises. At the beginning of the flight a girl is fresh and radiant with general friendliness, but soon she seems ready to explode with the forces of attention she has absorbed. She is blown up with it; she probably has a temperature—she certainly looks as if she has, with flushed cheeks and glazed excited eyes.

And she smiles. She smiles. She smiles.

One can imagine that when she gets back to her room after a flight she is restless, can't sit down, can't sleep, can't stop smiling, can't eat. She is too stimulated, she can't switch herself off. If she has a man, what can that poor nothing's love be compared to what she has been receiving from dozens of men all day. And imagine what happens when this victim marries! Which of course is bound to happen very soon: the marriage rate is high in the profession, like the divorce rate. But for one year, two years, three years—at the most half a dozen—that girl has been on show, the focus of hundreds of pairs of eyes, all day; every minute of her working time a receptacle for admiration and desire and envy, the producer of warmth, comfort, attention. Then she marries. It must be like walking off a stage where a thousand people are applauding into a small dark room. Very likely she has no idea at all of what is making her feel like a top that has been whipped and whipped—and left to spin there for ever. She cannot have been introspective or self-aware; for such a girl must necessarily be naive, to be prepared to do such work at all. Never during her entire life has this thought come near her: the monstrousness of putting up a girl to be a target for public love—drum majorette, airline advertisement, hostess—for months, or for years. She marries because to get married young is to prove herself; and then it must be as if she has inside her an organ capable of absorbing and giving off thousands of watts of Love, Attention, Flattery, and this organ has been working at full capacity, but she can't switch the thing off. What is the matter with her? She has no idea. Why does she feel so irritable, why can't she relax, rest, sleep? She is like a child the grownups have been admiring but now they have got bored with her, they have turned away and started talking and forgotten her, and no matter how she dances, and smiles and poses and shouts, Look at me! Look at me! they seem not to hear. At last they say, "Be quiet. Run along and play."

She has headaches. She is frigid and then makes frenetic love to a man who feels as if he has a rival. Soon there is a divorce. Probably she enquires for her old job, but she is too old. She has lost her easy puppy vitality, and her place has been taken by a girl just out of college.

It would soon be the middle of July. The conference would end in a couple of days, when the delegates would scatter while others came in: the hotel was to accommodate a conference on cholera.

Kate was smiling, smiling, in the beam of other people's appreciation, turning the beam of her own readiness outwards to warm everybody else; the thought that soon now she would be alone caused her reactions to become exaggerated. She knew it. It was panic. The smiling beam was too strong. Or perhaps that was not it: she was offering what she had available, as she had been doing since the start of the conference, but now it was too strong for a situation where they were all thinking about how they must pack up and go. She saw herself, through the reactions of Ahmed, as an efficient, high-powered, smiling woman, but spinning around and around on herself like a machine that someone should have switched off. He offered her cachets for headache, confessed that he suffered himself—at the end of such an event as this, he could not sleep, and his wife complained. Kate showed him pictures of her family; he showed her a quiet well-arranged woman with a stiff little girl on her knee; the taking of that photograph had been an occasion, Kate could see. This scene took place in an interval of work at the top of some stairs, standing up at a window. For Ahmed could not sit down, like a guest, as she could; just as she accompanied the delegates everywhere for meals and excursions, but of course Ahmed could not. So now she stood, with Ahmed beside her, and listened to how if she went to bed early tonight having taken this medicine, she would be less nervous in the morning.

Kate thought that this would not be true: what was waiting for her, the moment she gave it a chance, was not going to be patted and pushed out of sight by sedatives. She was going to have to return to London, to be alone somewhere for two months, and to look, in solitude, at her life. Of course, she had been invited to various countries by various men and women whose good friend she had become —friendship in the style of this way of living, casual, non-demanding, tolerant, friendship that was in fact all negation. It did *not* criticise. It did *not* make demands. It took no notice of national or racial differences which, inside these enchanted circles, seemed only for the purposes of agreeable titillation. And it was sexually democratic. Hearts did not get broken. Of course not, careers were more important than love, or sex: probably this was the sexuality of the future; romantic love, yearning, desperations of any kind would be banished into a neurotic past. Such friends, such past or future lovers, could part in Buenos Aires after intensive daily contact, not exchange another word for months or years, or even think of each other; and meet again in Reykjavik with discreet and carefully measured pleasure for another bout of adjusted intimacy. Rather like actors and actresses in a play, who suffer or enjoy such intense closeness for a short time and then scatter, to meet again, wearing different costumes, ten years later.

Perhaps she ought to go to Sierra Leone with the charming Madame Phiri? Why not? Or she could stay here; she had not done much more in Turkey than eat very good food in many restaurants and see two mosques and a church. But Turkey is not a place for a woman by herself. If this had been Paris or Rome, then perhaps . . . She would not be able to drive to inland cities alone here, or rather, she could not, equipped with her kind of personality, that of a long-married woman, without a man beside her.

She was in the hotel lobby waiting for Madame Phiri, who had asked her to arrange an appointment with a hairdresser. Of course, the hotel staff could have, should have, done this; but dear Kate was so clever at getting things done.

She stood waiting, while people went past nodding and smiling. Dear Kate. Chère Katherine. Sweet Katya, Katinka, and Kitty. Darling Katy, my own Cationa. Lovely Katlyn, Caterline, Kit, and Catherine. Ekaterina my love, my angel Katy. Karen, I don't know what I shall do without you.

I shall miss you, Mrs. Brown.

She was smiling, smiling, while she was humming, but silently, inside herself, not without hysteria:

I shall miss you Mrs. Brown!
How I shall miss you Mrs. Brown!
You have fed me, you have led me,
You have given me all I wanted,
But now you are supplanted
And I shall miss you Mrs. Brown. . . .

She was having to wait considerably longer than she had expected for Madame Phiri, who was saying goodbye to someone many floors above, when she noticed a young man whose face she recognised coming up to her: before she knew it he was inviting her on a trip to Konia with him the next day. He had hired a car.

They had seen each other first a week before, outside this hotel, on the pavement. He, a slight dark youth in a pale summer suit, was standing with his back to the rush of the traffic, looking up and down the height of this hotel as if measuring it. He looked as if he was a guest of the hotel, even a delegate, for his pale-suited elegance put him beyond the mass of casually clothed summer tourists. Later she had seen him in a café. He was at the next table with a group of young people, and some conversation had been exchanged. Now he was dressed like a tourist, and looked hot. His dark hair, which was cut to be smoothed back, and shining, was in loose locks. And he was not a youth; she had been misled. He was telling her that he was American, was visiting Europe by no means for the first time, and that he planned to go soon to Spain, where he was always at home. She could believe that: he looked Spanish, and in any Latin country he would seem a native.

He was not staying in this hotel, he said: it was far, far beyond what he could afford. So his asking her to go with him tomorrow could not be an impulse, but something planned? He was saying that having seen her at the café, he had deduced—after all, that was not so difficult!—where she was likely to be, had made enquiries, and here he was. At the same time as he was offering his casual impulsiveness: "It would be so lovely if you did have the time, it would be such a pity to waste the free place in the car," his eyes engaged hers in mockery—of the situation, of himself —and were not at all anxious. For of course there would be only the two of them in the car. Her duties would be ending this evening—formally, that was; she had no doubt she would be kept busy until the last minute if she allowed herself to be. She said she would like to go with him, even as the image of Mary Finchley suddenly appeared and told her she must be out of her mind. In obedience to Mary, she was about to put limits to her acquaintanceship with this young man—not so young as he looked, just as she did not

look as old as she was—but here came Madame Phiri sweeping towards them, all long lithe brown limbs, and immensely
long jewelled fingers fluttering her fervent apologies at
keeping Kate waiting.

Kate saw the young man's scrutiny of the beautiful
woman. It was not concealed, or apologetic, or ashamed of
itself; it was not aggressive, but an honest appreciation,
which she acknowledged by the faintest of amused smiling
nods before she swept on and out of the foyer: "Kate,
darling, I'm going to be so late . . ."

"Very well," said Kate. "And I don't know your name
yet."

It was Jeffrey. And he said he would ring her that
night, making a step forward into having claims on her
with the same straightforward honest declaration of intentions, or at least desires, given the chance, with which he
had gained a smile from Madame Phiri.

They never got to Konia. The trip (which was hot,
uncomfortable and lengthy, because the car broke down
twice, and then, finally) brought these two people rapidly
"together," as they say, precisely because of the many discomforts, and then because of wondering whether to get
onto a bus and continue, or to hire another car. Which
discomforts, or something like them, of course the young
man had been counting on, and expecting her to count on,
when he had suggested it. He did not mind about not reaching Konia. She did but not much—it was really very hot,
very dusty. They sat talking in the back seat while the
driver left to organise other transport.

They talked about him. He was in advertising and
publicity, New York, born in Boston. He was good-looking, intelligent, amusing, educated. He also had the attractions of non-conformity: four years ago he had decided to

leave what he was only too prepared to mock himself in calling "the mammon of advertising," thus sending himself up twice, once for being a part of mammon, and once for turning his back on it, which he had done after only three, but highly successful years. It was the success, the ease of it, that had terrified him more than anything. So he had "dropped out." Not to indigence, and hippiedom, already rather dated, for he had considered himself too old for that. And he had well-off parents. But he had turned his back on a career and a way of life. Since then he had spent much time hitchhiking and tenting around Europe. He was now thirty-two years old.

It was clear to Kate, listening as she would to one of her sons, that he was full of disquiet and conflict. The "dropping out" had not been a final decision. His decisions were ahead of him. It was all very well to "drop out" at twenty, or at twenty-five. All very well to live with a girl he fancied or who fancied him through a summer on Mount Shasta—he had done that; or in Vermont—he had done that. All very well to live on his dead grandmamma's money; he hastened to point out that it was "his" money and not his parents'. But he was over thirty. He did not know how he wanted to live: that was the essence of it. Like the Lord only knew how many millions of young people—which did not include, thank goodness, any of hers, or not yet, unless Tim was going to turn out like that—he did not know what to do with himself. Young people, that is, of affluent countries, the rich third of the world. The young people of the uneducated world, the hungry world, did not have choices. They had to grab and steal and starve to live. Not knowing how to live was a prerogative of the rich youth of the world.

All of these ideas he had elaborated in his dry amusing

way during the trip to Konia, and then in the back seat of the car while they watched the traffic swirl past to Konia, and then while they sat on the side of the road—it was too hot in the car. It was not until midafternoon that their driver got a lift for them back to Istanbul in a taxi driven by a friend of his. The taxi was very old. It bumped and jerked. They drove through a settling haze of yellow dust which inflamed an already wonderful sunset. He talked. Then they went to a restaurant. It had to be a cheap one, since he was asking her out, and he was not currently the employee of an Organisation. After the restaurant there was a nightclub, where he ignored belly dancers and singers, and talked, and talked. Kate listened. Above all, she was a skilled listener. While he talked she wondered whether she was going to decide to go to bed with him or not. She exchanged in imagination ribald remarks with Mary. She knew that the men who would have made approaches to Mary, had she been here, would in no way have resembled this young man. Mary would not—she would certainly say this with a rather brutal impatience—have looked at Jeffrey. There you go again, Kate, Kate imagined her saying. What's wrong with you? For God's sake, if you are going to get yourself screwed, then do it!

If Mary had been in this hotel, there would have presented himself in her room late one night a doorman or waiter or porter or perhaps even a fellow guest; they would have noticed each other in a corridor, a lift, a lobby; signals would have been flashed. After a night which Mary would pronounce on favourably—her instincts were infallible—she would not think of him again. Or: "There was that man I saw on the beach at Hastings," she might say. "I told you, did I? Well, *he* was all right!"

Kate was agreeing with the ghost of Mary; she already

knew that this lover, if she decided to turn things that way, had chosen—a listener.

This was the time for thought on a subject she did not think very much about . . . but here was a lie, another. False memory again. She must consider, honestly, the place infidelity had had in the successful and satisfactory marriage of the Michael Browns.

The blueprints of their defining conversations had in fact matched with the realities—well, to a point. The small ironical grimace did not have to do with the gap between formula and what happened. Or did it? Kate felt as if one pattern of memory was jostling another out of her mind; meanwhile she persevered with the one she was used to. This was a happy and satisfactory marriage because both she and Michael had understood, and very early on, that the core of discontent, or of hunger, if you like, which is unfailingly part of every modern marriage—of everything, and that is the point—had nothing to do with either partner. Or with marriage. It was fed and heightened by what people were educated to expect of marriage, which was a very great deal because the texture of ordinary life (surely that was a new phrase? It had supplanted an older one? What had they used to say, that life was a vale of tears?) was thin and unsatisfactory. Marriage had had a load heaped on it which it could not sustain. All of this had been thoroughly discussed right back in the beginning. No, not exactly in "Phase One," dedicated to delight, nor perhaps in "Phase Two" . . . she was belittling both of them when she mocked their youthful naiveties; they had not reached Phase Three, let alone Phases Ten or Fifteen—they had very soon grown out of such solemnity. Very well then, but it was not long after marriage, to the credit of them both, that they had agreed not to blame each other for not filling the deep hungers. What, then, did they hunger for? They did not know; they were always too busy to ask themselves.

There was the crisis when Michael had fallen tormentedly in love with a younger colleague at the hospital. By then the marriage had accommodated very many strains and surprises. It was ten years old; the children were born. This affair had been so shattering to the emotions of Michael and Kate, if not to their intelligences, which were quite easily understanding everything that was happening, that it was not repeated. Or rather, not in that form. Later she had understood—he had allowed her to understand—that he was having, occasionally and discreetly, and with every care for her, the wife's, dignity, affairs with young women who would not be hurt by them: affairs of the kind that blossomed among the delegates and the machinery of conferences in the great Organisations of the world. She had accepted it, and with not more than a tolerable pain. The pain was more what some part of her which she felt she ought not to approve of believed was owed to the situation. But the marriage continued quite well. To the surprise of them both, since they were surrounded by divorcing couples, marriages which had not been able to withstand an infidelity . . . at this point, the pattern of Kate's thought, or memories, quite simply dissolved. Some of it was true: they had been right in making sure they did not expect too much from each other, or from marriage. But for the rest—the truth was, she had lost respect for her husband. Why, when he was doing no more than "everyone" did, men in his situation? But she was feeling about him, had felt for some time, rather as if he had a weakness for eating sweets and would not restrain it. He was diminished; there was no doubt about that. She felt maternal about her husband; she had not done so once. To have fallen in love, and painfully—that she could understand, she had done the same herself. But to arrange his life, consciously and purposefully, as he had done, "clearing it" with her, of course, while he did it, so that he might have an infinite series of casual friendly sexual encounters with any young woman who went by—that made him seem trivial to her. And the way he had been dressing and doing his hair—when he came back from abroad somewhere, the first time, having tried to turn the clock back by at least fifteen years—she had suffered a fit of trembling anger and disgust. Soon, of course, she had been persuaded—not least by what Michael was not saying so much as indicating—that she was envious: it was petty of her.

But from the time she understood that this was what he was doing, and that this was what she could expect until old age did for him—unless, like a granny who dyed her hair and wore short skirts so that people could admire her legs, still unchanged, he would keep on till he died—she felt that her own worth, even her substance, had been assaulted. There was no explaining this, but it was a fact. Because her husband—who was in every possible way a good and responsible husband—had decided to experience an indefinite number of "affairs" that were by definition irresponsible, and would have no point to them but sex, she, Kate, felt diminished. She would have preferred him to confess—no, insist, as his right, on a real emotion—a real bond with some woman, even two or three women, which would deepen and last and demand loyalty—from herself as well. That would not have made her feel as if a wound had been opened in her from which substance and strength drained from her as she sat in her house in South London, knowing him to be (only in the intervals of his real work, his real interests, of course) pursuing this or that sexual titillation. She felt about him—against all reason and what her carefully constructed blueprints told her she could feel —as if he had lost his way, had lost purpose.

It was stupid to feel like this. It was unworldly, it was unsophisticated, it was ungenerous. She knew what Mary would say if she told her: that it didn't matter. But she did feel like this. She wasn't going to pretend she felt anything different. A few days ago she would have said that whatever emotions, or thoughts, or new blueprints of truth were standing offstage waiting for the chance to come on —once she had decided to stop being so busy nannying other people, talking, smiling, smiling, smiling, and now busy in the foothills of a love affair which she already felt she had to climb, like the kind of mountain peak that everyone has to climb who is interested in mountaineering at all—whatever these truths were (and she was so afraid of facing them that she was doing everything possible not to) they surely could have nothing to do with the fact that her Michael had trivial affairs by the dozen with anybody he could? *That* loss had occurred years ago. But perhaps this is where she should begin (when she gave herself time for it!) her feeling, childish, irrational, but absolutely undeniable, that because of Michael she felt like a doll whose sawdust was slowly trickling away.

She was feeling like this now, as she watched the young man sitting in front of her, leaning forward in his desperate need to receive from her—from anyone who would give it—whatever it was that kept him talking, talking, and not seeing her at all; after all, she had already done this climb, older woman, younger man!

Popular wisdom claims that this particular class of love affair is the most poignant, tender, poetic, exquisite one there is, altogether the choicest on the menu. With the possible exception of its counterpart, older man and girl. (If she was going to have this affair, the one in front of her, the one on her plate, was it because of Michael? Her will-less, drifting behaviour, not being able to say no, not being able to do what she would, was because she had been set in motion, like a piece of machinery, by Michael?) Popular wisdom was right. But she had done it already. The ingredients had been perfect: she had been thirty-five, he, twenty. And it had been secret; not a soul had known. It had been marvellously frustrated by circumstances, bittersweet, doomed—the lot.

It was Goethe, or rather Goethe as interpreted by his alter ego Thomas Mann, who said that the kiss was the essence of love. He had "wormed it" enough in his time, he said; but it was the kiss that was the thing.

One has to be a married woman of thirty-five with a husband and watchful children around every minute of the day and the night to achieve the circumstances where a kiss has to be enough. No, there had in fact been a delicious weekend, achieved at the cost of God knows what organisation, and arranging and lying, but looking back, it was certainly not sex that had been the thing. For apart from anything else, no sane woman goes to a boy for sex, an area where ripeness is all: her sex life with her Michael was everything fantasy would choose. Or it had been . . . what was it now, then? Physically admirable, of course. Emotionally? But why should that matter? Mary would have yelled with laughter at the suggestion that it should. (She was thinking more of Mary now than she did when she lived opposite to her.) The fact was, sex with her husband, these days, now that she knew that his sexual realities were in the so-carefully-planned-for adventures with girls, was something that—not bored her, no, but which certainly she was becoming more and more reluctant to have at all. It was like being faced with a heavy meal when you aren't hungry . . . it was not that her sexual appetites were less—or were they? If they were, why did she feel as if to admit it would be confessing failure? But what she did have an appetite for was something in the past, that time when she and the marriage—what he still found in marriage and in married sex—had been his need, his aim: what he was then making sure he would get, despite children, the weight of household management and care, in spite of everything. Once upon a time she had known that her husband's life had been sustained by her, by what they found together, and the centre of that was bed.

This affair, staring her in the face, certainly would not be a question of delicate emotions and rare anguish. This youth was too old. He was too worldly. He was too self-critical.

But she liked him. And he was so very amusing, particularly when being consciously tormented by the multiplicity of his choices of life style, by the texture of ordinary life, by this vale of tears.

But that night, they separated by mutual consent: his demand to come up to her room was being postponed to the following night.

She went to bed alone, thinking that in rooms all around her delegates were saying goodbye to each other, after weeks of pleasant sexual or other companionship: delightful goodbyes no doubt, as she would have been doing too, had she been like Mary . . . Jeffrey was too young for her; no, too old; at any rate, he was not the right age. Twenty to twenty-five—yes, he would be "young man" still, to her twilight condition. From thirty-five on, he would be nearing her status "agewise," to use his jargon. But thirty-two . . . should one judge people by the attitudes expected of them by virtue of the years they had lived, their phase or stage as mammals, or as items in society? Well, that is how most people have to be judged; only a few people are more than that. He, at thirty-two, according to the laws of his society, ought to be obsessed by "making his way in the world," by making a satisfactory marriage if he had not done that already, by starting a family. He was doing none of these things, but he was not free of what was expected of him. And he was seeing it as a straight choice, an either, or: "Either I take a proper job and get married and make a home and have children, or I go on drifting about. Half my friends have jobs and wives and children; the others have no responsibilities and refuse to acquire them. Which shall I be? Freedom or the gins and traps of commerce"—there was something old-fashioned about him, about his dilemma. This was because he could have a job if he chose: he did not have to be among the legions of the unemployed. And he had a private income still.

But she certainly did like him.

She ought to go straight back to England, ask for a room in a friend's house . . . or rent a room for herself—of course, that was it, in friends' houses she would be occupied again, every minute of her time, helping and nannying— and sit quietly and let the cold wind blow as hard as it would.

She was feeling dragged, as if by an undertow—this was something to do with her husband, but why blame him? She could not go on blaming him for what she was, what she had become—she ought not to go to Spain with Jeffrey, she ought not to go to bed with him. She already knew that Jeffrey Merton, in retrospect, when she looked back, would seem to her all dryness and repetition. But she did not seem able to summon up the effort to return to London, find a room, and stay there quietly by herself.

She dreamed as soon as she went to sleep. She was sitting in a cinema. She was looking at a film she had seen before—had, in waking life, seen twice. She was watching that sequence of the poor turtle who, on the island in the Pacific which had been atom-bombed, had lost its sense of direction and instead of returning to the sea after it had laid its eggs, as nature ordinarily directed, was setting its course inwards into a waterless land where it would die. She sat in the dark of the cinema and watched the poor beast drag quietly away from the sea, towards death, and she thought: Oh the seal, my poor seal, that is my responsibility, that is what I have to do, where is the seal? As she thought this she knew she was dreaming, and in the dream searched about, as it were, for the other dream, the dream of the seal; for while she could do nothing for the turtle, who was going to die, she must save the seal, but exactly as if she had strayed into the wrong room in a house, she was in the wrong dream, and could not open the door on the right one . . . where was the seal? Was it lying abandoned among dry rocks waiting for her, looking for her with its dark eyes?

The next day she spent helping delegates with the business of returning to their families; she did not really have to do it, her time was up, but her nature demanded that she should. On the night after everyone had scattered across the world, she joined that class of hotel guests who slip from their own rooms into others; returning discreetly before the sun rises and the corridors admit the maids in to work.

She spent the night with Jeffrey, and agreed to go with him to Spain for the month of August. Madness of course to go to Spain in August; but then it was madness to move around Europe in August at all. Sensible people did their travelling in adjacent months. But it would be easy to go into the interior of Spain, avoiding the coasts. There they would find waiting the *real* Spain, which was indestructible, according to Jeffrey, who knew it well.

The Holiday

On the 31st of July she walked out of the tall, gleaming, multinational hotel in Istanbul, thus leaving, in one step, the world of international organisation and planning, of conferences, of great Organisations—the atmosphere of money, invisible but so plentiful it is not important. The coffee and cakes she had eaten before leaving the hotel had cost two pounds, but she had never thought of asking the price. On the pavement, she was already in energetic altercation in three languages with the taxi driver, who showed signs of wanting to overcharge her by a few pence.

She had with her one suitcase, for she was adept at packing in small spaces, because she had spent so many years buying and packing for four children of that class of the world's citizens who have the best of everything, and from all over the world, available on the counters of their local High Streets. She had given some of her new smart dresses to Ahmed for his wife, having ascertained they were the same size: from the trembling incredulity with which he handled these garments, mixed with only just-controlled resentment—not at her, she hoped, but against circumstances—she saw how much tact and self-control had gone into Ahmed's working with her for the past month.

She stepped onto the aircraft wearing a shocking-pink dress that was in discord to just the right degree with her dark-red hair, and with a white skin that could not tan— already provocative where everyone was brown by nature, or getting brown as fast as possible. She carried *Paris Match, Oggi, The Guardian, Time, Le Monde.* Jeffrey had *The Paris Tribune, The International Times, The Christian Science Monitor.*

By the time they had read their own and each other's newspapers, they were in Gibraltar, and in a couple of hours were sipping apéritifs in Málaga.

Again her ears were painfully reproached, by the Spanish much more than by the Turkish, since she knew the language closest to it. All around her were languages being spoken that found their way easily into her understanding: outside this central stage of drinkers and waiters was Spanish, but in offstage mutters again; the Spanish were extras and bit players on their own coasts.

Ever since early June that sun-loud coast had been filling. It was now so loaded that one could easily imagine that if seen from the air the peninsula must seem pressed down and the waters rising around it—the blue of the Mediterranean on one side, the grey of the Atlantic on the

other. Soon these millions would submerge with their coloured clothes, their umbrellas, their sunglasses; their hotels,
nightclubs, and restaurants.

At a table between a tall hibiscus bush and some plumbago that was moth-grey and not blue in the artificial
light, a couple who were turned away from the crowd, and
demonstrating their preference not to watch it, from time
to time touched hands, even held hands. Once or twice
they even kissed; but lightly, even humorously, certainly
decorously. They might have been observed, too, giving
many glances and indeed long looks away from each other,
not into the crowd of which they were a part, but away
and down on to a beach where flocks of many-nationed
young people were playing. Not *in* the sea, no; that, alas,
had become too problematical a pleasure; the waters that
glittered so appropriately with moonlight held too many
questions. Flesh was being withheld from it. Or almost.
One or two did swim there, making their statement of
confidence, or of indifference: to submit one's body to the
waters of these coasts had become a manifesto; one could
deduce people's attitudes to the future by what they chose
off a menu, or by whether they decided to swim, or to let
the children put their feet into the sea. In a restaurant a
man would order a dish of local fish with exactly the same
largeness of manner and a glance which circled the room,
I am feeling reckless tonight, that once would have gone
with an order for champagne in a restaurant that didn't
take champagne for granted. A girl who walked into the
sea on a warm morning would draw glances and grimaces
and shrugs: *She isn't afraid, that one. But not for me. I
wouldn't take the risk.* But if bodies were being withheld
from these warm waters where once people had swum and
played half the night, now the youth of a dozen countries

danced to guitars for hundreds of miles along their shores.

The glances of this couple were definitely wistful; he because he wished he was part of the scene, she because she was thinking of her children. She also watched the man, in the way one does watch someone else's longing—only too ready to offer ointment and comfort, if one felt that could help.

He was a slightly built young man, good-looking but not remarkable, for his colouring classed him with the natives of this coast, brown eyes, sleek dark hair, olive skin. It did, that is, until he spoke.

The woman, older than he, was the more striking because he fitted so unobtrusively into the scene. She was category Redhead. She had dead-white skin. Her eyes were brown, like grapes or raisins. Her face was humorous and likeable, and around it her hair that was so beautifully cut and shaped and brushed lay in a solid sculpted curve, so thick that looking at it put a weight of reminiscent sensation in the palms of one's hands. Rather, that is what the amorist might have felt; the waiters knew what that haircut had cost, what her clothes had cost, and were automatically extending their expectations to a large tip.

This couple might have been observed . . . this couple were indeed being observed, closely, expertly. They had been minutely observed at the airport, when they descended from the plane, and then on the little bus where they had sat side by side among their fellow passengers from the plane, and then from the moment they booked in at the hotel. Their room had been reserved by telephone from Turkey by Global Food. They had been examined, ticketed, categorised, docketed, by experts whose business during the summer months was to do nothing but observe and weigh their visitors.

Which visitors fell, roughly, into three categories. First the package tours, the groups that had been parcelled up in their home countries—Britain, France, Holland, Germany, Finland—had travelled as a unit by coach or plane, lived as a unit while here, and would return as a parcel. These were the most predictable, financially and personally. It was enough for a hotel manager or waiter to give such a group five minutes' skilled attention to understand, and "place" each individual in it. Then came the category *international youth*, who moved up and down the coast in flocks and herds, like birds or animals, in an atmosphere of fierce self-sufficiency, of self-approval. These were decorative, always provocative of violent emotions—envy, disapproval, admiration, and so on—but on the whole pretty nonrewarding financially: they could, however, be counted on to grow older and join groups one, or three. The third and smallest class was that which once all travellers had been—the lone wolves, or couples, or families travelling together and making their own arrangements, their passionately individual arrangements. These, for those experts in the tourist industry with the temperaments of philosophers or gamblers, were the most rewarding, because they might turn out to be anything, rich or poor, eccentric, criminal, solitary. It was among these, of course, that occurred most of the love-couples—that is, if you discounted "the youth" who were by definition bound to be in a state of love, or sex. And, of course, the couples who travelled together without being married were more numerous than they had been. Just as, not much more than five or ten years ago, bikinis or even bare knees or bare shoulders had been banned, and by public notice and order at that, even on beaches and terraces—the *guardia civile* marching about to make sure these orders were being obeyed—and now all these don'ts and can'ts and prohibitions had melted away under the pressure of Money, so too had dissolved that silent NO which had made it difficult for unmarried couples travelling together to simply enter a hotel and order a room. It had been possible; it had been done, but with much discretion and often deception on the part of the unwed. Now, up and down that red-hot coast, during the months of bacchanalia, while "the children" frolicked and loved on the sands—or, if they were gamblers by temperament, in the warm, treacherous, increasingly odiferous waters, sometimes copulating as openly as cats and dogs—it had become normal for a hotel manager, a good Catholic and a good family man, who would in his own life, from his own choice, refuse to speak to a woman suspected of such a crime, throw his own daughter out if she dishonoured him by making love unwed—this man welcomed into his clean and honourable premises, his beds, his bars, women with men not their husbands, would smile, bow, chat, wish them good day and goodnight and a good appetite, with never an inflection of disapproval, not a shadow of reproach—well, just the slightest shadow perhaps, a *soupçon*, enough to suggest that the pressures of economics might be forcing this on him, but at least he (the manager) was still aware that it was immorality, even while he was housing and feeding it. So much honour and propriety remained to him—all this he might convey, in nuances so slight the couple could choose not to notice it at all.

This couple had been classified as an immoral one by these experts in the social condition.

They had also been classed as that time-honoured pair, older woman, younger man. The desk clerk at the hotel had been surprised at the large difference in age, when he had taken in the passports, to write down details for the police files. They were not a frivolous or an embarrassing couple; they behaved with taste and discretion. But there are conventions in love, and one is that this particular sub-classification—older woman, younger man—should be desperate and romantic. Or at least tenderly painful. Perhaps —so those unwritten but tyrannical values of the emotional code suggest—a passionate anguish can be the only justification for this relationship, which is socially so sterile. Could it be tolerated at all in this form, which was almost casual, positively humorous—as if these two were laughing at themselves? They were indifferent to each other? Surely not! For their propriety was due to much more than good manners—so decided these experts, whose eyes were underlined with the experiences of a dozen summers, enabling them to flick a glance over such a couple just once, taking in details of class, sexual temperature, money. Perhaps this was after all not a pair of lovers? They could not be mother and son—no, impossible. Brother and sister? No, one could not believe that a single womb had produced two such dissimilar human types. They were an unlikely marriage? No, their being together lacked the congruence of mood and movement by which one recognises the married—and then, there were the documents, at the desk. There was nothing else, they must be lovers.

So they were judged, as being in a category which demanded the utmost in tolerance from this country, whose own standards were still strict—men still owning women's sexuality, and as eccentrics within that category. They seemed to be non-loving lovers, though they did seem to pay homage to their condition by holding hands, or with a light kiss. It was this that caused the slight chilliness, the reproach, of the waiters—(who were, of course, unaware that they showed these reactions)—which was

sixties, there had been a pride, a dignity; there had been a readiness to proffer small services, unasked, without wanting money; there had been a dimension in the Spaniards, even on the already developed coasts, which went far beyond commercialism. There was a humanity in ... a stature ... a depth ... He began to laugh at himself, when she did. There were tears in his eyes, certainly not for the Spaniards.

As for her, she had come by car with her husband and the four children, for a prolonged camping holiday—she found this hard to say, but made herself—getting on for twenty years before. They had been among the very first tides of tourists. Along this coast, now loaded with hotels and holiday camps, had been nothing—nothing at all. Sand in which some thin grass grew stretched from headland to headland; camping under the pines, they had seen no one for days at a time. She too had memories of all sorts of spontaneous kindnesses from the natives—she was more than able to match his words—dignity, pride, and so on and so forth.

She started to tell how, in those days, when the rare foreign car came into a town, an army of young men and boys would fight to earn sixpence for keeping watch on it for the night; how, when the Browns ate their frugal-enough meals in restaurants there would be a dozen hungry faces pressed to the glass, so that the Brown children had their fairy tales illustrated for them—those where the poor little boy gazes in at riches, but is noticed, and is brought inside by the kind family, or compensated by a fairy god-mother—sometimes by being taken away altogether from his poor streets into heaven. She was telling him of children in rags and without shoes, children with sores and with flies crawling on their faces and into their eyes, children with the swollen bellies of malnutrition. But as she talked she was thinking how once and not so long ago these things had seemed like surface symptoms, soon to be corrected by the use of a general common sense, they had not yet presented themselves as the general condition of man which would soon worsen and darken everywhere. She was thinking how once talk of this kind sounded almost like a blueprint for a better world, or like a statement of concern. Now it sounded like callousness. In a moment they, Jeffrey and she, would be outbidding in each other in that most common of middle-class verbal games: which of them had acquired more grace by being close to other people's sufferings.

That was not her own thought: it was her son James's. He got into a fury whenever poor people anywhere were mentioned—usually by Eileen, or by Tim, who engaged themselves in welfare work of different kinds. James saw the solution as simple: it was revolution. Anything less was insulting to the suffering poor, and a waste of time. The classic revolution—like Castro's.

But the four children had all evolved their own positions, quite different from each other's. They had evolved, too, individual attitudes towards tourism, towards travelling so indefatigably in so many countries.

Stephen the oldest was in advance—it was a way of looking at it—of them all. His attitude that all governments were equally reactionary left him free to travel everywhere, exactly like the selfish and the indifferent, whom he spent much of his time attacking. Eileen, uninterested in politics, travelled without scruples of conscience, like Stephen. James had a more difficult time than any: for instance, he would not have visited Greece, but had visited Spain last year because he was, he had said, adding to his political education, regarded Israel as too fascist to enter, but had travelled with equanimity through the military dictatorships of the Near and Middle East. Tim believed the end of civilisation was close, and that we should shortly be looking back from a worldwide barbarism formalised into a world-bureaucracy to the present, which would from that nasty place in time seem like a vanished golden age: he made journeys like someone tasting the last bottle of a rare vintage.

As for their mother, here she sat with (there was no other word for it, she supposed) a young lover, drinking apéritifs on a terrace in Spain: they were going to a bull-fight tomorrow because he adored them. For aesthetic reasons.

Before the two went to their room they descended to the beach along paths scented with oleander, sun oil, and urine, and stood on the same level as the throng of youngsters, their feet in churned sand. It being late, and the half moon standing up high over the sea, and the crowds much thinner along the terraces, some of the young ones had put themselves to bed for the night and lay in each other's arms—anywhere, in the shelter of a rock, on a stretched towel, on sleeping bags. Reed mats had been laid on the sand, and on these some still danced, their hair flowing, their eyes gleaming and drowsy. Near the sea's edge a group sang to a guitar played by a girl who sat on a rock like a mermaid.

Kate was now careful not to look at her companion; she knew that he would certainly, in the state of emotional sensitivity he was in, resent it: already she was making comparisons with her own children's reactions. But she was remembering—not her youth, no, that was too far off and too different to be matched with this context. She was thinking of that time ten years ago when she had been in love with that boy. *That* pain, a longing after something beyond a barrier of time, matched with what he was now feeling. She had lived through and out the other side—well, she had had no alternative. So, of course, would he. But despite what people said about the poignancy of that class of experience, and what she said herself, she did not like remembering that time. It had been false memory again, she had dolled it up in her mind, making something presentable of it to fit the convention "older woman, younger man." But really it had been humiliating. Yes, looking at all these beautiful young creatures, all moving, or lolling, or sleeping in their postures of instant grace, she said to herself that that time had been horribly humiliating. The reason had been simple, and why old Goethe (or Mann) had talked of "worming it." Long marriage, long, gratifying sex, had absorbed sex, the physical, into the ordinary and easy expression of emotion, a language of feeling. But the boy had had practically no sexual experience, understood only fantasy, the romantic. Her sexuality for him had been horrifying—or would have been; she had, of course, damped it, learning that the conversations of the flesh were for the mature, learning, with the first inklings of unease, of her dependence on this long married conversation. She had felt when with him as if she had a secret or a wound that she must conceal. Young, as that girl in a white dress (another convention, like an old-fashioned portrait: "Girl in a White Dress with Lilies"), a kiss had seemed a gateway into a world which had in fact turned out everything she had imagined—until she had had to look at it through the eyes of a twenty-year-old from public school and English university, a virgin as far as women were concerned.

She knew that she ought not to add to her companion's wild misery, which was mixed with so much animal shame—like her own with that boy—by letting him know how easily she was able to share what he felt.

As they stood there, not twelve paces from the young ones, but absolutely separated from them, a girl went past, smiling to herself, and dragging naked feet in the sand for the pleasure of the sensation. She glanced at Jeffrey; the smile was blotted out while she presented to him a blank face, and went on, smiling. Kate recognised that face: it was what one shows to someone outside one's own pack, herd, or group. She tried to put herself in the girl's place— she was about seventeen, with thin brown arms and legs and long black hair and what seemed like an absolute self-sufficiency—in order to see Jeffrey as a man old enough to be so looked at. She managed it with difficulty. So she herself had looked at men over twenty-five when she had been that age. She could just remember that the godlike creatures had had above all the glamour of responsibility, or power in the adult world. Returning herself to her own stage or stratum in the human community, she could see only a young man whose strength was all going into recognising his own weakness and not collapsing under it. He turned to her and said, "Good thing you are here or I'd be dragged back into it again."

At this most frank statement of why she was here, with him, her heart did give an obligatory gulp, or grimace of pain—but nothing much, for it was much too occupied with painful reminiscence for small considerations: the official memories of all kinds were wearing thin, were almost transparent. If she had been asked, let us say in late May, on that afternoon when her husband's casually met acquaintance had come to her garden—when the series of chances which had brought her here had begun?—if she had been asked then what scene or set of circumstances would be best calculated to bring home to her a situation, a stage in life that she *must* recognise, no matter how painful, then she might have chosen this: to stand on the edge of a mile of soiled and scuffed sand that glittered with banal moonlight, watching a hundred or so young people, some younger than her own children, beside a young man who—it was no use pretending otherwise—made her feel maternal. Almost she could have said: There, there, it will be better soon, and hugged him. She was actually thinking, like a mother, Off you go then, you'll have to live through this, much better if I am not anywhere around—except, of course, that I have to be watching and guiding from somewhere just out of sight. . . .

Their hotel was not in the glittering strip along the luxurious part of the little town. It was set back in the older part which in normal months was inhabited only by Spaniards. But they entered a foyer as lit and as lively as in day, for this was holiday month and sleep could be postponed. Couples of all nations sat about drinking. The dining room was open, and people were still at dinner—it was past one o'clock. The desk clerk handed the key over to Mr. Jeffrey Merton and Mrs. Catherine Brown without any dimming of his smile, but his body expressed offended disapproval without knowing that it did.

They ascended to a bedroom which was not the best the hotel had: she had a lot of money because of the highly paid job, but was scaled down to him, who was making sure that his grandmamma's money would continue to preserve his independence for him—none of it was invested, he had insisted on putting it into jewellery and pictures, which were in a bank's keeping. It was the kind of hotel she and her family might have chosen: unpretentious, old-fashioned. The room had a balcony, which overlooked a little public garden; from it came a gay churning music, the sound of voices. She went to stand on the balcony. He joined her. They kissed, expert lovers. He departed to the bathroom. Down in the moon-whitened street people sat on doorsteps, talking. Their children, even small ones, sat with them, or played nearby. It was warm and soft and the small isolated music intensified a general stillness. People had slept all afternoon and would not go to bed until the sky lightened. The town felt more awake, more flowing and alert than it ever did in the day. In the cities of southern Spain, at night, in the biting summer, another vitality awakes, holding together in a web of sociability that runs from street to alley to garden the cries of children, the barking of a dog, music, gossip. This is the time for sitting and watching, for talk, for living. From everywhere in the quiet dark, from the pools of light where the street was lit, arose voices.

Jeffrey had come back into the room. She left the balcony and went towards the bed to turn it back as he pitched forward on to it, prone. At first, her femininity rose and shouted that this was an insult: they had made love only once, and they were supposed to be lovers. Next, she found herself laying two fingers on his pulse and a hand on his shoulder, to assess his condition and his temperature. His flesh was hot, but then the air was. He looked exhausted. What she could see of his face was a beaded scarlet. His pulse was slow. She used all her strength to turn him over, to lay him in bed, to pull the sheet up. The flush was rapidly draining from his face: now he was pale, sallow. He might not have a temperature but he certainly wasn't well.

While her femininity continued to shout, or rather, to

make formal complaint, that it was outraged, and that she ought to feel insulted, she returned to the balcony, on the whole with relief. She fetched a straight chair from the room which seemed stuffy as well as unwholesomely dark compared with this light airy night over a street that still moved and laughed, and she put the chair in the corner of the balcony, and sat herself there. She wore a white cotton robe that left her arms and neck bare to receive what breezes there were. There she sat, in that most familiar of all situations—alert, vigilant, while a creature slept who was younger than herself. The block of moonlight on the balcony soon shifted. She moved her chair out of it, in such a way that her legs and arms might lie in it but her head would stay in the shadow—exactly as if the moon were a sun.

Some fifty feet down, on the opposite pavement, two men were talking. They were two papas, stout men, in creased light summer suits that from here looked dazzling —like the sand on the beach in moonlight. The creases showed black. Beyond them boughs waved: the square where the music had stopped. Occasional cars went past, noisy, saying that the music had been louder than it had seemed. In the intervals between the roarings and hootings she could hear the men's voices quite clearly. The Spanish was coming into her ears in lumps or blocks—unassimilable. It was a veil between herself and Spain which she could not pull aside. But it was a semitransparent veil, unlike the Turkish of only that morning. It had moments of transparence. The Portuguese that was in her, like an open door to half that peninsular, a large part of Africa, and a large part of South America, sometimes fitted over the sounds she was listening to, sometimes not. A language she knew nothing of, like German, was all thick and impenetrable.

But this listening to the Spanish was like seeing something through trees off a road one is rushing along. The conversation nagged, on the edge of meaning. When she leaned right over the balcony, receiving moonlight all over her, in a cool splash of white, so that she felt so prominent and self-displaying she could not prevent herself glancing this way and that along the face of this hotel—no, she was the only person out on the balconies—when she leaned right over so that she could see the gestures, the poses, the positions of the two portly bodies, then she was able to understand much more. A set of the fat shoulders, or a flinging open of a palm added to the messages sent out by the intonation—*almost* she was understanding Spanish. They were talking about business, that was clear. Yet she had not heard one word that told her this. Their voices were those of men talking about money; their bodies talked risk and gain. The shriek of a passing car swallowed the talk, spat it out again: it was a near intelligibility, like windows paned with sheets of quartz instead of glass. The voices stopped. A smell of tobacco. She looked over and saw them lighting cigars. The smoke drifted away in small mists and sank into leaves. One fat man went away; the other lingered, looking about as if the night might offer him a postponement of sleep; then he went too. In a few minutes they would be in striped pyjamas. The pale suits would be heaped on a tiled bathroom floor ready to be picked up by their wives and put into the wash. The men would be sliding into bed beside two fat pale women.

Darling! Chéri! Carissimo! Caro!

She inspected the bedroom, so dark because of this blaze of cold light outside. On the bed, her lover lay sprawled. She could hear his breathing. She did not like the sound of it. If he had been one of her sons, she would be thinking about calling the doctor in tomorrow—*she must stop this at once!*

It was getting on for four. At last the streets were emptying, though in the square people still reposed on benches, breathing in the night, dreaming, smoking. The steps below were empty now. But two children played quietly against the hotel wall, while their father sat by them on a stool, his back against bricks which were probably still warm. The mother came out and said the children should go to bed, and they set up a wailing protest; one did not need Spanish to understand what everyone was saying while papa was being stern, mamma exclamatory, the children clutching at the life their parents wished to bury in sleep. Then mamma brought out a chair and sat by her husband; one child sat on her lap, the other on his. The children were drooping in sleep; the parents talked quietly: hotel employees, from the kitchens perhaps? The cars were few now. The town was as quiet as it could be in these frenetic months of the tourist.

Kate was far from sleep.

She was tempted to slide into the big bed and sleep simply to avoid—what she had to do, at some point.

Besides, she was still able to savour moments like these, without pressures of any kind, after the years of living inside the timetable of other people's needs. She could still hug to herself the thought: If I don't go to bed until the sun rises it doesn't matter. I needn't get up till midday if I don't choose.

It had not been until three years ago that this freedom had been regained by her—of course, that was where she was going to have to look, at the time of the children's growing up. But she could have claimed the right to freedom years before. Years before. What about Mary Finch-

ley for instance? If she felt like staying in bed till mid-
afternoon she did, and shouted at the children to bring her
food or tea. In between Kate the girl who had married
Michael, and Kate of three years ago which was when she
had become conscious there was something to examine, the
rot had set in.

The climactic moment of three years ago had been
when Tim, then a tumultuous sixteen, had turned on her
at the supper table and screamed that she was suffocating
him. This had been wrenched from his guts, it was easy to
see that. All the family were present, everyone was shocked
—oh yes, they had understood that this was an event of a
new quality, destructive, which announced a threat to that
unit which they were; all had rallied into tact, smoothing
this moment of real misery and fright for both herself and
the boy. For it *had* been wrung out of him, and he was
shocked at the hatred he had shown. Normally, in this
well-tempered family—so they had thought of themselves,
well-adjusted, with effort spent to keep them so—such
conflicts were out in the open, discussed, bantered away.
Sometimes brutally. It could be said that the spirit of the
young couple's "Phase Two"—discussion to soften the
painful limits of "Phase One"—had been taken into use by
their growing family, years later. No one could have said—
who? Kate was imagining some sort of critic, a welfare
worker perhaps—that this was a family in which things
were smothered, hidden, and had to go underground.

Yet that the boy had had to crack himself open in that
way, before them all, and under pressure, showed that perhaps all the banter and psychologising and criticism was
not the healthy and therapeutic frankness she had imagined,
they all had imagined, but a form of self-deception? A
family *folie*, like the madness that encloses lovers who de-

stroy themselves. If there is a *folie à deux* then there is certainly a *folie à*—as many as you like!

Looking back at a typical family scene, during the adolescence of her four, she saw herself at one end of the table, tender and swollen like a goose's fattening liver with the frightful pressure of four battling and expanding egos that were all in one way or another in conflict or confluence with herself, a focus, a balancing point; and her husband at the other end, being tolerant, humorous—a little weary. But not really implicated, not involved, for he worked so hard, had so little emotional energy left over to give to the family, to the four children—monsters. They called themselves so: we four monsters. Five monsters: she had been so involved with their growing, the continual crises, their drive up and out from herself, all the emotions, that she had found it hard to separate herself from them. She still did. Yet the monsters' pressure on her, the insistent demands, had ended. Well, nearly, except for the youngest, Tim.

On that particular occasion she had retired from the table as soon as she could without it seeming as if she were a little girl going off to sulk or weep. Even so she had been like a cat or a dog that has been kicked inadvertently by a friend. She knew that as she went. She was conscious of five pairs of eyes deliberately *not* looking at her. She had gone to her room while the boy fled in shame because he had shouted, having kept his head down over his plate to finish his pudding.

In her room she had sat and thought, had tried to think, while emotions rioted. She had felt nearly crazy under the pressure of her old feeling: It's not fair, what do they expect of me?

It was her fault that Tim was very hard, on himself,

on the others—on her? The three others had stepped imperceptibly from being "children" into being adolescents. All stormy and problematical, certainly, but Tim's explosion into adolescence shook everybody. Everybody discussed, understood; much verbal display went on among these clever modern children. Tim was judged by them all to be more monstrous than any; and Kate as his victim. But the one thing that had *not* happened—she had to come back to this point again and again—was evasion, secrecy. During those years when she felt as if she were locked for ever in a large box with four perpetually exploding egos, she had consoled herself with: But nothing's being hidden, everything's being said. And she had contrasted her own family with others—not with the Finchleys, they were beyond comparison, they had their own laws—and all families with adolescents were like this. At the hub of each was a mother, a woman, sparks flying off her in all directions as the psyches ground together like pebbles on a beach in a storm. She had been overanxious about dominating, controlling, keeping them younger than they should be? She had been as anxious about giving them too much freedom, treating them like adults too soon—but perhaps that was the fault, and Mary was right, who never gave a thought to *how* she should behave—she simply followed her mood. But it wasn't a question of domination or not, it was all to do with involvement. She had been too involved with everything, had sunk herself into it too far, so that the children had not had some strong fixed point to rely on? But surely the man, the father should be that? Perhaps after all Michael had been right all the time, she had been wrong in criticising him: his degree of involvement had been the right one. For why should it be necessary for a mother to be there like a grindstone at the heart of everything? Looking back it seemed as if she had been at everybody's beck and call, always available, always criticised, always being bled to feed these—monsters. Looking back at her own adolescence she could see nothing similar. Of course, she had had a close, a very close, intimacy with her mother until she died, the year before the trip to Lourenço Marques; and her father had been away for most of the war, leaving the two, mother and daughter, together; but she could not believe it had been the same thing at all.

But what was the use of her sitting here balancing and sifting—making excuses? For Tim had cracked, shouting that she smothered him, she had made him into a baby, and the fact that this had not been just routine "love talk"—the family's own name for their criticisms of each other—was shown by everyone's reactions.

Very well, then, she had been too dominant with him.

But the remarkable thing was that just as now, sitting on this moonlit balcony, she was quite aware of her current situation, standing as it were on a cliff with the north wind blowing straight into her face that would strip her of flesh and feature and colour, then, too, she had been aware, right from the start, of the danger to the last of a family when he was growing up. Clearly it was not enough to *know* a thing, otherwise he would not have screamed out: "For Christ's sake leave me alone, you are suffocating me!"

All she had done was to tell him not to forget something, she couldn't now remember what—had that been the point, it had been the *what*, and not the *how* of it?—but she couldn't remember, that had gone. Gone because she didn't want to remember, had arranged the incident so it could take its place among her official memories, memories that had stood in her mind for ten, fifteen years; a quarter of a century? But certainly there *had* been a girl all vital energy and individuality, and much wider experience than most (for instance, there had been the year in Portuguese East Africa spent self-consciously, if not theatrically, as a *jeune fille*); a girl with the temperament that goes with being a redhead (she had been congratulated on possessing this temperament from her earliest girlhood, *that* she could remember very clearly); a girl who had stood out, she knew she had, wherever she was, among others, not only by virtue of that dramatic colouring, but also by her style and her manner—well, had any of that been untrue? She was deceiving herself in this description? She did not think so. This girl, much coveted by a variety of men, had married her Michael. After first living together for a year (Phase One). They had become an attractive young couple, and a centre for others not yet married, or soon to be married, or married and lacking their—charm? Personality? This marriage had, however, been offered up as a charming, almost whimsical sacrifice to convention; they had continued to behave like a couple living together, in love, loving, lovable. The first baby had altered this, but not much. The baby (now Stephen) had been fitted into the life of an attractive young couple doing things rather more vitally than others. The baby accompanied them to parties, had travelled with them, had not prevented her from attending a course of lectures on Saracen influence on Provençal poetry. It was true that to continue living as if there had been no changes, with the wakings in the night, and the having to get up early, and the always-being-bound to the infant timetable had been hard. But at the time this wrench in her habits had not seemed—as it did later—the important thing that was happening. When this first baby was a year old, she was pregnant. In the minds of both parents was the notion that they could continue living in this way with two children.

Anyone could have told them this was nonsense.

The real sharp change came not with the first but with the second baby (now a young woman called Eileen). With one baby they had been a young married couple, still radiantly paying unforced tribute to foolish convention, to social demands. With the second the emphasis had sharply shifted. Seeing how different their life had become, they decided to have the third "to get it over with," a very different spirit; and they soon had a house, a mortgage, a small car, a regular charwoman, a regular life, all for the sake of the children. It was extraordinary for how long this couple continued to think of all these extraneous objects, car, house, and so on, as having nothing to do with them personally—not for their sakes at all, but only because of their children.

As for Kate, she was acquiring hard-to-come-by virtues, self-disciplines. Looking back now at the beautiful girl, indulged by her mother, indulged and flattered by her grandfather, treated always with that very slightly mocking deference which is offered to girls, and contrasting her with the same young woman of only five years later, she was tempted to cry out that it had all been a gigantic con trick, the most monstrous cynicism. Looking back she could see herself only as a sort of fatted white goose. Nothing in the homage her grandfather paid womanhood, or in the way her mother had treated her, had prepared her for what she was going to have to learn, and soon.

With three small children, and then four, she had had to fight for qualities that had not been even in her vocabulary. Patience. Self-discipline. Self-control. Self-abnegation. Chastity. Adaptability to others—this above all. This always. These virtues, necessary for bringing up a family of four on a restricted income, she did slowly acquire. She had acquired the qualities before she had thought of giving names to them. She could remember very clearly the day when, reading certain words that seemed old-fashioned, in an old novel, she had thought: Well, that's what *this* is—getting up several times in a night for months at a time, and always good-temperedly; and that's what *that* is—not making love with Michael when a child was ill. And as for being a sponge for small wants year after year, so that anything that was not a child seemed a horizon too distant ever to be reached again—what was the word for that? She had been amused by big words for what every mother is expected to become. But virtues? Really? Really virtues? If so, they had turned on her, had become enemies. Looking back from the condition of being an almost middle-aged wife and mother to her condition as a girl when she lived with Michael, it seemed to her that she had acquired not virtues but a form of dementia.

On the morning after her youngest's outburst, it happened that she was out with a shopping basket in the High Street, and she was held up in a brief traffic jam. She watched a young woman walk up the street with a baby in a push chair. This girl, perhaps nineteen—about her own age when she had her first child—wore a brief skirt, had wild dark-red hair, green eyes, a calm energy. She looked, however, like a little girl playing at being mum. She was pushing the baby along with one hand while she carried a vast bag of groceries in the other. She strode along like a viking's woman. From this girl Kate had turned her attention to others. It seemed as if the street was filled suddenly with young women, unmarried girls, or girls with babies, and they all of them moved—yes, that was where you could see it, in how they moved—with a calm, casual, swinging grace, freedom. It was confidence. It was everything that she, Kate, had lost in excesses of self-consciousness, in awareness of the consequences of what she did.

Then, having most conscientiously absorbed the truth of these young women—it was painful, the contrasting of herself with them—she looked at the movements, at the faces, of her contemporaries. Twenty years was the difference, that was all it needed, to set these brave faces into caution, and suspicion. Or, they had a foolish good nature, the victim's good nature, an awful defenceless *niceness*—like the weak laugh that sounds as if it is going to ebb into tears. They moved as if their limbs had slowed because they were afraid of being trapped by something, afraid of knocking into something; they moved as if surrounded by invisible enemies.

Kate had spent the morning walking slowly up and down, up and down that long crammed street, taking in this truth, that the faces and movements of most middle-aged women are those of prisoners or slaves.

At one end of some long, totally involving experience, steps a young, confident, courageous girl; at the other, a middle-aged woman—herself.

Kate had then gone home and spent weeks watching herself move, talk, act, but from this other viewpoint, and had concluded, quite simply, that she was demented. She was obsessed, from morning till night, about management, about organisation, about seeing how things ought to go, about the results of not acting like this or of acting like that. Watching herself, listening to herself, she turned her attention to the women of her own age, who were her friends. All, every one, had had a long education in just one thing, fussing. (Not Mary Finchley of course. Not Mary. But she was going to have to understand what Mary meant to her, what she was standing for. Obviously one couldn't simply exclude her from every normal category

and leave it at that.) That was what all those years of acquiring *virtues* had led to: she and her contemporaries were
machines set for one function, to manage and arrange and
adjust and foresee and order and bother and worry and
organise. To fuss.

Her family, she saw now, were quite aware of it. She
was being treated by these independent individuals—husband, and young people only just free from the tyrannies
of adolescent emotion and therefore all the more intolerant
of other people's weakness—as something that had to be
put up with. Mother was an uncertain quantity. She was
like an old nurse who had given her years to the family and
must now be put up with. The virtues had turned to vices,
to the nagging and bullying of other people. An unafraid
young creature had been turned, through the long, grinding process of always, always being at other people's beck
and call, always having to give out attention to detail,
minuscule wants, demands, needs, events, crises, into an
obsessed maniac. Obsessed by what was totally unimportant.

That realisation had been three years ago. While continuing to run the large and demanding house, running
what she felt had become a hotel or resthouse for the family
and friends and friends' friends, she had tried to withdraw.
It had been an inner withdrawal, since it was hardly possible to announce her plan to do so without adding to the
family's irritation, to their feeling of being obligated to
herself, the servant who kept it all going. It was made
harder because her efforts were not noticed. Her husband
had been particularly busy, and she could understand that
he was arranging to be, for in his position she would take
any chance to expand out, to go out and away from the
narrowing of middle-age—he was older than she was, by

seven years. The children were quite naturally no more involved with her, her problems, than any healthy young adults are with their parents. But she found that they were always using mechanisms of defence against her in situations where she had been trying to make them unnecessary. She had been continually dragged back into—outgrown, she had hoped—patterns of behaviour by people who still expected them of her.

But why should she not announce to the family that she was going to change, was in the process of changing? She could not. They would see it as a claim on their attention, their compassion. As she would have done in their places—the point was, and here she was coming back to it again, it was all nonsense, the out-in-the-open discussion and the talk and the blueprinting and the making decisions to behave in this way or that way. (That was not how people changed; they didn't change themselves: you got changed by being made to live through something, and then you found yourself changed.) But if all those years of "love talk" had been any use at all, she now could have used it, could have said: And now, enough. I'm like a cripple or an invalid after years of being your servant, your doormat. Now help me. I need your help. But she could not say this.

Soon after the incident of Tim's screaming at the supper table, she had gone away by herself to visit old friends. She left her daughter in charge. She kept prolonging the visit, on all kinds of pretexts. She thought that if she could keep it up long enough, the pattern would be broken, the cage would be open—She went home earlier than had planned, because Eileen decided to go off on a visit of her own.

Even though she had almost at once slid right back

into what she had been flying from, she was able to look at herself, the worrying woman at whom the boy had shouted, as at a creature who had been really mad. Crazy.

That summer, the scene at the supper table, her going away, had been the begetter of this summer's event, for without them she would not have responded to Alan Post, not even with her husband's help—yes, his irritation with her for not leaping at the opportunity had been that. It is always a question, when in a cul-de-sac, a trap, of seeing what there is for you, one has to be listening.

But what had stopped her from saying that she wanted to take a room by herself somewhere in London for the months of summer? Nothing, except that it was inconceivable! It would have been so exaggerated a thing to demand that she wouldn't have thought of it; yet it was what, probably, she should have done.

She had needed a springboard.

She now sat on a balcony from which the moonlight had quite gone, looking up at a sky where stars stepped back into a cool grey, looking down into a street that was now really empty, at last. Now if she were alone, really alone, in this country, able to please herself . . . yes, that is what she could have arranged for herself; it had never crossed her mind, of course.

She could have sat here while the dawn came up, then slept all day if she wanted, then wandered about this town, which was after all a Mediterranean port, as well as being a provider for tourists. She could have wandered on her own will, and returned home in two months' time, by herself, having been really alone—that is, a person operating from her own choices.

But now she sat in a cool dawn, thinking that she should go to bed because he would wake up fresh just as she was ready to collapse in sleep. And unless she was very much mistaken, she would be faced with a man on the defensive because he had keeled over the night before and gone to sleep and not made love as circumstances and convention demanded. Almost, she was able to hope that he was a little ill—not much, just a little.

At the end of the street a man came into sight. He was fair, a northern man—a tourist, like herself. He had been on the beach with the youngsters? Drinking? Dancing? He had been sitting talking in a café? In one of the cool cellar-like bars? He came level with her balcony as the street lights went out. She saw him as a night figure caught out of his time by dawn: the sky was beginning faintly to flush and tingle. He was looking up at the sky. He was not young enough to have been with the young people. He was hardbodied, in strong middle age, and his face was lined. No, he was older than that, his hair was quite white, it wasn't blond: he was a Spaniard, probably just finished with some night work. He pushed his way through oleanders, and stopped at a fountain to splash water over his hands and face. He swallowed a mouthful or two by directing the flow with the edge of his palm straight to the back of his throat. Then he moved his hand so that the jet played on his lowered head. He shook his head energetically and walked to a bench and lay on it, his face turned to its back, away from the street and from observers. He was a poor man, then? Homeless? She was conscious of an upsurge of concern. This small spouting of emotion was like the falling tinkle of the fountain. Derisively she watched herself think, or feel, that she ought to go down into the square, and touch his shoulder—carefully of course, so as not to startle him—ask him if he needed something, offer help. In what language? She ought to learn Spanish!

The feeble spurt of emotion was the same as that which had led her, the winter after that dramatic scene with her son Tim, to take in a stray cat. Her emotions about this cat—while they had lasted—had been strong. She would not have been the product of all the years of "love talk" if she had not been able to say to herself: that cat represents me, is myself. I am looking after this poor cat because I feel I should be looked after. But by whom? By my family, of course! Who no longer need me, and who find me intolerable.

The family were aware of the cat's role, and her thoughts about it; aware of their part in it, their emotions. They had been humorous and indulgent. "Oh go on, you've taken in that smelly old cat just because we aren't being nice to you!"

"He's hit it on the head, mother. You're just *showing* us, that's all."

Sitting on that balcony, hundreds of miles away and over two years later, she wanted to spring up and shout out her rage and bitterness to them. At the time she had smiled, of course, been "humorous." Now she wished that she had slapped them hard, her delightful daughter Eileen, her charming Michael, Tim—all of them. "I wish I had hit him," she heard herself mutter. "I do, I wish I had hit them all hard!"

She had seen Mary Finchley scream abuse at her husband, at her children: afterwards she collapsed in laughter. She had done what she had felt like doing, at the time she felt like doing it.

The family had treated Kate like an invalid and the cat a medicine.

"Just the thing for the menopause," she had heard Tim say to Eileen.

She had not started the menopause, but it would have

been no use saying so: it had been useful, apparently, for the family's mythology to have a mother in the menopause. Sometimes she had felt like a wounded bird, being pecked to death by the healthy birds. Or like an animal teased by cruel children. And of course she felt she deserved it, because she disliked herself so much—oh, that had been an awful spring, to follow a bad winter; she had feared she was really crazy, she spent so much of her time angry. Then the two older ones had started to give their time entirely to university, to friends, and she had been delighted. Absolutely delighted, though of course she then felt guilty that she was delighted. Feeling guilty seems almost a definition of motherhood in this enlightened time. It was a lot of nonsense, it was all a lot of rubbish, all of it—somewhere along the line they have gone wrong—Who? Herself? Not the children, of course not! Society? But *why* so much tension and antagonism and resentment—it was over though. Eileen was busy with men; there was only Tim who still had his sights on her—that was how she felt it. So the nasty time was past. She looked back on it . . . but if that were really so, why was she here now, with this young man who Mary Finchley at least would have seen at first glance was going to offer her what she already knew, what she did not want . . . she did not leave the balcony until the sun's rim shot hot rays over the sea and into the town. She was really tired. Inside the room a blackness filled eyes that were adjusted to the day. Her eyes cleared and she saw that Jeffrey lay looking at her. She smiled, prepared for speech—saw that he was not really awake. He scrambled up, crouched on the bed, stared, a surprised animal, his dancer's limbs expressing the dream he must still be in, his face alert, suspicious, ready to turn itself aside. She said, carefully, "Jeffrey!" but he made a hot confused denying sound, and shot into the bathroom. She heard him being sick. She went on standing where she was, wondering if he would be awake when he came back. He came into the bedroom by dragging himself on the door frame, then the edge of a chest. He must feel himself alone, then: he saw her, lurched forward, clutched the bottom of the bed, stared. She was, she understood, outlined against the door onto the already dazzling balcony; she must seem a dark watching shape to him. At last he smiled: he knew he ought to know who she was. It was an effort, because he was three-parts asleep, but he was a polite person, he had been brought up to please, to offer courtesy. The smile was courtesy offered to a situation which demanded it and did not warm into pleasure. He manhandled himself into bed, and collapsed, asleep again immediately.

She sat by him in her white frilly robe that had on it the sweet coolness of the night air she had brought indoors away from this day's heat. She was swearing to herself that when she woke she would not be maternal, she would not suggest a doctor, she would not be concerned. Lying beside this young man, whom she knew was at the least "off-colour," if not ill, she tried to put herself into the frame of mind of a woman who had come here to be with him for love. Suppose that she were still "a love woman"—this was how she put it—and not a maternal woman, as a result of a quarter of a century's nursery work—if she were this "love woman" then how would she be feeling? That was easy—she had only to remember Michael. She would be waking Jeffrey to make love—she and her husband had enjoyed making love when she, but particularly he, had fever. He had tended to run temperatures for the least thing; and for years they had made the most of this con-

diment for eroticism—or so they had seen it. But she could
not imagine approaching Jeffrey erotically. For one thing
(as of course literature and all sorts of experts, marriage
counsellors and the like, could have told her) if a woman
is attuned well and truly for one man, then a new one
doesn't come so easily. (For which reason she had never
been able to believe in the easy pleasure of wife-swapping
and amiable adultery.) And after all, her sexual experience
had been with Michael, and, at second hand, through Mary.

Of course, if she had been madly in love as the occasion demanded, as even an aesthetic sense, a sense of the
appropriate demanded, she would not be lying here trying
to imagine herself erotic.

She leaned on her elbow and examined him with all
the caution of a mamma with sick child. He managed to
suggest, even while his flesh flung out heat, that he was
cold. There was a chill damp coming off his forehead. He
smelled sickly. No, not even a woman madly in love could
choose this moment to approach him. There was something
about his present condition which was antipathetic to sex.

It was of course possible, indeed, likely, that *he* was
antipathetic to sex, at least in his present mood of worry
about the future, or at least, with her . . . the degree of her
uninvolvement with him was confirmed by her coolness as
she came to this conclusion.

She fell asleep and was at once on a rocky hillside.
Yes, there was her poor seal, slowly, painfully, moving
itself towards the distant, the invisible ocean. She gathered
the slippery creature up in her arms—oh, she ought not to
have left it there. It was weaker; its dark eyes reproached
her. Its skin was very dry; she must get some water for it.
In the distance was a house. She staggered towards it. It
was a wooden house, its roof steeply sloped for snow

which—she knew—would soon fall, for it was already autumn. The house had no one in it, but people were living there, because in a tiny fireplace were embers of a fire that was going out. She laid down the seal on the stone before the fireplace and tried to blow the fire into life. There wasn't much wood, but she made the fire blaze at last. The seal lay quiet, its sides heaving painfully. Its eyes were closed. It needed water badly. She carried it to the bath house and splashed water on it from the wooden buckets that stood along wooden walls—the dream's flavour was still, was more and more, that of another time; myth, or an old tale. The animal's eyes opened and it seemed to revive. She thought that there were many things she must do: she had to clean the house, to fetch wood for the fire from the forests before the winter snow came down, to get food, to take warm clothes out of the chests and lay them ready for herself and for the people in the house who, she knew, were her family, but transformed and transfigured into myth creatures, larger than themselves, representing more than they were in ordinary life. In an upper room of the house she saw a tall fair young man with blue eyes. She knew him. He was her lover. He always had been. They made love. They had been waiting for years and through waiting and wanting made this love perfect . . . she remembered the seal. The seal needed her, was lying abandoned on the floor of the bath house, waiting for her. She left the fair young man who was a nobleman of some kind, perhaps a prince, saying, "I am sorry, I want to stay with you, but I must take the seal to the sea first."

She woke to find herself assaulted simultaneously by a blaze of sunlight and by Jeffrey, who was making love like a ten-year-old who has been dared by his gang to climb a high wall, or like a Soviet factory worker over-fulfilling a norm. While her experience—limited, as has been said—had not included love with an American, literature had of course acquainted her with American male sensitivities in this field. Besides, Mary Finchley had once spent a fortnight with an American airline pilot and had reported—in detail, of course. (There had been no need to listen, Kate had often chided herself.) But the situation last night had demanded sex; he had failed to provide it; his masculinity was now in question.

She thought of making a joke or two about conditioning—as he did, continually—but understood from his bloodshot eyes and his sullen body that on this subject jokes were not possible. It was six; she had slept for less than one hour. Now that his aggression was spent, it was clear that he was ill: they ought, as reasonable people, to part amicably and go their separate ways across the world?

Lying in a welter of now crumpled white frills, the very picture of a woman seductively dishevelled, she regarded a surly eighteen-year-old who, if he had any sense, would go to the doctor.

An effort of will enough to fuel a decent-sized moon rocket kept her from suggesting a doctor.

They had got dressed and were breakfasting on the terrace, which was already crammed, lively, multi-tongued, when, having had to depart to the lavatory three times, he confessed he had the tourist trots, and would go to the chemist.

She sat on alone and watched a man of fifty or so sitting against a background of plumbago with a girl of about twenty. He, like Michael, had his hair cut straight around neck and face without a parting, growing from a centre point at top back; on women it had been known as the urchin cut. Kate had worn it, but some time ago. The man's haggardly handsome, burned face, which was being kept ironical out of self-respect, wooed the girl's heart-breaking freshness; she was flattered, and rather bored. The man looked intelligent; snippets of conversation—in English this time—caused Kate to say to herself, Well at least *mine* is not stupid. She supposed she must be feeling ashamed? *Mon semblable*, she was silently addressing him, while she remembered that not more than twenty-four hours before, she had said goodbye to Ahmed, the world's servant, another facet of herself, whom she had addressed also, but privately, as *brother*. Somewhere in the States her Michael—urchin haircut, lean attractive face, experience—was probably protecting himself with irony while youth itself, capsuled in delicious flesh, sat opposite being flattered and bored. If so, Kate did not know him: she had never known him urbane, ironical—vulnerable. Nor did his woman have to be very young; Kate didn't really know what he looked for. Of course, Eileen was around, which meant he wouldn't be free to do as he liked; perhaps the young girl sitting opposite him was his daughter, and he was looking proud and cherished, as middle-aged men did with their female children. If there was one thing certain, it was that when Mary did this—had the affair older woman–younger man—there hadn't been any mysterious indispositions or sweet-sour mirror encounters on sunny Southern terraces with middle-aged gents and their popsies. Birds. Of course not. For about four years Mary had intermittently had it off with a waiter in a Greek restaurant. He had been about twenty-three when it began, was handsome, and "ever-so-keen," as Mary said. He had adored her. He was prepared to marry her, and wished to move in and become father to her three children. This being vetoed by Mary, they had conducted an affair remarkable for its good temper, its sweet reasonableness, and its mutual liking until he had gone back home to Greece.

When Mary had wept. This was the only time Kate had known Mary to weep. So even Mary paid tribute to the altogether high quality of this category of affair.

Jeffrey was easing his way through packed tables, cumbered with many packages: pills of all kinds. They spoke for some minutes of various possible plans, but he was looking critically at the holiday scene around him and soon he said that he wished to go inland, to the "real" Spain.

The question of money now confronted them. He did not have the money to fly inland, nor to hire a car. Coaches and trains were what he could afford and were what she, too, was committed to. Besides, she would enjoy them.

Beyond the terrace the beach still lay empty, ploughed by last night. Two men with great rakes were smoothing the sand ready to accommodate the young, who were all still in bed; though some lay asleep along the edges of the beach where it met the terrace wall. They, she knew, would not have any "hangups" about money; they shared what they had. The fact that Jeffrey could not take money without feeling it—as he said himself—in his guts, would have put him beyond "the children's" company, if nothing else did.

"There is a cheap place up the coast," he said. "And there are no tourists. You can get a room for a dollar a night."

He sat leaning back into the thin shade from the oleanders, his hand on his chest, as if protecting it, his eyes half-closed. Under his hand his chest was rising and falling very slowly, like a sleeping man's. He kept subsiding into long silences, while his other hand went loose on the table, even twitched a little—he was falling off into dozes and making himself wake again. A wasp settled on a minute patch of jam on his forefinger. He watched it for a while, then he shook the beast off in a movement enough to startle an elephant.

"I think you ought to go to bed and stay there till you are better." These words spilled out of her mouth, and he jerked his head up and glared.

"Why?" he enquired, cold.

Less than twenty-four hours after their arrival in Spain, they were again on a bus, rolling up the coast—north, and against the tides that flooded south. They were on their way to the unspoiled village. Not so much a village, he said, as half a dozen houses used by fishermen whose wives were happy to welcome travellers, and had to be persuaded to take money. They reached the place in late afternoon, to find a large new hotel, and the beach swarming.

Jeffrey, who had slept all the way, his head on her shoulder—a fact which she took care he did not suspect—regarded this scene without comment and got back onto the bus.

"But where are we going?"

"Up the coast. There is another place."

"Shouldn't we have supper first? Or perhaps go on in the morning?"

"No, no, no, it's just near here, it's only twenty miles, come on!"

He jumped back onto the old bus, now nearly empty, for it had already shed its load of working people who were going back to their homes across fields.

On they went. Down below, on their right, the Mediterranean's blue curved and looped against the brown coast, against the pale beaches which for mile after mile were filled with bodies.

Sometimes a woman who had been somewhere to visit a relative or for a day's shopping got in with a full basket. Children got in at one little town and got off an hour later on a hillside where there was not a house or even a light to be seen. They ran off into the dark holding hands, exchanging loud comments or information—the Spanish words, like unknown birds, flew away over the sea.

Jeffrey slept. At midnight they reached the end of the bus's journey. They were past Almeria, in a small town, a mile from the coast. There was a hotel which had not been done up for the tourist trade. The man behind the desk watched them register, but did not comment, and then showed them to the dining room where local travellers, not tourists, were still eating dinner. Jeffrey ordered one heavy dish after another, frowned as he lifted his fork in an attempt to convey the food to his mouth, but as the smell of it came to his nostrils, laid the fork down again. It was as if he had never heard of illness, or of the condition of being nauseous. He looked worried: why was it that his hand, as it were of its own accord, kept returning the laden fork to his plate? When the dessert came, he ate some peaches and called for more. She, having eaten well, this being her first meal of the day, watched him gulp down a fifth peach, and then bolt from the dining room.

She found him collapsed on the bed, the light glaring down on his face. His hand shaded his eyes as if he was in sunlight. Seeing her, his frown deepened. She saw herself in a green dress that left her white arms and legs showing, she saw her heavy curve of red hair, her warm brown eyes.

From under his hand he frowned at the stranger who stood smiling at the bottom of his bed.

"Jeffrey!"

"What do you want?"

"You need a doctor."

He turned his face over to one side, like a soldier ordered to look *Right!* and lay with his arms down at his sides, rigid. Then he flung his body over, dragging the sheet up over him as he did so. He was fully dressed still, even to his shoes. As for her, she was asleep at once, having slept so little the night before.

She woke early; he was up, throwing the pills the chemist had given him into his mouth in handfuls. At seven she was confronted by an efficient young man who said, "We'll go inland to Granada. We're close."

She agreed, of course.

But while she drank coffee and ate sugared rolls, and watched the wasps at work in apricot jam, he was avoiding the dining room, was standing with a glass of soda water in his hand conferring with Reception. No bus left here direct for Granada. They would have to return to Almeria, and find another bus. A full day would be needed for the journey.

He came to the door of the dining room to call her out: he was, she could see, protecting all his senses from the presence of food. He had decided to go on up the coast. There was a good place further on; he remembered it well. Obviously, the effort of returning to Almeria in one bus, and then hanging about to wait for another, and then a day's journey inland—all this was too much. Yet he had to be in movement. That was what he needed, she could see.

"We'll go to Granada later," he announced, and car-

ried her suitcase and his to the bus that stood waiting to go
north, up to Alicante, which city it would reach about
three in the afternoon. But they would not actually get to
Alicante, for the village he remembered came before Alicante.

This bus was full of the country's inhabitants, not of
tourists, though there were one or two young people from
the coasts, travelling cheap. It was a gay companionable bus-
load; people talked and exchanged news, though of course
she could not understand, she understood nothing. It really
was the oddest experience, odder even than the absurd
situation she was in with this young man whom she could
not leave because he was ill, or breaking down or something, and who was obviously determined to go on riding
north indefinitely along the garlanded summer coast: for
weeks, a period which had ended two days ago, as she had
to keep reminding herself, since it seemed such a long time
ago, she had been like a multilingual machine, and all the
languages, or most of them, spoken around her had been
like doors or panes of glass. Before she had arrived in Spain
she had even imagined that the competence of the world
of conferences would follow her, would have imbued her
in some way, so that she would find herself effortlessly
speaking Spanish; but she was like someone waking from
a dream in which she has been flying, unable to believe
that in reality she can't just step into the air and soar off
and away. It seemed almost as if she *did* understand it; as
if she had at one time understood, and was suffering tem-
porary amnesia. On a smile from a woman across the aisle
of the bus, or when the driver came around to collect fares,
she opened her mouth to speak—her brain shuffled the
phrases of other languages to find a useful one, her tongue
was useless in her mouth. She had to stretch the muscles

that moved her lips into a smile to communicate willingness to love and share. And she sat listening, listening, to the heavy sounds that would not give up their meaning—until she turned to look, taking in meaning as it was easy to do, from gesture, and from the set of a head, a shoulder. Meanwhile, as she sat like an invisible person in this chattering and laughing crowd, Jeffrey, who had gone to sleep again at once, slid down in his seat and lay heavy against her.

At midday the bus allowed a longer pause than usual so that passengers could get a drink or a sandwich. She left him lying there, found herself lemonade, smoked a cigarette, and returned to find the driver examining the sleeping young man. He pointed down at him, indicating his sick look. She nodded, and smiled, her tongue paralysed, her ears *almost* receiving. With a final shake of the head the driver went back and started the bus. It was abominably hot now. Everything shimmered and dazzled and both she and Jeffrey were soaking. His sweat had a sallow smell to it, and he was very pale, with a yellow tinge. Jaundice? But with his colouring he would be bound to look yellow in illness.

They reached Alicante in mid-afternoon and Jeffrey woke. He was wet with sweat, and shivering. But he was determined to continue north. She took him by both shoulders and said, "You are sick. Do you hear me? You are ill. You've got to let me put you into bed and get you a doctor."

He pulled himself away, as if she were a spider web he had walked into, or a snag of wood he had caught a sleeve on. He walked to a bus that stood nearby and got into it, without looking to see where it was going. She stood wondering whether she should call for help—who? The police?

Instead she lifted the suitcases that now stood on the curb, their bus having turned itself around to return along the way they had come, and carried them to the second bus. The fact that this super-polite American had let her carry heavy suitcases and had not even noticed it said everything about his state.

The bus had a board which had a name on it; she had no idea where it was going, or how far. But did it matter? She bought soda water from the café and took it to the bus. Jeffrey drank the liquid, but in the now familiar way of someone with a connection arrested in his brain, like an animal at the same time very hungry and conditioned to find food disgusting or dangerous. He kept bringing the glass up to his lips in a frantic thirsty way, swallowing without thought—then holding the water in his mouth with a look of agonised suspicion. He swallowed the water as if trying to remember what he had been told about it—something terrible!—then his hand took the glass up to his lips again, fast, desperate. In this way the soda water got drunk, and he did not bring it up. So he wouldn't collapse of dehydration, that was something. He fell back into the seat. It was even hotter now. The streets were empty, for it was siesta time; the cafés, and the benches around a dusty square, were full of somnolent people. The town was crushed by the weight of heat, and when the bus started it was almost empty.

Now Jeffrey sat limply jerking and sliding with the movements of the bus. It had resumed a northwards progress, but after half an hour, it turned inwards from the coast. It seemed that he did not notice the Mediterranean no longer accompanied them. But after a time he said with a pleased smile, "Oh yes, this is the way, I remember, the village is here." The bus was driving through flattish land which was lightly cultivated. Then it began to climb through low hills. Now that they were lifted up the sea appeared behind them, a distant blue plain. Then it was gone, the hills concealed it. They were on a rough unmade road on the side of a hill, winding up. Jeffrey sat jogging, jerking, dozing. She kept her arm around him to keep him upright. Once he woke, not out of the sullen personality of a sick man, but having returned in sleep to an earlier one, who had chosen her as a companion. He smiled delightfully into her face and said, "Kate! Isn't this just great? Isn't it wonderful? Isn't it just . . ." But he drooped off to sleep again.

The sun was coming into the front part of the bus. What passengers there were moved back, and the driver was trying to keep his head shaded by lifting it and holding it back in the shade under the roof, his chin up: he looked as if he were holding it out to receive a blow.

The sun went behind a range of hills, much higher than those they were driving through. It was already early evening. At a village that looked as if it might be in North Africa—poverty-cracked houses, poverty-shaped people— the bus stopped, dropped a wire cage with some thirst-crazed fowls, a barrel of sardines in oil, a crate of oranges. It picked up two nuns, who looked fatigued to the point of illness by the heat, and waited for Kate to return from a café with more soda water for Jeffrey. Then it drove on into the interior.

Kate was now quite passive. Quite soon, clearly, this awful journey would end. Not because Jeffrey wanted it to end: he needed to move, to be going somewhere, to be travelling—she could feel that, understand it. But he was by now a bit lightheaded: he kept waking into moments of gaiety, he chattered, he giggled, then fell abruptly into a doze. Even he would soon be forced to see that he was ill and must stop. Or some driver would refuse to take them on any farther. At eight in the evening, with a moon swelling towards full flooding everything, they stopped in a village square. It was a small place. There was a fountain trickling some dispirited water into a basin that had a cracked white china cup, lying on its edge. There were some dusty trees. A building across the square looked as if it might be a café; there was a large window covered across from inside by some material, to exclude the sun, and two tables stood outside where men sat drinking. There was also a solid-looking old-fashioned building that said it was a hotel. She found the village on her map. They were about fifty miles inland.

She left Jeffrey sitting in the bus neither asleep nor waking, and went into the hotel. The manager came out of the dining room where he had been at table; she indicated in various languages that she was travelling with her husband, who was ill. French released her, and Señor Martinez came with her to the bus, and helped her pull Jeffrey out. It was like handling a bundle of clothes damp from the washing machine: he was so wet that his hands were slippery and his hair was soaked to his head. They supported him upstairs—there was no lift—and laid him on a small bed in a room of the kind common anywhere in Europe. It had a double bed for mamma and papa, and three smaller ones, for the children.

Señor Martinez went out and returned in a moment with a bottle of mineral water: a good family man, he did not have to be told that this young man was in danger of dehydration. He supported Jeffrey, and she held glass after glass of liquid to his lips. He drank avidly, but with a look of furious distaste.

Señor Martinez departed to say he would try and reach a doctor.

"But you must understand, madame, il faut que vous comprenez, oui? This is a small village, it is a place without resources, we do not have a doctor here—pas de medicin, oui?—he comes from twenty miles away and perhaps he is on holiday, I do not know. But I will do my best."

He descended to the office and she sat on a hard chair by a window through which again she watched a wide starry sky and roofs and trees white with moonlight from a hot and stuffy room. Jeffrey spoke sternly of the necessity of getting onto another bus at once, then laughed at something funny he remembered from the day's bus ride, but which he did not succeed in telling her about before he fell asleep again. Señor Martinez returned to say that the doctor's aunt reported he would be back in three days: if affairs were urgent, it would be best to contact the nuns.

"This is a small place, you understand? They are poor people. When the doctor comes it is for a serious illness. The nuns at the convent attend to small sicknesses."

They stood on either side of the bed, and looked down at the invalid, whose clothes were sticking to him, whose skull was shaped by dank strands of hair.

Señor Martinez, the Spaniard, at fifty or so was what Jeffrey would look like. He was all sloping prominences: sloping bald skull, small sloping shoulders, an unexercised sloping stomach. Jeffrey, the American of German immigrant parents, must have in him a gene or two from these shores, for Señor Martinez could easily be his father.

But how ill was he?

Kate was thinking that if this were her son, she would not be worried at all, she would diagnose that condition of *opting out*: there is a temperature or a cold or a lowering of vitality that merits a doctor's visit and some days in bed, but the point is the days in bed. Why, she used the evasion herself, quite consciously, when life got too much of a good thing. It is a state of affairs like winter for the earth: it feels as if all heat has retreated inwards, the fire is deeply hidden under rock, the sun is too far away. One lies huddled or sprawled, according to one's temperament, far away, behind surfaces of flesh, hair, eyes that do not seem to have much to do with one, like a dog lying in the sun to get winter warmth.

Señor Martinez, father of children, did not seem more perturbed than she was. Yet on the face of it Jeffrey was ill enough not to see them; he stared past or through them, and he shivered convulsively in great spasms that seemed self-consciously dramatic. Señor Martinez, his lively dark eyes full of support and warmth, said, "Alors, ça va mieux demain, oui oui, madame, j'en suis certain," as if he were a doctor and she a worried mother. He went off saying that she would find a meal in the dining room but of course this was not a fashionable hotel like the ones they were used to; she must take what she found.

The dining room was no larger than one for a bourgeois family, which was probably what it had once been. There was heavy dark furniture, heavy white tablecloths. The meal was bread soup, a piece of fried meat, fruit. She was served by a girl who cleaned rooms as well as waited at table and helped in the kitchen. This hotel was used by visiting government officials, by the police, whose local headquarters was some miles away, and by the priests who came to confess the nuns and serve them sacraments.

She went to bed quietly. This was the first silent place since she had left her large garden in Blackheath. The Spanish coasts, Istanbul, Global Food in London—

all had rung, hammered, shouted, or chattered with noise. Here, towards midnight, she woke to hear a horse or a mule clop past under the windows. But Jeffrey was wakened too, and just as if he had not for so many hours been not there, been absent from ordinary life, he sat up and demanded in a normal voice what he could have to eat—and where were they?

She explained. They enjoyed a normal moment of reunion in the silent hotel in the village where now nothing was moving. He said, "I must have been sick, then?" She confirmed it, and went downstairs in her robe, as if in her own house, to see if she could find something to eat in the dining room, for she knew that the maid and Señor Martinez—whose wife and children were away visiting relatives in Barcelona—were in bed and asleep. She found a loaf of bread and some butter, covered against flies, on the great sideboard, and brought slices of bread and butter and some fruit up to the room. And there was Jeffrey, who had in the interval plunged in and out of a bath, had combed and dressed, demanding that they should go out and find a café or a restaurant. He seemed full of energy—suspiciously so. His extreme irritation, his restlessness, were a warning. She explained again that in this village everyone must now be asleep; that they were far from tourist country; that in the morning they could leave. He devoured the food as if he hated it, and was sick again, just as he was demanding to go out for a walk and enjoy the moonlight.

He held on to the bottom of the bed, swaying, yellow, saying that he was quite recovered. He crawled back onto the bed, lay down, slept.

He would probably be better in the morning.

And indeed he woke early, and they descended together to the hotel dining room, where Señor Martinez was drinking coffee. She confessed her theft of the night; but of course he had already noticed it and understood it. He was charming, but she noted the change in his manner. She had left the passports on the hotel desk the night before: the fuss over Jeffrey's sickness had prevented Señor Martinez taking down the details for his records. This morning he had done this. Last night she and Señor Martinez had been like parents conferring over a sick child's bed; now he had to think that his guests were in some sort of scandalous relation. He was exuding reproach, sadness. As it were a philosophical reproach. While his kind, fine eyes rested on the lovers, it was as if he said, We are poor people here. We cannot afford such things.

But he made the girl bring them good fresh coffee, and heavy bread, toasted in the English manner—he knew all about this custom, oh yes, for his younger brother had been a waiter in a restaurant in Manchester; and he said over and over again, as a nervous person repeats himself, that he was sorry there would be no bus until tomorrow: his nervousness, if it was that, said what he was too polite to say, that he wished their sinfulness and irregularity could be removed from his hotel earlier.

What his courtesy said was that he regretted the limited resources of this place: for of course these two were on holiday, and it was unfortunate that such experienced and travelled people were confined to a village that had so little to offer of what they were used to.

And so he went on; while Kate sat silent, knowing she was putting this nice man in a false position, but hoping that the shadiness of the room was hiding her embarrassment. Señor Martinez continued to speak French, and to her; by now he knew that Jeffrey understood a few words

of Spanish, but he was ignoring him. His disapproval was
directed at the man, then? He felt none for the woman?
He did not like Jeffrey, but did like Kate in spite of her
immorality?

When the meal was over, they went out into the little
square. It was empty. A dog lay in some shade. Already
as hot as it would be at midday, the August sun whitened
the sky. The fountain trickled silently. The large rectangle
of screened glass opposite drew them towards it; the door
stood open to admit air. It was a café, but it was for the
people in the evenings: no one here had time to sit about
in the day. There was no one in the café, not even a waiter.
They walked into a street off the square, passing a black-
smith's and a shop. This was the village shop. It sold
onions, coarse sausage, olive oil from barrels, sardines that
had lost all individuality, being crushed together with salt
crusted on them, large greenish-red tomatoes that smelled
strongly of the vine and the fields, enormous loaves of pale
bread, green peppers. There were, perhaps, a hundred
families in the place; and after a few yards the fields began,
where maize stood turning yellow among olive trees and
stones.

They returned in silence to the square. Señor Martinez
had observed their attempts to reach the amenities of the
café, and had set a wooden table under a tree outside the
hotel's main door. He waved them towards it, and brought
them glasses of mineral water with slices of lemon. There
they sat, and knew they were being watched. The few
houses of this village had shuttered windows, and the
shutters had eyes behind them. Once or twice a farmer,
or a labourer, walked through the square, wishing them
Good Day. These men were full of dignity and reserve.
Just as Jeffrey remembered. Here it was, what he had

been looking for, in the withdrawn reproachfulness of Señor Martinez—who nonetheless was at this moment in the kitchen conferring with the cook to produce a meal more the style of the visitors than that of the village—and in the women who sat or stood behind windows, not showing themselves, in the men, who as the morning passed, came to cup water from the fountain.

But it was like a punishment sitting there, exposed.

They were surrounded by a poverty so deep that even their clothes, ordinary enough according to the standards of their own countries, were out of reach of anyone here; her handbag—she had taken it for granted until now, when she couldn't stop looking at the elegant shining thing lying on the scrubbed wood of the table—was probably a month's wages. She had bought it as a treat for herself, in the hotel shop in Istanbul. But that wasn't important, it wasn't the point, for she knew that no one walking past or looking from windows grudged the clothes, the bag, the shoes. It was what they were, she and Jeffrey, that was intolerable, their casual travelling, indolent enjoyment, ease of movement, casual relationships.

They were only fifty miles from the coast; on the coast they, what they were, was the norm. Everybody there, or at least, the visitors, moved from country to country by car, coach, train, plane, bus, on foot, crossed continents to visit a music festival or even a restaurant, had a freedom of friendship, love, sex that to the people in this village must be truly unimaginable.

There they sat, Kate Brown, forty-five-year-old mother of four, wife of a respected doctor at that very moment probably lecturing at some conference on a tricky condition of the nervous system, and Jeffrey, who almost certainly by this time next year would be unhappily but dutifully at work in his uncle's law firm in Washington—"lovers," and with so little emotional disturbance that when they looked back on this shared experience, the "love" would be the least of its ingredients. There was not a woman or girl in this place who was within a hundred years of such freedom. Madame Bovary would still describe their excesses; and if the men, like Señor Martinez's brother, did go to Manchester to be waiters, one could be sure that the manners and morals of that wildly sophisticated town would not be brought back here. But the men were mostly peasants, they worked on the land. They grew maize and made flour out of it. They grew olives and sold some. They grew tomatoes. They worked on the estate of the rich nobleman who spent most of the year in Madrid or in his villa on the coast, as his father and his grandfather had done; and the wages of these men kept the village thin and parched.

By twelve the sun was thinning the leafage of the tree so that it was like lace above them; they retreated into the hotel, and Jeffrey fainted away onto the floor. Again she and Señor Martinez lifted him upstairs and laid him on a bed.

And again Jeffrey had withdrawn behind blind eyes that had a look of indignation or astonishment: Why are you expecting so much vitality out of me? they asked, whether they looked at ceiling, walls, the square of blinding light that was the window, or Señor Martinez. Again he was soaked with sweat. Now Señor Martinez, with an apology, turned up the young man's eyelids: inside the flesh was sulphurous. And he pointed silently at the flesh of the arms which lay yellow on the white of the counterpane. Shaking his head, he trod off downstairs to telephone the aunt of the doctor.

Who said that when the doctor made his regular telephone call to receive her report, she would tell him that there was a young American with fever, much sweating, and yellow eyes and skin. In her opinion, Señor Martinez said, it was a case of yellow fever: she had a relative in South America who had died of it. He shrugged: of course the good woman was not to be taken seriously.

She went upstairs to find that Jeffrey had as it were collapsed inwardly. He lay on his back, so loose and relaxed that when she lifted his arm it slid onto the bed with a thump. He looked as if the bones in his flesh had collapsed, or had shrunk. His eyes were half open. He looked corpse-like, but she kept saying to herself—silently, of course, as one does for children or the people who *choose* to put a distance between themselves and the world of imperatives—"Yes, but he's got to choose either one or the other, he's got to be a lawyer or a vagabond, for no other reason than that he sees it as a choice. For if he didn't, he wouldn't be lying there with a temperature, yellow in the flesh—but not ill, no, not ill as someone is ill with cholera or even with measles."

Yet of course Jeffrey was ill, really ill, even if, had he been a Spanish labourer or a small farmer for whom a day's work was the difference between eating and not eating, he would not have been ill at all. Not, of course, that she grudged it to him! She did not, even if she could not help wishing that he could have gone home to the States to enjoy this spiritual crisis. Which, of course, it was. . . . As for her, she was muttering to herself, ribald, being out of sight of Señor Martinez, she was here for physical reasons. That was what she had contracted for— the body, the pleasures of the flesh; wishing there was someone with whom she could share the joke, she sponged Jeffrey's forehead and lifted him to drink.

In the dining room there was an obese man in uniform with a gun in his belt. It was a military uniform.

The gun monitored the meal, while the girl served cold jellied soup and cold meat and salad and bread.

Kate returned to the room, found Jeffrey exactly where she had left him, made him drink more water, and then collapsed herself and slept. And slept and slept, listening as it were to something just out of hearing; the inner tutor was wanting her to understand something, but she was being too obtuse to understand. She was dreaming of the seal, or had dreamed of it, for she could feel the heaviness of the animal. It was still damp from the water she had put on it. Behind her a low and sullen sun had moved in a low arc sketched across perhaps a quarter of the horizon. It was a small sun, it had no heat at all, everything was getting very dark; she seemed to be walking on and on in a permanent chilly twilight.

Next morning, when the sunlight withdrew from the room, it was as if it had left a stain of colour on Jeffrey's flesh. She sought Señor Martinez and asked if he would make another attempt at the doctor. But the aunt was not answering the telephone: it appeared that her mornings were spent at her devotions in the church at the convent. It happened that as Kate and Señor Martinez stood conferring at a window, a lorry stopped in the square. It was a battered old Ford, and the driver was filling the radiator from the fountain. At the same time a horse drew into the square a cart of a kind that must have been seen in Spain for many centuries. The horse was thirsty, for it went straight to the fountain and drank while the lorry driver was dipping his empty oil can right under its nose.

Señor Martinez's frown disappeared; he ran out, conferred with the lorry driver, and returned to say that this man—he was a roadworker—would take Jeffrey to the convent to be nursed, if he could be got ready quickly.

Kate and Señor Martinez attempted to dress the

patient, who was unresisting, but so heavy in his limbs that they gave up, and wrapped him in blankets. They carried him downstairs naked but cocooned, and helped him to the high cab of the lorry. Señor Martinez got in with Jeffrey; for the nuns spoke no language but Spanish. Unable to remember the French for "jaundice," they had agreed on "la maladie jaune," which layman's diagnosis would be transmitted to the convent.

The lorry jerked out of the square, Jeffrey lolling like a shot man between hotelkeeper and roadworker.

That was at ten in the morning.

Señor Martinez, who had reported the nuns' willingness to keep and care for Jeffrey, telephoned on Kate's behalf at five in the evening, was told he was sleeping, that they believed him to be very ill, but were awaiting the arrival of a doctor from Alicante who came to them for serious cases.

Though there was nothing she could do there, Kate decided to walk to the convent. The way led along a street she had not before noticed: it was a lane, or alley, rather than a street, very poor, lined on either side with rooms, each room for a family. The room's front doorstep was in one alley, its back door in another. The doors stood open, and each room contained children of all sizes, and the children's mother, probably Kate's age or younger, but looking like an old woman. There were many old people as well sitting on chairs in the lane, among chickens and goats. There were no young or middle-aged men; they were absent at work. Kate walked down this street, smiling: she felt ashamed, and no amount of reason could dissolve that emotion. She said to herself in every second breath that fifty miles away on the coast she would be absorbed unnoticed into the throng of humanity, an item of morality among hundreds of thousands—indeed, in this month, millions—of her kind. But it was no use. The smiles and greetings of these poor women, in their poor women's shabby black, the swarms of children, the deadly, desperate rock-bottom poverty, were accusations shouted at her who so amiably walked there with her smart white dress, her fashionable dark-red hair (whose parting, however, was already showing a band of grey) her smart bag, her creamy, white, cared-for limbs.

She reached the end of the lane a hundred yards after its beginning, on a stony slope of olives through which a horse track ran—the lorry had jolted that way this morning—and looked back to see the lane packed, crammed, solid with black-dressed women and barefooted Murillo children staring after her.

She walked on, her face burning, through olive trees and then maize plants, until she turned past a eucalyptus that shed its dry scent even more powerfully than the olives. There was the convent. A tall stone wall curved back on either side of ironwork gates, and inside the gates was a clean-swept yard which had some flowering bushes in it, and a whitewashed double-storied building. As she crossed the yard, another great gate—the main gate, obviously, the one she had come in by being a secondary entrance—showed the church dominating everything: the convent building, wall, ornamented gates; olives, fields, stony earth. Its cupola glittered to answer the fire of the sunset. Kate knocked on what she now saw must be a back door, and was smiled at, was made welcome by, first one blackrobed woman, then two, then three, then a small flock of them, all of whom knew about her, and that she must have come to see their patient. She was accompanied into a small room off a courtyard in which Jeffrey lay on an iron bedstead under a shiny picture of the Bleeding Heart. A crucifix stood on a low table; an ivory cross was on the whitewashed wall.

Since that morning, some drug had taken Jeffrey even further away. He was absolutely still, chill and damp to the touch, his flesh looked as if it had been painted. She might as well not have come, but she sat for a time on a rush-seated chair, while the nuns brought her coffee and cake, and then a glass of wine, always smiling, delighted that she was there giving them opportunities to serve God. At last she thanked them, and left. She went into the church. It was quiet, and smelled of incense, and she would have liked to sit for a while and think, or even perhaps to wonder what prayer might be, but it was no good, there was enough gold and precious stones in this small, unimportant, undistinguished manifestation of the Church to feed and to heal thousands. This thought, here, could have little force behind it: it was an alien thought, had in it the peevish uselessness of the lost cause—but she rebelliously kept it in her mind, and left the church to walk back through a scented, warm, intimate dusk, to the village.

In the lane of the many families the men had come back from the fields, and she was pleased of the dusk, made heavier by the crude glare of light from each room. It was good evening, good evening, buenas tardes, buenas tardes, all the way, while the children ran with her in crowds through the dust until she stepped into the hotel when they were checked like birds swerving away from an obstacle, and fled away shouting into the dark.

In the dining room she ate—in the company of an elderly priest who, she learned, was none other than the doctor expected at the convent—hot thick soup, fried eggs, peppers and tomatoes, and stewed quinces. She asked the priest to telephone when he had examined "her husband," accepted his cold regard, which he believed to be uncondemning, and went up to her room to wait for the call. The priest was to walk to the convent, as she had done, then of course he would talk to the gay friendly women in their stuffy black, then he would examine Jeffrey. It was after midnight when the telephone bell shrilled downstairs, and Señor Martinez came up to report that Father Juan believed the young man to have jaundice, but there were certain features of the case which contradicted this diagnosis. There would probably be something more definite in three days' time when the local doctor made his regular visit to the convent.

She went to bed and slept lightly, just below the surface of wakefulness, in a shallow lake of dreams where shadows of ideas moved as cool and light as fishes, a very far place from the dark northern country where she and the seal were making their painful journey. She woke early, when the day was still a fresh greyness flowing across the dark. She sat at her window to watch the waking of the village.

Soon a man came to the fountain, held his hand to direct the water in a spray across his face, then dipped his head to the flow point, drinking sideways, weak sunlight colouring his brown cheek.

A black horse wandered in from a side street, and stood with its head down, blinking flies away from its eyes.

A woman came out of her door, and set a wooden chair in the dust. She went back inside and came out again with a knife, an enamel plate piled with green peppers, a plastic bowl. She wore the shabby black of the poor women of Europe. She sat herself carefully on the chair, as if sitting were an act that could hurt her, and put the bowl between her knees. Holding the enamel plate balanced on the bend of her elbow, she sliced peppers into the bowl. She was old, an old tired woman, with greying hair pulled tightly back. Just as Kate was thinking, No, probably not, probably I'm going to see she's not old at all, it's going to be brought home *again*, the woman looked straight up at Kate, who sat in white frills at her window. The woman smiled, and Kate smiled back, knowing she could not match the smile: and of course the woman was no older than Kate, but she was as worn out as the horse.

Kate retreated from the window and dressed. A tray arrived with coffee, the sugared buns, jam. The sun now crashed in. She shuttered the room against the dazzle, and, having nothing to read but the magazines of not quite a week ago, which looked every bit as false and silly as she expected they would, from here, this village, she sat idly through the morning until she could eat. Then she slept again, and walked to the convent. Jeffrey lay in his white-washed cell whose floor was pooled with fragrant water. The nuns threw down scented water several times a day to take the dryness from the air and to settle the dust that lay around the convent like bleached cloth.

She walked back again, making herself do it, through the poor people, and sat in her room until dinner at ten, and afterwards wished she could go to the café, which at this hour had people in it. But of course she could not, it was full of men. Even with Jeffrey it would have been impossible or awkward, for they would be disturbing people who came here every night, for whom the café was an extension of their family lives.

She was wishing that she could find some activity to end what she had been telling herself so long she needed: time to think. But she wasn't thinking, she was feeling.

She was wanting her home, her life in it—which was the past, of course. But it was as if she were building a future in her mind, and the continual effort to check herself, to say, That's over, that's finished, was bringing on attacks of emotion she could not control.

She was longing for her husband.

Her condition up to the time she had left her home in May, the constant swings of emotion from needful love to irritation at her need, from the desire to have more freedom to the coward's need of being confined, had passed now into a passion of desire which was however being postponed until the future—the autumn. She longed for her husband's body as once years ago, when she was still a girl, she had longed for a lover; but of course this present longing was a thousand times more intense, since she had accumulated so many memories to feed it. While she was engaged in spending all day, half the night, in holding her marriage up to the light between finger and thumb to analyse it, a small object with neat outlines which she could even now reject altogether, the rhythms of her flesh, her memory, had made an appointment with her husband. Whom her intelligence was regarding bleakly, as someone who had made a conscious choice to enjoy the flesh while it lasted—bleakly but rather wearily, in an effort towards decency, almost in the spirit of: *I don't agree with what he thinks but I'll fight to the death for his right*—etc. Whom her emotions were deriding because they felt him as a small boy who was indulging himself with sweets.

Her sexuality—in a vacuum, and unsupported by what she thought, what she felt, by what she expected of the future—was a traitor to her conviction that now, at this time, she had only one duty: to think about what her life had become, what it was going to have to be. This, though, was not the hunger of someone who is having to do without food: she was not tormented, or needy; for her sex, apart from the odd twinge, like a contraction of the mouth when smelling food or seeing chocolate on a counter, was as it were postponed. To the autumn. To the future which would not take place, or would not in the shape that her husband, herself, her children, had been visualising until that famous afternoon in May when everything had changed. The future was not going to be a continuation of the immediate past, with this summer seeming in retrospect like an unimportant hiatus. No, the future would continue from where she had left off as a child. For it was seeming to her more and more (because of this sexuality, something displaced, like an organ lifted out of her body and laid by her side to look at, like a deformed child without function or future or purpose) as if she were just coming around from a spell of madness that had lasted all the years since that point in early adolescence when her nature had demanded she must get herself a man (she had put it romantically then of course) until recently, when the drug had begun to wear off. All those years were now seeming like a betrayal of what she really was. While her body, her needs, her emotions—all of herself—had been turning like a sunflower after one man, all that time she had been holding in her hands something else, the something precious, offering it in vain to her husband, to her children, to everyone she knew—but it had never been taken, had not been noticed. But this thing she had offered, without knowing she was doing it, which had been ignored by herself and by everyone else, was what was real in her.

Even now, with all the pressures off her, alone, in the condition which had so often during her years of immersion in the family seemed out of reach, she was not able to rest, and to think, understand, absorb—for she continually felt herself streaming towards the future, into her husband's arms, into a sea of intimacy which included her past. Which her mind was judging as being a kind of madness. She was longing for the past, obsessed with it. Sitting alone in her hotel room, a fever of want transported her to her bedroom at home, her husband's arms, and leaves being swept about their house in a cold wind, but the warmth of their home closing them in: the past.

She sat at the window until she was the last person awake: all the lights in the village were out. The cluster of lights up on the mountainside which Señor Martinez said was another convent had become a distant twinkle, like that which a hurricane lamp sends across miles of country, and the twinkling is because a wind is making it swing. But this flickering was because of the swaying of leaves across the single light at the convent gate. She found this out when she walked up the hilly roads next morning: there was a little white building all by itself among orange trees, where hens scratched. A nun was hoeing among the orange trees, the black sleeves flung back to expose her wrists, dust settling on black skirts.

This bride of Christ smiled at Kate; Kate smiled back. Mad, she was thinking. All of us, the whole bloody parcel of us, the whole thing, crazy, men and women both, we're all mad, and don't know it. Here was this woman in her self-chosen prison, here was she, a prisoner of her memories; and there was Michael, engaged in—not so much eating as sampling a box of chocolates, taking a bite out of one, swallowing another, discarding a third without tasting it.

The lantern on the gate was of iron, and looked old. Probably deliberately made to look old. The leaves that made the light tremble at night were on an ancient olive tree.

Back at the hotel Señor Martinez said that she should

not walk by herself in such heat; he was sad for her that she had nowhere to amuse herself, but perhaps she would like to use the courtyard which was not open to ordinary hotel guests, but could be for her.

The courtyard had a small pool where goldfish could be seen with difficulty through a film of dust and many water plants whose leaves were crowded with bubbles. Across the court, in a corner of shade, sat an old woman, an aunt of Señor Martinez's wife. She was reading a holy book and knitting a black garment.

In the evening Kate visited Jeffrey again. He still had not said anything to anyone, the nuns reported, but now he opened his eyes, appeared to recognise her, and said in a normal voice, "Oh, hi there, hi, how is it?" and fell back into his sleep, or stupor, again.

That night the local doctor came to the convent and the nuns rang Señor Martinez to say that Jeffrey might have typhoid, it was a possibility, but no one was to worry.

Next morning typhoid was ruled out, but jaundice had not been confirmed. A day passed, another. She visited Jeffrey, sat with him, walked through the poor streets and alleyways and olive fields to the convent; she sat in the courtyard, she fought her emotions in a fury of irritation with herself—and she dreamed about the seal. She was becoming drawn into the air of the dream so that even when awake she recognised atmospheres, flashes of feeling —if that was the word, that came from the dream, from the seal. She had always been on good terms with her dreams, had always been alert to learn from them. Ever since she was very small, five or six, she had been able to reach her hand into the country behind the daylit one, to touch a familiar object that lived there, or to walk through it at ease, not astonished, or afraid. Nor was she surprised

by a dream that developed like a fable or a myth: she accommodated several such long-running dreams, and when
a new stage of development of a familiar theme was presented to her, she would lie awake for as long as she could
before letting it be seen that she was awake, thinking of
the ideas that were taking shape in her, and which she
could not see except in these reflections like firelit shadows
on the walls of her sleep.

But this dream, the dream of the seal, was of a different quality from any she had known. Not because it
seemed so "real"—many of her dreams did, as real as waking life. No, it was because of its atmosphere, so particularly its own that she could enter into it even when the
seal was not there—when it was, as it were, offstage for
the time, busy elsewhere, on its own affairs. She could
enter the place of the dream and know it to be "the
dream of the seal." Going to sleep and entering this dream
was as much her business for this time in her life as being
in this hotel in the poor dusty village in a blazing August,
as visiting Jeffrey and waiting for his recovery, as wrestling
with her emotional self, which seemed like a traitor who
had come to life inside her. What she was engaged in was
the dream, which worked itself out in her.

One hot afternoon, in siesta, she was in an arena with
the seal: in the northern landscape was a Roman amphi-
theatre. She was at ground level, down on the floor of the
arena. Suddenly wild animals leaped from cages that had
been opened in the arena walls. Lions, leopards, wolves,
tigers. She ran with the seal and climbed as high as she
could up the stands, while the animals came after them
both. She made an effort and climbed up onto the arena's
edge, which was a flimsy wooden rail that shook under her
weight and the seal's. There she clung, pulling her legs up,

trying to lift the seal up and away from fangs and claws. There was an awful noise of snarling and roaring. She thought she would not have the strength to hold on, to keep the seal safe for long. Her strength was going, and the animals were leaping up and snapping and snarling at her feet, only inches away from the seal's scarred tail. Then the frenzied leaping became less, and soon she and her burden were a long way from the animals, who dwindled, and thinned, and vanished.

It was now a week since Jeffrey had been taken to the convent. No, he most certainly had not had typhoid, though the convent, and the authorities, had had a bad forty-eight hours. But they now did not think it had been jaundice either, the yellowness notwithstanding. The yellow had gone, completely, and he was running rather high temperatures. What was certain was that he was ill, and too weak to travel.

Kate visited him daily, sometimes twice a day. Now he recognised her, and they spoke, not much, but were friendly, and likeable to each other, as they had been at the beginning, in Istanbul. His fever kept flaring up, and subsiding. He said he was happy where he was; lying in that austere room, looking out into sunlight that held a tree, and a bed of petunias, some jasmine, was what he had been needing for—he did not know how long. He did not believe he was ill: he had forgotten his days of being semiconscious and did not know he had been for many days unconscious. He saw his sojourn in the convent as this: lying quietly in a white bed, in a white room, looking out at foliage and flowers.

When she was not at the convent, Kate sat through the hours in the courtyard at the hotel. At night she sat at the window, an area of alert vigilance against the treachery of memories, wants, false hopes, and watched the moon that was at its full.

One evening the walk to the convent was beyond her. It was too hot, she had slept too long at siesta, she felt a little sick with all this heavy unseasonable food, she believed that the night before it must have been dawn before she had been able to leave the moon-filled window, the stars, the convent light that flickered down the mountainside through its moving screen. She asked Señor Martinez to ring the convent and tell Jeffrey she was not coming that evening, and remained in her bed. She did not go down to dinner, sent back her breakfast tray untouched, and when Señor Martinez arrived in her room to enquire after her, saw from his face that she, like Jeffrey, was ill.

Oh, so that was all it was? She had been feeling so—she did not know how to describe it, but to be told that she might be getting jaundice, or whatever it was that Jeffrey had, was reassuring. All last night she had lain on her bed—sitting at the window had been beyond her—watching the moon's movement across the square of stars; but she had been walking northwards with the seal in her arms. She believed that somewhere ahead must be the sea, for if not, both she and the seal would die. Snow had begun to fall softly, drifting into the cracks and the hollows of the sharp black rocks. She shivered, and was glad the seal's body was against hers, shielding it. The seal had its head on her shoulder, and she could feel the soft bristles of its hide on her cheek. The seal's life was very weak, she knew that. She knew that walking into the winter that lay in front of her she was carrying her life as well as the seal's—as if she were holding out into a cold wind her palm, on which lay a single dried leaf.

Señor Martinez said that she should authorise him to

ring the doctor's aunt, who would tell the doctor to come and diagnose for her. Kate saw that she was at the beginning of a process that might lead her to lie in a whitewashed cell beside the one Jeffrey was in. If she was ill, or going to be ill, then she should go home. While up to this minute it had seemed impossible to leave Jeffrey here alone, an act of coldness or of irresponsibility, now she was saying to herself that he was after all a man of thirty, that he would continue to live and probably even to prosper if she were not waiting at the hotel to sit with him once or twice a day for an hour—which in any case she could no longer do. She might leave him. She sent him telephone messages through Señor Martinez and the nuns, and, with paper from Señor Martinez—the hotel did not have its own paper—wrote to him. It was a small, humorous, regretful letter, full of the ironies of the situation—writing it she understood she *was* ill, for the effort was enormous. In due course he would write a similar one to her. By then, this little village and their two so very different experiences in it would have slipped into the past like films which had however begun with the same sequence—of a man and a woman sitting side by side in a country bus that had stopped somewhere. They were looking out into bright moonlight. It was a village square. On the edge of a small cracked fountain shone a white china cup. Men sat drinking outside a cafe. There were some trees that did not look right. They were diseased? No, they were thick with dust.

She stood by the fountain with her luggage, having paid the unbelievably modest bill, and Señor Martinez pressed her hands in his and his eyes had tears in them. She felt tears in her own. And she was embarrassed again, for while Señor Martinez liked her, oh yes, indeed he liked her very much, and understood why that unfortunately ill young man should have chosen her, although so much older than he was (passports say everything), all the same he was shocked, he was still shocked, though regretfully: he knew the world accommodated many such relationships nowadays, but he did not think the world to be better for it—all this and a lot more he conveyed in the pressure of his hands, the wetness of his fine lively eyes, as the bus stood shaking gently in the sun of an early morning waiting for two passengers, Kate, and a young girl who Señor Martinez said was the daughter of a man who grew tomatoes on a field she passed walking to the convent. The girl was going to work as a maid in a hotel on that lucrative coast for a month, before coming back to help her mother with the six smaller children.

Señor Martinez put her suitcase on the bus and told the driver that the señora was not well and should be treated gently. As indeed, she needed to be: the drive to the coast was all nausea and heat, and the glare of the coast when she reached it made her dizzy. It was midday. Her head ached, and she should be in bed, but now she was set on one thing, to return to London as fast as she could.

At the coast she found another bus and was soon in a town large enough to have a tourist office, and by five that afternoon had reached a doctor: a few miles inland, among those very poor people, getting a doctor had meant days of waiting, and the intervention of religion.

This doctor heard all she had to say about jaundice and typhoid, examined her, and said that in his opinion she was anaemic. He advised her to see her own doctor the moment she arrived in London, though for his part he believed she would soon find herself quite well. He prescribed a sedative, and charged her something like five pounds. Of course, in Full Flood Time, while rivers of gold poured up and down the coasts, and when the señora was obviously rich—look at her dress, her handbag, her shoes!—what could be more just?

The señora, recognising in the doctor her own attitude to Jeffrey, that to begin with at least his illness had been a sickness of the will, nevertheless felt too weak for buses and for coaches, and re-entered the world of the rich by hiring a car to take her to the airport.

There she drowsed in a chair, waiting for a cancellation, and then as time passed and passed, she laid herself down on a long seat, shutting out the curiosity or disapproval of other passengers. She was deep inside the cold nausea that characterised this sickness, whatever it was, and when at last, but not till next morning, she was on an airplane, knew how great a mistake it was to be there at all: she was sure she would die, hoped that she would, and by the time she reached London was sustained only by thinking of her own bed, in her own room, with its flowered curtains beyond which summer branches could be seen sifting sunshine, or cloud light, or moonlight—oh, she could not wait to be back in her own home, with possibly even one of the children back from somewhere and able to help her. She had already given her address to the taxi man when she remembered that she had no right to it: her home was full of strangers. She asked him to wait while she considered. He did so, and the clock measured her predicament while she thought that to freelance for a hotel room in London in August was insanity. But she did not want to approach friends, and particularly not Mary, who she knew would take her in with enthusiasm. If, that is, she was not engaged in some affair or other—*her* children were away too.

At last she told the taxi man her trouble, and indicated

that his devotion to her concerns would be rewarded. He drove her into London, turning to examine her from time to time to see how ill she was, and if he ought to be taking her to hospital, and then drove to hotel after hotel, leaving her while he went to put her case to one, two, three, four receptionists. At last, at a hotel in Bloomsbury, one much more expensive than Mrs. Michael Brown would use, he came to say that if she was able to wait for an hour or so, there would be a double room with a bath: the price appalled her, but she had no choice.

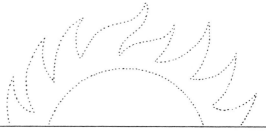

The Hotel

Paying off the taxi man, she paid herself in at the hotel and was asked if she were well enough to sit in the foyer and wait. The question, the solicitude, were delightful, but of course she had to go on sitting there, unless she took herself to hospital, which alternative had been turned down by the taxi man and the desk, in their consultations—which must have taken place—about infection, epidemics, that sort of thing. No, the desk, the taxi man, and herself, had decided she was sick rather than ill, and so she sat weakly in the foyer trying to make her mind steady itself by concentrating it on the scene around her. Surely, looked at from a

geographical vantage point—a pair of particularly strong
binoculars on top of the Alps, for instance?—it must seem
as if in August all of Europe swaps populations, exchanges
blocks of populace? In this foyer, set off by banks of
flowers—artificial, but trumping nature so magnificently
that real flowers would have seemed puny and out of place
—the uniforms of the many attendants, the holiday clothes
of the visitors, at first disguised the really interesting fact:
that she was probably the only British person there. The
couriers and porters that ran about, the nannies, of the kind
she had recently been herself, smiling and sympathetic behind their desks, the waiters, as well as the guests, were
from every part of Europe. She might as well still be in
Istanbul, she might be in Málaga or Alicante—she might be
anywhere, though not, of course, the village which she had
left yesterday. And her ears were still attempting to make
amenable lumps of sound to which she did not have the
key, while they absorbed other sequences of sound which
sank easily into her brain. A young couple near her were
speaking German; they turned to stare at her, and Kate
wondered why they did. They kept on her a steady, quite
friendly, but attentive gaze. They were very attractive and
obviously rich. He wore, although it was a muggy London
summer's day, a full-length fur, like moleskin, in a soft
mauveish colour. Or perhaps it was a very supple suede. It
was buttoned up all the way, but open at the collar, showing a gleam of white silk. His eyes were dark and affec-
tionate, his hair cut like a page's, in supple black locks. The
girl was himself, his double. Her hair was dark, and cut like
his. Her eyes and smile were equally delightful. She wore
long white crêpe de Chine that was fastened with a couple
of hundred minute covered buttons along the sleeves and
up the front. She wore very long glittering crystal beads,

and white lace-up boots. Their hands, which looked capable and quick and intelligent, had rings on every finger. Even in this well-fed, well-tuned crowd, these two stood out, radiating a harmony of sensual fulfilment. They had only to walk into a room, these two, and everyone must know that their eating, their love-making, their conversation, their sleep, must be a feast. They looked as if all their lives they had been licked all over by invisible tongues dipped in honey . . . Kate was not the only one who was staring. Of course, that was why they were looking at her: "Yes, we are used to being stared at, we know it is the price we have to pay for being so beautifully dressed, for being so beautiful ourselves, but enough is enough!" Kate turned her gaze elsewhere, and listened to their German instead—no, now they were speaking French, and were deciding whether to take a car to visit friends who lived in the country in Wiltshire, or whether first to give themselves some lunch—no, at a restaurant, not here in this hotel, where it was obvious, the food could not be expected to be up to much . . . the sounds seemed to be going away and coming back, they seemed almost to be fanning her, her forehead was cold and wet: a smiling young woman in a bright black-and-white outfit was bending over her and inviting her in accented English to accompany her. As Kate stared, the invitation was repeated.

"I'm sorry," said Kate, "I'm not well." And she tried to get up, staggered, was supported by the girl. Warmth and concern were already being poured all over Kate: oh yes, the girl knew her job, who should recognise this better than Kate, who had done it herself, and so very recently.

"Oh, I am so sorry, they told me you were not well, and you don't look it, but let me take you to your room, you should certainly be in bed, one can see that."

One had to wait for the attention, for which one paid so highly—it was midsummer, it was August; but when the attention was switched on, then it was of the very highest quality.

In a cocoon of love and warmth, Kate was soon in her room, and the girl, Anya from Austria, here in England to put the finishing touches to an obviously admirable training as a hotel manageress, helped Kate undress, saw her into bed, drew curtains to make a soft dark, called the floor service to bring lemon tea and dry biscuits, prescribed rest, peace, silence, and departed, having handed Kate over to the care of another girl from Italy, equally delightful and solicitous, here to perfect her English and to further her training—she was not as advanced towards managership as her colleague Anya. For while Anya's loving sympathy and devotion were spread over all the floors of the hotel, Silvia's were only for this floor.

Silvia withdrew, smiling, having offered Kate her services whenever Kate chose to push the appropriate button.

Kate was lying in a room the size of the smallest bedroom in her home. It was planned and fitted like a workbox. The bed she was in—a single—was the size she and her husband had shared for their early years, when they could only afford the smallest size in double beds. The twin to it stood at a hand's stretch away, still covered in its dove-grey skin, in which two rosy cushions lolled to suggest home, comfort: there was nothing else in the room that was not functional. The curtains were thick, rose-colour, would wash in a washing machine, would not need ironing—what was the use of being in a hotel if you brought with you the housewife? She continued, however, with her inventory: the carpet was dark grey, would not show the dirt. The walls, she decided, had not been intelligently surfaced: they were white, papered in a blistered or pockmarked stuff that held dust easily; these walls would probably have to be vacuumed at least twice a week? There was television and radio, and a board behind the bed full of switches and buttons to press and turn. But it wasn't quiet, no: traffic raged and swore below windows which of course had to be open, in this weather, and not far off along the corridor there must be a working room of some kind: there was much clattering and laughing coming from it. She could have the dark, immobility, rest—but she was not going to have quiet.

She should, however, submerge herself in sleep until the malady, whatever it was, had passed. Jaundice? No, she was not yellow at all. Nor was her flesh cold; on the contrary, it burned, as if the dry heat of Spain was in her body still. She felt as if she had a fever, and her head ached. Yet she was nauseous, and felt as if inside her she was cold, very chilled, despite her burning surfaces. She was realising how awful had been that long journey on jolting buses, and in the air, and then again in the taxi—a nightmare of hot, sick movement that had in it a cold nausea.

She needed to be sick. She was sick. And again . . . holding on to a basin with both hands, she saw in the mirror a greenish-white face that had flaring scarlet on the cheekbones, and lank slabs of tarnished red hair falling over it. The grey was pushing up into it fast. The bones of the face were prominent, the skin creased and shabby. If this face had walked through the village, the women would have recognised kindred flesh: she staggered back to bed, and dozed. She was conscious of a discreet knock, and the entrance of Silvia, and the smiling face, bent over her. But Kate did not move; and there followed a long, slow, underwater time, in a room that showed if it was day or night by whether it was like a dark noisy cave that had painfully brilliant vertical streaks of light from which she had to turn herself away, or a dark cave lit by a horizontal streak near the floor from which, again, she had to screen her eyes. Silvia came in often, with a drink her training prescribed for Kate's condition, of lemon, that had white of egg whipped into it. It was delicious, and Kate drank each glass as it arrived beside her—and was sick when Silvia had left. For she knew that Silvia was a spy sent by the management to make sure that Kate was not suffering from some disease that would earn the hotel condemnation on the part of authorities higher still: Silvia was reporting on Kate—as of course Kate would have done in her place; she did not blame Silvia, on the contrary, she merely took care to hide how often and how thoroughly she was sick, and that the noise was an affliction worse than the nausea. For Kate, who lay neither asleep nor awake, felt the noise washing all about her, felt it crash on her, making her bones ache; a screech of brakes from the street hurt her back-bone, and the voices in many languages from the corridor, the thudding of feet, vibrated and shook in a lake of sensation that filled her head.

Several times there was a heavy trundling sound; and apparently she had asked Silvia about it, for the information in her mind was that a trolley carried cleaning materials for the rooms, and that others bore meals and drinks and cigarettes, and that these trolleys journeyed up and down and around all day and most of the night. They clanged, and they rattled, and they shook, and the thin walls trembled, while the windows vibrated with the traffic.

She must have had other conversations with the always kind and gentle Silvia. For instance, she knew that Silvia came from near Venice, in the country, where "my father has an inn, the family are all in the business." Silvia had worked in every capacity in the family inn, as waitress, maid, and cook, even substituting for her papa when he had gone on a holiday with her mother to Sweden last year. Next year she would be in Lyons, in a hotel where she would be fulfilling the function that Anya was in now: she would have moved up a stage. And the year after that? She would be married to her fiancé, who was this summer in Zurich, learning the wine trade. They would get a job in the same hotel, perhaps in Italy, but it did not have to be; France, Germany—even here, in Britain. After all, these days, it could be anywhere, not so? She saw herself as a manageress, he as manager, and in a good hotel, of course, something of this class or even better. This hotel was very good, yes, she had been pleasantly impressed, but in due time she would like a country hotel, like her father's only on a higher level, for the very rich, who could afford perfect simplicity, perfect quiet, the ultimate in everything —and, it went without saying, attention of the highest quality. By which time of course Silvia herself would not be the one who would allow sympathy and love to flow forth whenever it was needed; other people would be employed for that function.

But in the meantime she was so very good at what she did that her face, bent over Kate in the darkened room, had become a symbol of reassurance, of kindness—ridiculous, absurd, yes, of course, even in her illness Kate knew that—but in the meantime how very pleasant. And no wonder that handsome couple in their fur as supple as silk, in the white crêpe de Chine with the hundreds of minute buttons, each one clothed separately in a silk of a slightly different texture to the crêpe, so that you had to look and look again to see if a different material had in fact been used to make the tiny buttons more glossy than the gown, seem almost, at first sight, like ivory or a polished bone—no wonder they were so confident, so assured, so effortlessly in command of themselves: the self-immolation of Silvia and a thousand like her had made them so. Where were they by now? Switzerland? Greece? But they wouldn't have to confine themselves to Europe, they might already be in South America, or in Iceland.

Kate found herself awake, and in a real silence. Nothing trundled along the corridors, and the traffic was absent. She was hungry. Telephoning, she discovered it was four in the morning; but decided that if she was in such a hotel she might as well get the benefit of it. Room service brought her a cold meal, and some pleasant wine, but it was too soon. She ate a little, and was sick again, but was still clear in her head, and ready to start living. The day began, in its din, the light blazed and hurt. She got up and dressed. Her clothes dragged around her; she had lost, the scale said, fifteen pounds. In how long? She tried to remember, but could conclude only that now it must be early in September.

She stood in front of a glass, the curtains pulled right back at last, showing the square packed with the hot glitter of traffic, and the heavy damp weight of leafage above. She saw a woman all bones and big elbows, with large knees above lanky calves; she had small dark anxious eyes in a white sagging face around which was a rough mat of brassy hair. The grey parting was three fingers wide. She looked nothing like the pretty cared-for woman of the home in South London; and the people who had been so happy to see the kind, the smiling, the elegant Kate in Global Food and in Istanbul would not have recognised her.

It was her hair, her hair above all, but nothing was easier than to put this right. She telephoned for an appointment in the hotel's hairdressing salon, discovered that she would have to wait until late afternoon, and discovered too that she had not enough energy for what she had planned to do, for what she had got herself out of bed and dressed: she had meant to walk across the mile or so of streets that separated this hotel from Global Food and pick up the letters that should be waiting there for her. In fact, she fainted, found herself on the floor with a bruised shoulder, got herself back into bed, and asked for the hotel to send a messenger for her mail. It came; there was not much of it. It was the letters from her husband that she longed for. She had sent him many postcards and one real letter from Istanbul, saying that she planned to "drop over" to Spain, knowing that he would certainly think she had found attractive company, but deciding it was better to say it in so many words now, so that he would have had time to digest it. There were two letters from Michael, warm, humorous, full of information about everything, including the doings of their daughter, who was staying with some friends in Philadelphia and who might be seriously in love. These letters cancelled every critical thought she had ever had about her situation, about her marriage. She lay in bed, feeling very sick again, but longing for her husband, the familiarity of their knowledge of each other, their intimacy. Now it seemed to her that she had been childish ever to resent his affairs—they could not matter compared to this—that if she held out a hand to him, or he to her, in that gesture was contained a quarter of a century's being together. The empty bed a hand's stretch from hers diminished her; her being here at all, her having left even for one moment the pattern her life was set in, seemed a mistake chosen by a madwoman. The violence of these reactions, her reluctance to get out of bed again, her need to weep, her need to send a telegram to Michael asking him to come home—all this told her she was still ill, and that she might even be sensible to call a doctor. But having decided that this was what she would do, she slid down and away again from her daylight self, as much to lose her miserable need for her husband as for anything, and dreamed she was in a country where pine trees and spruce stood around her in thick clean snow. The sky was a sunless grey. She approached a village built all of wood, and people streamed out of it towards her; among them—taller than they, dominating them—the young king, he whom she had met in the wooden house where she had laid down the seal while they made love. He was fair, with a handsome bony face and strong blue eyes. But he had grown older since she saw him last. He bent to kiss her, claiming her, and then whirled her off in a dance. The people of this village were all dancing, old and young, men and women, holding hands and swinging each other around, or with hands on either side of each other's waists. He and she, the young king and herself, danced on a raised wooden platform, so that the people of the village could see them clearly, for, as these people danced, they kept their eyes on their king and on herself, his chosen consort, and they smiled and laughed because of their pleasure that she was there with the king. The music was loud, and she could not see where it was coming from. Then the young king stepped down from the platform, leaving her without a look, and, taking by the hands a young girl who had been dancing with a boy who seemed to be her brother, he drew her smiling up onto the platform and took up the dance with her. Her long gold plaits, each tied with a red ribbon, flung out as she spun about and around, guided by his hand on her waist, and she laughed up at the smiling face that was coming close down towards hers in a kiss. Kate was running away, in a desolation of grief. The people of the village came after her, shouting: she had become an enemy, because she had been discarded. They caught her and held her; meanwhile the young king ignored them, ignored her, while he danced with the girl. They put her in a pit that was framed with wood, so that she was surrounded by fragrant planks, and she could not get out of it: her eyes were above the lip of the pit, and she could see the young king dancing with the girl on the platform. She shouted out that she was unjustly imprisoned, unjustly deposed, and the king, his face turning sharply from smiles to anger, came swiftly across the snow, pulling his partner by the hand, to stand over the pit and chide her for her lack of generosity, her niggling and critical spirit, her failure in communal feeling, but above all, for her lack of understanding for the laws that governed life: it was necessary for the king to dance with one woman, one girl, after another, until every one of them had been singled out, and had danced with the king on the raised platform in the eyes of the village. The dance was going on, the loud music, the singing, the laughter, the kisses. Overhead pine trees swung and hissed, as a cold wind blew faster, began to wail and shriek. Kate had to get out of the pit, she knew that. Somewhere not far away the seal was, alone; and it was again trying painfully to make its way along the ground towards the sea. It believed she had abandoned it.

She woke, very cold. Trying to get out of bed to look at herself, to see if she were yellow or red or some colour that would be a diagnosis, she fell back into it, and rang the bell for Silvia. In came a girl she had not seen before.

She was a plump dark girl in a short white dress. She had
a plump face and friendly black eyes. Her mouth smiled;
over it was an infant moustache that sketched the handsome authoritative woman she would become. She moved
on a centre of self-assurance and self-appreciation, and this
was caused, as with Silvia, as with Anya, by her knowing
that she was doing this job of hers so well. She bent smiling
over Kate, laid her fresh hand on Kate's, and demanded
how she felt today. She sat on Kate's bed, and held Kate's
hand, and said that she too was Swiss, and from the French-
speaking part, and was training for the hotel business; she
too had a fiancé apprenticed to wine; she was taking Silvia's
place while Silvia took Anya's—for Anya was manageress
for a fortnight, while the manageress went to visit a mother
suddenly taken ill. Her name was Marie, and she smiled
and she laughed, and she said that madame did not have
a temperature, but perhaps she was worried about something? This made Kate laugh, and they both laughed,
Kate's tailing off in a tearful wail that was like a demand
for instant love. There was nothing wrong with her; both
of them thought this. Yet she was lightheaded, nauseous,
and the flesh was melting off her. Marie brought some
soup, which Kate at once vomited; the girl was in the
room, and able to help Kate to the bathroom in time. Now
it seemed to both of them that the ritual act of calling the
doctor should be performed. One came, and like the doctor in Spain, he was full of negatives. Kate did not have
jaundice. No, she did not have typhoid. No, she was not
anaemic, or if so, only a little. She probably had flu in one
of its many manifestations, and she ought to stay in bed
and take these pills. . . Kate went back to sleep.

Far behind her, the sun slid up sideways over a horizon of dark lowering mountains where ice never melted,

and after a crab's scuttle very low down, a few inches above the peaks, fell back into its day, leaving this dark land to cold shadows. She was in a heavy twilight, only just able to see the dry hummocks she was picking her way among. The seal was inert in her arms, its head on her shoulder. But it slid about as she walked, for it was in a coma, or dying. She could hear its dry harsh irregular breathing. She should wet the seal's hide again. But everything was frozen, and the seal needed to have on its dry hide some salt water. She laid the animal down on the snow and searched about in the dark for something to help her. She found a black rock that had salt crystals in its seams. In a hollow between this rock and another she saw ice and broke the surface. A little water was congealing there. She broke the crystals off into this water and made a saline solution. She carried the half-dead seal near this pool which was already trying to freeze over, despite the salt, and she splashed the animal with the liquid, quickly, even more quickly and frantically as the surface of the little pool froze and the water vanished. But before the ice was solid, she had been able to smooth the water all over the seal, over its poor dry hide, its face, its eyelids. Its eyes opened and it moaned softly, but in greeting. She knew the seal was now alive and was saved, for the time at least. She must pick it up and walk north, north, always north, away from the sun, which was so far down south in its eternal day. The dark about her was thick. It was snowing again. She lifted the seal, whose weight was now easier because it was breathing and alive, and went on her way north.

It was mid-September before she dragged herself out of bed. She had lost more weight. Her hair stuck out around a face all bones, stiff and frizzy, streaked with orange, grey-rooted. She could not get her brush through it. Of course, a little patience over an appointment, and in a couple of hours it could be restored to the heavy sleek silky shape that was "her" style. Or had been, for three months. When she returned home though, she would have to return to "her" style of before that summer, pretty and discreet waves, a total lack of provocation. What was the point of doing either, when her body was all bones: this thought, analysed, turned out to be that she could not face sitting under the dryer.

She tied her hair back off her face: this was too young for her, but she found she did not have energy to do more. She went out through the noisy lobby that smelled so strongly of perfumes that she felt sick again, into the street where every face was that of a busy tourist, seeking sensation. People stared at her. Seeing herself in a shop window, she could understand why. She saw she should have tied a scarf around her head, and another to make a waist around the sack that dragged from her shoulders. She went into the first shop that sold them, bought a large hat at random, and pulled it down over her face. Now she felt protected from stares, from criticism.

She found a bus and climbed painfully to the top, and sat rocking slightly from weakness as she was taken the several miles south to her own home. She wanted to look at it. No, not to go in, but just to see it. She had never looked at that house as she would now, when tenanted by other people. It would be like looking in at her own life.

She got off that bus, changed to another, and was at the end of her street. It was wide and tree-lined. There was nobody about. Mr. Jasper's spaniel was sitting on the pavement panting. It recognised her, but did not move. Its tongue was shaking off great heat drops. Seeing the over-heated dog in its mass of fur, she understood that it was very hot, and that she was sweating.

She walked slowly down her street. She felt as if only now she had returned home, to England, from abroad. Now she was really home. She had left cosmopolis. Young Mrs. Hatch was in her front garden, digging around her white rosebush. The girl glanced up at Kate who was walking past her garden, looked again, and as Kate was about to greet her, lost interest in the strange female, and went on digging.

Kate stood under plane trees at the foot of her garden, looking in. The large solid place stood silent under the mid-morning sun. The sky was clear, and the garden seemed overexposed, a bit limp. Things needed watering. A dove was cooing in the tree under which they had sat on that climactic afternoon. The lawn could do with some cutting: the tenants would probably cut it, in the last-minute rush before they expected themselves, the real family, to come back. A deck chair lay on its side on the lawn, looking desolate.

Kate went on standing there, in the heavy shade. Perhaps someone would come out. But nothing happened. Mrs. Enders was cooking, perhaps? Had gone out shopping? But it was not Kate's affair. This was how her house, her home, would look very soon when Michael and she had left it to live in a flat somewhere. One says "my house," "my home." Nonsense. People flow through houses, which stay the same, adapting themselves only slightly for their occupants. And Kate was not feeling anything at all about this house in which she had lived for nearly a quarter of a century. Nothing. She did feel rather vague and light, as if she might take off somewhere, through lack of substance. Certainly it was foolish to get out of bed so abruptly, after being in it for three weeks and not eating for so long, to come halfway across London. She would go back to bed for that day. She left the shelter of the tree, and on the

opposite pavement saw Mary. Mary was wearing a hat and
gloves. She hated wearing both; she seldom did; what occasion could she possibly be returning from? Kate's mouth
had stretched into a smile, for the moment when Mary
would look at her. But Mary's frown did not change. Like
Iris Hatch, she glanced at the woman standing there, looked
again because of the creature's eccentricity—what was a
tramp doing in this respectable street?—and walked on.

And now Kate did feel emotions, violently. One was
fear, another, resentment. How *could* Mary look straight
through her? They had been close friends for years and
years? Why, Mary must be drunk or something like that!
They had shared crises, domestic and personal, each other's
children—perhaps their husbands? Kate knew that Mary
had at one time fancied Michael—being Mary she had said
so. And Kate knew that Michael found Mary attractive—
well, all men did, even if they did not want to, even when
they disapproved of her. Which Michael did. Kate had
even been a little jealous—damn it, she was doing it again,
using false memory: the truth was she had burned with
jealousy, had made herself ill with it. The intensity of her
relationship with Mary dated from that time. It was not a
memory that she could be proud of, to say the least.

Kate watched Mary's retreating back, a straight and
competent back, under a straightly set and sensible hat:
nothing of what she was seeing now was true of Mary,
who was in disguise.

She realised she was relieved that Mary did not know
her. More: she was elated, as if she had been set free of
something. She quickly left the shade of the trees, and
walked through deep wells of shade along the glaring pavement. She saw that Mary had already flung off her hat,
gloves, and shoes, and stood on her lawn, barefooted, her

legs planted apart, hands on hips, breasts flopping inside her dress. Her face was screwed up with the glare and she was staring across at Kate's house.

The screwed-up eyes made her look puzzled: this was characteristic. More often than not Mary confronted situations with this look of someone needing an interpreter.

For instance, the occasions they referred to as cow sessions. There had been, in fact, only two of these. The first was about a year ago, and it had followed a visit from Mary's ten-year-old son's teacher, who had come to get across to Mary that there was something the boy needed that he wasn't getting from what the teacher described as "his home environment."

It happened that Michael was away that weekend, Mary's husband working, Kate's and Mary's children variously occupied. Having exclaimed several times how remarkable it was that they both found themselves alone at the same time, they found they had created the atmosphere of an occasion, and they drifted to Mary's bedroom where they were drinking first coffee, then whisky.

Mary was telling Kate, detail by detail, in her way that sounded conscientious, but was the result of her puzzlement, the teacher's recommendations for the child's "better integration." The phrases followed each other: well-adjusted, typical, normal, integrated, secure, normative; and soon they were smiling, as hilarity mounted in both that was partly the prospect of two days' perfect freedom, and partly the Scotch.

Kate, putting in her mite, told Mary how a counsellor had once come on a similar errand about Eileen, then being "difficult" for some reason or another now forgotten. "She said," said Kate, "that Eileen's problems would be easily supported and solved in a well-structured family unit like ours." Mary suddenly let out a snort of laughter. "A unit," said Kate. "Yes, a unit she said we were. Not only that, a nuclear unit." They laughed. They began to roar, to peal, to yell with laughter, Mary rolling on her bed, Kate in her chair. Other occasions came to mind, each bringing forth its crop of irresistible words. At each new one, they rolled and yelled afresh. They were deliberately searching for the words that could release the laughter, and soon quite ordinary words were doing this, not the jargon like parent-and-child confrontation, syndrome, stress situation, but even "sound," "ordered," "healthy," and so on. And then they were shrieking at "family," and "home" and "mother" and "father."

But Kate began to feel uncomfortable; and her discomfort—Mary's instincts were acute—communicated itself; and Mary's face put on the familiar look of curiosity, of readiness to be instructed: why was Kate now reacting in some sort of disapproval, whereas she had not a moment ago?

A few days later, in Mary's kitchen, waiting for a dish to get itself cooked, they began laughing again, because of a word that had, without Kate's meaning it to, slipped out of its place in a sentence and been given emphasis. She had been saying that she had walked into her living room and seen her children and her husband playing some game of cards; but the word "husband" had isolated itself and they had to laugh. They could not stop themselves. They began improvising, telling anecdotes or describing situations, in which certain words were bound to come up: wife, husband, man, woman . . . they laughed and laughed. "The father of my children," one woman would say; "the breadwinner," said the other, and they shrieked like harpies.

It was a ritual, like the stag parties of suburban men

in which everything their normal lives are dedicated to upholding is spat on, insulted, belittled.

It was Kate's guilt, it goes without saying, that ended this occasion too; and Mary checked herself, quite willingly and promptly, when Kate did, and lit herself a cigarette, and sat smoking it, scattering ash all about the place, and smiling in her usual way: Well, so we have stopped doing that, have we? We've gone over the mark, I suppose? What mark? Do tell me, do explain?

Quite soon the two incidents, unrepeated, had gone into the past and Mary was referring to them like this: "When we laughed, do you remember, Kate? When we had our cow sessions." And the expression on her face was as it was now while she stared at the house opposite her own, the sun contracting her eye muscles: I don't understand, but if you say so I suppose I'll have to accept it, I'm doing my best to fit in with your ideas you know. I always do.

Mary stood among deck chairs, an outgrown children's climbing frame, bicycles, a garden table, a bird bath, hydrangeas, a lawn sprinkler, two cats, a watering can, and a small heap of colour lying on the grass that was her handbag, her hat, her gloves, her shoes.

Kate passed the spaniel that lay stretched out, its pink tongue gathering gravel, its tail lazily moving in greeting.

On the bus she was thinking, over and over again: Mary did not know me. That girl, Iris Hatch, didn't know me.

It being the middle of the day, and the traffic thick, it took over an hour to get back to central London, and all the way Kate was thinking: they didn't know me, they see me every day of their lives, but they didn't know me. Only the dog did.

Dragging herself up the hotel steps, trying to make herself invisible in the lobby, leaning against the wall of the dizzying lift, collapsing into bed in the noisy room, she was repeating: They looked right through me. They didn't know me. Far from being saddened by it, she was delighted, she felt quite drunk with relief that friendship, ties, "knowing people" were so shallow, easily disproved.

She slept through a hot afternoon, waking to tell the solicitous Silvia—back again on this floor after her flight into the higher regions of her profession—that she felt much better, yes, she felt fine, yes, she was probably cured. Although it was foolish to get up again—she had still not been able to keep anything down—she got the hotel to book her a ticket for a play.

She did not care which play. She wanted to see people dressed up in personalities not their own, that was all. Her closest friend had not known her: a loss of weight, a hat put on any how, probably a walk that dragged, the fact that Mary imagined her somewhere on the shores of the Mediterranean—these small things had been enough for Mary not to recognise a woman she had seen every day of her life for years; all that had been needed was that Kate should play a very slightly different role from her usual one.

The people at the desk were proud that they had got for her a ticket to *A Month in the Country:* they were able unerringly to choose right for her; that was what they were proud of.

At eight o'clock she was in her seat in the front row of the stalls. The theatre was packed. Normally this play would be in a smaller theatre for a choicer audience, but it was September, a month almost as much washed in gold as August. Dollars. The audience were mostly American.

They had come to see the leading lady, a famous name, in a famous play. This was a high-class and cultural experience; the atmosphere was much too heavy, because of the amount of respect it had to carry.

A Month in the Country is quite a funny play in its way. Funny in the high-class and lifelike way, a tear behind every second or third wry smile. You have to be in the right mood, though. In the frame of mind, in fact, that Kate had been in when she was here last, four years ago: she had come out, she remembered, as if she had eaten a particularly well-prepared meal.

Kate and Michael went often to the theatre. If they let time go by before going again, they felt remiss, as if not doing their duty to themselves. They usually came together, or with friends, because their children preferred the cinema. They went as easily to the new kind of play, where audience and actors mingled, or people wore no clothes, or the actors insulted the audience, or old plays, like Shakespeare's, turned on their heads to illustrate some director's private vision, as to plays like this, which were like hearing well-known poems beautifully read. In judging the experience: That was rather good, that wasn't very good, what made the judgment was the feeling of having eaten well or not, of having been filled, sustained, supported, or left hungry and needing some sort of confirmation. Confirmation of what? But this kind of play Kate had always found to be the most filling. Ibsen, Chekhov, Turgenev—the sort of play where one observed people like oneself in their recognisable predicaments.

"So very Russian," people around were murmuring. That they did meant this was an audience pretty low down on the scale of sophistication, otherwise they would be saying, "Just like us, isn't it?"

And indeed, Kate was thinking that the household of Natalia Petrovna was very like her own. Or, rather, that is what she had been thinking last time she saw the play. Perhaps it was a mistake to come to the theatre when just out of a long stay in bed?

A woman sat prominently in the front row of the stalls, a woman whom other people were observing. Some were looking at her as much as they did at the play. She seemed quite out of place there, an eccentric to the point of fantasy, with her pink sacklike dress tied abruptly around her by a yellow scarf, her bush of multi-hued hair, her gaunt face that was yellow, and all bones and burning angry eyes. She was muttering, "Oh rubbish! Russian my aunt's fanny! Oh what nonsense!" while she fidgeted and twisted in her seat.

Natalia Petrovna said: *And what, pray, am I hoping for? Oh God, don't let me despise myself!*—and this distressing creature, who must nevertheless be rich, to be able to afford such a price for her ticket, said out loud, speaking direct to the players in an urgent, and even intimate way, "Oh nonsense, nonsense, why do you say that?"

She was thinking that there must be something wrong with the way she was seeing things. For although she was so close in to the stage, she seemed a very long way off; and she kept trying to shake herself into a different kind of attention, or participation, for she could remember her usual mood at the theatre, and knew that her present condition was far from that. It really did seem as if she looked at the creatures on the stage through a telescope, so extraordinary and distant did they seem from her in their distance from reality. Yet the last time she had sat here she had said of Natalia Petrovna, that's me. She had thought, What person, anywhere in the world, would not recognise her at once?

Well, for a start, not the people in the village in Spain where she had just been with her young lover Jeffrey. Not them. What those women had in common with Natalia Petrovna was that she was supposed to be twenty-nine, or so Turgenev said, but she was behaving and thinking like—was being acted by—a woman of fifty. A woman who thought of herself as getting old, grabbing at youth. Obviously the nineteenth century, like the lives of poor people, aged women fast. You couldn't imagine a woman of twenty-nine behaving like that now; she wouldn't regard falling in love with a student as an expense of spirit, far from it.

In which case what were they all doing here? Well, what? Rubbish, it was all rubbish—oh, not the acting, of course, not the way the thing was done, it was all wonderful, wonderful. "You're marvellous," she cried out to the actors, feeling as if her powerfully critical thoughts might have damaged them, but they continued regardless, taking no notice of the mad woman a few feet away.

Yes, wonderful; and four years before she had squirmed, she had felt personally criticised; she had been full of discomfort at the self-deceptions and the vanity of the lovely lady, the mirror of every woman in the audience who has been the centre of attention and now sees her power slip away from her.

But no matter how she called out Wonderful!—or felt that she ought and refrained, for people were glaring at her and telling her to shush—there was no doubt that what she was paying a lot of money to sit here and look at seemed (it was the mood she was in, that must be it) as if a parcel of well-born maniacs were conducting a private game or ritual, and no one had yet told them they were mad. It was a farce and not at all a high-class and sensitive comedy filled with truths about human nature. The fact was that the things happening in the world, the collapse of everything, was tugging at the shape of events in this play and those like them, and making them farcical. A joke. Like her own life. Farcical.

But they would go home, these people here, across all those thousands of miles of sea and air and tell their friends they had seen *A Month in the Country*, and keep the programme in a box full of special memories.

"Oh do be quiet," someone was saying. To her. She was still expressing her feelings then? How very bad-mannered of her. Perhaps she ought to slip out and go back to bed.

I'm standing on the edge of a precipice, save me! cried Natalia Petrovna, and the audience vibrated with her emotion.

Kate now had her lips tight shut, so that nothing could come out of them; and she was thinking: She's mad. Nuts. Loony. Allowed to be. More, encouraged to be. She should be locked up. And here we are sitting and watching her. We ought to be throwing rotten fruit at them. At us. Yes, that was it, if she had an apple or two or a banana, rotten if possible—but for God's sake don't think of food. Don't look at the stage either, much better not.

She looked at the people around her, knowing that it was with a cocky aggressive sideways cast of her eye, as if expecting them to hiss back at her, "Don't stare!" But look at them, all these tourists, just as she herself had been till a week or so ago, with their good clothes, and their solid flesh, and their grooming, their carefully arranged faces and their hair—good Lord, look at the heads around her, there were parts of the world where a family could be kept alive for fifty pence a week. Some heads here would keep a dozen families alive for months. This was a

ridiculous way of thinking, because it was no more than
what people had been thinking for the last two hundred
years. The French Revolution. Two thousand years. Chris-
tianity. Probably thousands of years longer than that, if one
only knew it. For many thousands of years people had
looked at expensive heads of hair and thought of how much
food and warmth they represented, so obviously it was a
thought of no use at all, so why bother to have it? But
thoughts of this sort did go ticking on, useless or not. The
old woman next to her was a fat old thing with dead-white
hair carefully puffed and curled to hide a shining pink
scalp. Her carcass with its diamonds and its furs would feed
hundreds of families for years and years. As people had
probably never stopped thinking. But what a remarkable
thing it was, this room full of people, animals rather, all
looking in one direction, at other dressed-up animals lifted
up to perform on a stage, animals covered with cloth and
bits of fur, ornamented with stones, their faces and claws
painted with colour. Everyone had just finished eating animal of some kind; and the furs that were everywhere, despite the warm evening, were from animals that had lived
and played and fornicated in forests and fields, and everyone's footcovering was of animal skin, and their hair—no,
one had to come back to this again, it was impossible not to
—their hair was the worst: mats and caps and manes and
wigs of hair, crimped and curled and flattered and lengthened and shortened and manipulated, hair dyed all colours,
and scented and greased and lacquered. It was a room full
of animals, dogs and cats and wolves and foxes that had got
on their hind legs and put ribbons on themselves and
brushed their fur. This was a thought even more useless if
possible. There had been a caricaturist, hadn't there, who
drew people as animals, so what was the point of thinking

like this, *he* hadn't achieved anything by it, for it all went on and on.

Natalia Petrovna was saying with measured flirtatiousness: *Well, if the word "morbid" doesn't appeal to you, then I'll say that we're both old, old as the hills.*

Oh for God's sake, thought Kate—but alas, had said it, too, for a woman several seats down leaned forward to give her a contemptuous stare. The woman looked like a cat, an old pussycat that has gone fat and lazy; but enough now, stop it, she should keep her attention well away from the stage since she couldn't behave properly—really, why was it that no one but she could see, couldn't anyone *see* that what they were all watching was the behaviour of maniacs? A parody of something. Really, they all ought to be falling about, roaring with laughter, instead of feeling intelligent sympathy at these ridiculous absurd meaningless problems.

Unhappy woman, for the first time in your life you are truly in love!

And soon off went the audience, jostling and pushing and heaving to get their glass of something or other, and Kate went to the cloakroom, where she was not surprised to see that a monkey looked back at her from the mirror. The attendant was a fat old pig, and women coming in for a wash or a pee were cats and dogs. One was a pretty little fox, all sharp nose and bright observant eyes. Returning to the audience, now getting themselves uncomfortably back into their seats, Kate saw that they had all become what a few minutes before she had fancied they might be: she was in a room full of animals, each one dressed more ridiculously than the next. Was this how that old artist had always seen humanity? It had been no fancy of his, but he had lived always in the state she was in now? He had been served in shops by pigs and monkeys, had loved women with the faces of cats and little bitches, had evaded wolves, looked into mirrors hoping that one day a human face would at last appear there, dissolving the animal mask that always confronted him, no matter when and how he crept to the glass, trying to take himself by surprise, hoping that the light of an early morning, or a break in his sleep, or a sudden turn away from his easel or sketchbook would let him see the face of man with the eyes of a man looking back into his?

And he thought that perhaps one day when this happened the animal masks would dissolve away from all the people around him and then—well, what?

Then the Lion would lie down with the Lamb no doubt, and all these ridiculous thoughts could stop running around in people's heads, the old "progressive," "liberal," "intelligent"—or socialist or what-you-will—thoughts, because they were useless, they did not change anything, that lot on the stage there had been swept off the boards by a revolution, and what of it, there they were still at it, and nothing had changed, and the same thoughts went revolving and revolving in their grooves in people's heads, and quite soon they would sound loudly for what they were, like a lot of old scratched gramophone records, because people would find what was grinding around and around in their heads intolerable because of its repetitive meaninglessness. They would put an end to it. They would have no choice.

Natalia Petrovna, in an exquisite green gown—the third that evening—was on the point of tears. Tears came into Kate's eyes in sympathy.

To do this so well, to portray ridiculous shameful behaviour that everyone should be hissing at and condemning, men and women of the highest intelligence and talent spent years of aspiration, hard work, devotion, study, humiliation, living on hope or tuppence-halfpenny in the provincial rep. They sweated and suffered for this, the moment of high art, when Natalia Petrovna sweeps languid skirts across dirty boards and says to a girl who fancies the same young man: *When you think that our secret—entirely my fault, I know—that our secret is already known in this house by two men—instead of mortifying each other, shouldn't we be trying to rescue ourselves from an impossible situation? Have you forgotten who I am, my position in this house?*

Ah yes, that was the kind of talk people should make pilgrimages to hear.

Well, what she was thinking was going to have to be wiped from her mind; because who was she to find a great con what everyone else found marvellous, and anyway, she had always found it wonderful in the past, so presumably she would again, once normality had set in, and habit, and she was back in her family, sweeping her skirts all about the place and unfurling her exquisite lace parasol with a flick of her white wrists.

One last effort and I shall be free. Freedom and peace, how I have longed for you both, and very soon everyone stood up to applaud and applaud, in the way we use in our theatre, as if the need of the actors to be approved, the need of the watchers to approve, feeds an action—palms striking repeatedly together in a fusillade of noise—which is a comment quite separate and apart from anything that has happened on the stage, nothing to do with whether the events shown are ugly, beautiful, admirable or whatnot, but is more of a ritual confirmation of self-approval on the part of the audience and the actors for going to the theatre and for acting in it. A fantastic ritual. A fantastic business altogether.

Kate applauded with the rest, and shouted out Bravo! as some enthusiasts were doing from the back stalls and the gallery, grimaced back at the catlike woman who was frowning horribly at her—presumably because she was now making noises of approval whereas before she had been critical?—and was swept to the pavement by people who had lost their animal masks and were men and women again.

She waited obdurately for a taxi, observing that more than one chose not to stop for her, the crazy creature on the pavement's edge. Finally a taxi did stop, and the driver said, "But that's only a couple of hundred yards away!" and she said, "Yes, I know it is. But I've been ill." So she was driven to the hotel, and went through the foyer like a criminal, hoping that no one would notice her. But of course they did, heads kept turning after her. She got to her room, took up her hand mirror—she certainly could not have found the energy to sit upright a moment longer —and fell into bed and looked at her face.

Since that morning, the dry brassy crinkly mass of hair had got worse, and her face was an old woman's. Natalia Petrovna would not have put up with that face for a moment. She could be imagined sitting in front of a glass in a delicious white morning gown, smoothing cold cream made with cucumbers—the Russians were very strong on cucumbers—into the bruised flesh under sharp, defensive red-rimmed eyes, and saying: I'm standing on the edge of a precipice, save me! Or, while she got her maid to undo the hundred little covered buttons down her back: Can anyone ever have been so unhappy?

Long ago, a young girl lay on her back in a bed, with

a hand mirror held close to her face, and she was thinking: That is what *he* is going to see.

What *he* very shortly did see was a face that could only be described as "elfin" or "piquant," despite eyes of a depth of brown that could not be anything else but a spaniel's.

For years Kate, who spent the requisite amount of time in front of many different mirrors, had been able to see exactly what *he* was seeing, when his face was close above hers. Oh it was all so wearying, so humiliating . . . had she really spent so many years of her life—it would almost certainly add up to years!—in front of a looking glass? Just like all women. Years spent asleep, or tranced. Did a woman choose *him*, or allow herself to be chosen by *him*, because he admired that face she had so much attended to, and touched, and turned this way and that—she wouldn't be surprised, she wouldn't be surprised at all! For the whole of her life, or since she was sixteen—yes, the girl making love to her own face had been that age—she had looked into mirrors and seen what other people would judge her by. And now the image had rolled itself up and thrown itself into a corner, leaving behind the face of a sick monkey.

Those actors were absolutely right. They didn't allow themselves to be shut inside one set of features, one arrangement of hair, one manner of walking or talking, no, they changed about, were never the same. But she, Kate Brown, Michael's wife, had allowed herself to be a roundly slim redhead with sympathetic brown eyes for thirty years.

Kate was now grimacing into the hand glass, trying on different expressions, like an actress—there were hundreds she had never thought of using! She had been limiting herself to a frightfully small range, most of them, of course, creditable to her, and pleasing, or non-abrasive to others;

but what of what was going on inside her now, when she was ill (her skin was burning again, a shell of heat over the cold lake of sickness), when she was seething and rebelling like an army of ants on a carcass? But she still had a few weeks, she had a long span of freedom ahead . . . how long? She rummaged for Michael's letters, which had sent packing all emotions but one: the longing for him, for the comfort of being with him, the family, for her home. Now she saw that he had said he would not be back until the end of October, possibly even the middle of November—if she didn't mind? He would not accept the invitation to extend his visit if she would rather he did not. He gathered from her letter that she was finding her summer interesting too— well, good luck, he was delighted, it was about time she had a break. He would see her in the autumn if he did not hear from her at once. But of course he had *not* heard, because Kate had not taken in this part of his letter: now, to make sure, she sent a telegram to say that he must please himself.

As soon as it was light she bathed, put on a dress that swung around her, brushed her hair this way and that, and, failing to control it, tied it into a scarf, ordered, but could not eat, a lavish cosmopolitan breakfast, and left the hotel without knowing where she was going.

The hotel bill had left her funds pretty low. Low, that is, for Kate Brown of the world of conferences, but high for an ordinary woman who had some weeks on the loose waiting for her family to come back to her.

Maureen's Flat

She got onto a bus and sat on it until she saw a gleam of water—a canal—and the word, scarlet on dead-white paint that shone in the heavy September sunlight, *Ristorante*. The rest of the street was all London, basic London, and she got off, and saw a noticeboard by a cigarette shop. As she approached it, she saw that the proprietor of the shop, a small old man wearing overalls, and a young man, were together putting up a new card on the board. The old man held up his thumb in that gesture which in some countries means: Good, that's fine, that's spot on, but on its blade was a thumb tack, and this he applied hard to the centre top of the white square. The young man had long Jesus-hair and his feet were bare. His face was sweet, childish, and open; and when the old man had gone back into the shop, he stood looking at the hundred or so bits of white card, among which his was now lost.

It said: Room in private flat to let until end of October five pounds a week share kitchen and bath.

Kate said to the young man, "Where is this room?"

"Around the corner."

"Is it yours?"

At this he grinned, politely, but with a small what-else-can-you-expect nod, which grin was making a statement she was meant to notice, for he followed it with, "*Mine?*"

It having thus been made clear that like all her generation she thought in terms of private property, while he, being of his age, was free, his grin became natural, and he followed it with, "Among others."

"If I took the room," said Kate, using the humorous adaptable tone that came easily after years of use with "the children," "would it be mine, or would I have to share it?"

At this he consented to laugh, and said, "Oh no, it would be yours. I'm going away for a bit, and most of us will be away."

"Then could you show it to me?"

He examined her. What he was seeing, of course, was an old woman. That she was ill, or had been, was being absorbed into "an old woman." Then he turned, to set himself beside her, thus indicating that she was possible, and they walked together along the pavement by the canal. He was giving her glances which she interpreted as: But we didn't want an old woman in the place.

She said, "I am clean, careful, housetrained."

He laughed, again in his way of making it clear that it was after careful consideration, and said, "I'm not hung up about that." Then, interpreting, "I don't mind what you do. But there's someone in the flat who . . ."

"I have to be approved, is that it?"

The flat was a basement flat, and rather dark, after the yellow September glare. The young man went ahead of her along a wide hall that was furnished with piles of cushions and some posters. There was the dry tang of marihuana. Kate followed him thinking she would be shown the room that was to let, but she was led into a large room that had French windows open onto a small patio, crammed with plants of all kinds. On a hard chair by the windows sat a girl in the sunlight. Her bare brown feet were planted side by side on rush matting. Quantities of thick yellow hair fell all around her face—fell forward over it, so that it was not until she lifted her head that Kate saw a brown healthy face in which were round blue candid eyes. She was doing nothing. She smoked.

She considered Kate, then looked at the young man. He said to Kate, "I didn't ask your name?"

"Kate Brown."

"This is Kate," he said to the girl. To Kate he said, with the formality that must have come from his upbringing, which included a small stiff nod, like a curtailed bow, "This is Maureen." Turning back to the girl he said with the naive awkwardness of his acquired manner, "I put up the card and she was there and said could she come along?"

"Oh," said Maureen. She pushed back hair, jumped up from her chair as if meaning to do something, but then sat down again, with the instant relaxation of a cat. She wore a very short brown skirt and a blue checked shirt, like the girl you see on a poster advertising milk or eggs.

At last she smiled and said, "Would you like to see it?"

"Yes," said Kate.

"You think she will be all right, do you?" said the young man to the girl—his girlfriend? This struck his upbringing as rude, and he even reddened a little, as he explained to Kate, "You see, I wanted to make sure that Maureen was all right before I took off."

Maureen's eyelids lowered abruptly; two white half-moons on brown cheeks. Kate thought that she stopped a smile.

"I'm fine, Jerry. I told you," said Maureen.

"Well in that case I'll just . . ."

"Yes, do."

Jerry nodded at Kate, gave Maureen a long steady

look which was meant to impress something on her—but what, Kate could not decide—and went out of the room. And that was the last Kate saw of him.

Maureen considered. She was wondering if she should ask about Kate's qualifications to pay? All she said was, "It's the room at the end of the passage on the left. It's Jerry's but he's going to Turkey."

She did not come with Kate, but sat on, planted on her chair, in a cloud of blue smoke that smelled of other states and climates. The blue ripples and whorls and waves lay all about her as if she were sitting in sunny water.

The room was small, and had in it a narrow bed and a cupboard. It was many degrees colder than the front of the flat, which was on the south. This room had a chill on it that connected with the cold that lay permanently around Kate's stomach. But it would do.

She went back to the girl and said the room was all right, and that she would stay in it until the end of October—hearing herself say this, she realised she had made decisions her conscious self knew nothing about.

As Maureen said nothing about money, she put down five one-pound notes on a red cushion near the girl's feet.

At this Maureen allowed a smile to appear from behind her blind of yellow hair. "Thanks," she said. "But any time."

"The key?" prompted Kate.

"Oh yes. It's somewhere, I suppose. Yes, I remember." She jumped up, straightening herself into the perpendicular in a single movement, bent without bending her knees, in another sudden movement, and picked up cushions at random. Under one was a key. This she handed up to Kate— she had not straightened herself, and then, neatly folding her legs, jumped into a sitting position on the same cushion.

"You're a dancer?" said Kate.

"No, I'm not a dancer. I do dance." She was frowning —lost among the rigid categories of the old?

On the way out Kate stopped in front of a long old-fashioned swing mirror in the hall. She saw a thin monkey of a woman inside a "good" yellow dress, her hair tied into a lump behind her head. She pulled off the scarf and the hair stood there, stiff and thick. She noted that she was in the grip of a need to do something for herself—get her hair done, buy a dress that fitted; this was because of the girl with her healthy young flesh, and her fresh clothes. She noted, too, that this impulse had something to do with her own daughter: Maureen was about Eileen's age. She saw that the moment of returning to her own family was going to be a dramatic one, whether by that time she had pulled herself together—in other words, returned to their conception of her—or had decided not to . . . surely she couldn't stay as she was? Could she? What an interesting idea! But the family would, as it is said, have a fit. The idea was making her prickle pleasurably, with exactly the same sensation as if she had swallowed too large a mouthful of water ice, and her mouth and throat were being paralysed by it—as she had felt yesterday, when Mary Finchley did not recognise her, and as she had felt while derisively watching Natalia Petrovna at her tricks of self-deceit.

This pleasurable sensation faded and left another, not nearly so agreeable. Now she was again in the grip of vanity. If she were to go home looking as she did now, all that her husband and four children would say was that she did not look herself—for they knew what she could look like. But Maureen, that girl sitting on her red cushion dreaming in the tangy blue-swirling clouds, had never seen her in any other guise but that of a sick monkey . . . there was no doubt at all that she was mad. What on earth did it matter to the girl, or to herself, what she looked like? Or, for that matter, what she was—if she, or if anyone, knew what that was. She, Kate, had hired a room from Maureen, that was all. It was a neat reversal of a recent situation for Kate, who, earlier that year, had let stay in her house a young girl who was the Belgian friend of James's best friend: the girl wanted to learn English. What Kate had cared about was that the girl should fit into the family atmosphere, adding to it because of her humorous friendly nature which was also a trifle persnickety and old maidish— her upbringing had been conventional—but not disturbing it too much. This she could have done by falling in love with her own husband—not that Kate had thought her husband would have fallen in love with the girl . . . here Kate pulled herself up short and shouted to herself, Don't start that again, remember the *au pair* Monique, there was hell to pay because you thought Michael had fallen for her.

Kate finished the list of the requirements she had had for the Belgian girl in the mode of the gloss: that she should not fall in love too much with any one of the three sons, unless the son in question fell equally in love with her. That she should not get pregnant, requiring her, Kate, to deal with the problem—like Monique, whose abortion had had to be paid for by the Browns, since the foetus's father, a young Frenchman met at a language class, had no money. That she should not take drugs like Rosalie, a former *au pair* from Frankfurt—that is, it would be all right if she smoked pot, but not anything stronger. That she should not play the hi-fi too loudly. That she should not . . . but in the tone of her present self, Kate summed it all up: that she should not do more than conform comfortably to her, Kate's, way of life because while it went without saying Kate would not claim any particular virtues for the way of life as such, she did not want to suffer the annoyance of it being disturbed.

Maureen had come into the hall, like a milkmaid in a nursery rhyme, on bare feet. Seeing Kate standing in front of the glass, in a semidark, she switched the light on, and walked in her springy energetic way quietly along the passage until she stood just behind Kate, reflected in the same glass.

Maureen pushed back her yellow hair and looked at herself and then at Kate. She frowned. The frown was the result of perplexity, the need to understand the situation?

Maureen smiled dazzlingly, all white teeth and red lips, and began dancing. It was an energetic hopping springing sort of dance, and she watched herself in the mirror as a child watches itself do something for the first time. She decided to be delighted with her dance, she smiled. Then, flinging back her head, flinging out her arm, she circled round and round, her feet pattering about under her as she got dizzy, when she slumped against a wall laughing.

All this had been self-absorbed, almost a private performance. But now she pushed herself up from the wall, using a heave of her shoulder, and came to stand by Kate. Kate caught the smile on her own face; it was a middle-aged smile, a bit sad, humorous, shrewd, patient. This smile was what had provoked that perky provocative dance?

Maureen leaned forward and looked at herself carefully past Kate's shoulder. She stuck out her tongue at Kate. This was out of resentment, of self-assertion. Then, equally disliking, she stuck it out again, but at herself. Then with a false jolly smile at Kate, she returned rapidly to her sunny room.

Kate felt assaulted. No matter how her mind said that

it had been friendly, a sharing—the girl had come to share her moment at the glass—she felt it as aggression, and this was because, quite simply, of the marvellous assurance of the girl's youth. Of her courage in doing what she felt like doing. Yes, that was it, that was what she, Kate, had lost.

But it was no good standing on and on here, in this large hall full of cushions—which were all tumbled and disarranged, as if they had been slept on the night before, simply because she did not want to go out into the street, to expose her weakness. And she had to rest soon. She should start eating.

She went out again into the sunlight, up cement steps. She stood under the heavy trees that lined the canal and was two steps from the *Ristorante*. She had decided that she ought to be hungry, or at least, that the demands of the coming weeks meant she must be fed—but why, with nothing to do, with no claims on her, did she think of demands, claims, strain? She would go and eat well, keep the meal down, enjoy it if possible . . . She went towards the *Ristorante* that had little bay trees on either side of the entrance. Through the glass of the frontage she could see a waiter bending attentively over a woman of about her own age, who was absorbing his flattering deference and smiling—"like a silly old fool," Kate thought. At the door she was thinking that before her flight into the international elite, she would have gone into such a restaurant on special occasions; that she would as automatically have passed this place and looked for a cheaper one as now she singled this one out as being the only possible one in this road. Now, as she turned herself away from it, it was with a feeling of real deprivation. A hundred yards on she went into a restaurant of the kind that occurs in every street in London at intervals of a few yards. It was nearly empty. The lunchtime rush had not started. She sat by herself and waited for service. In front of her stood the unvarying British menu. At the other end of the room, a waitress was talking to a customer, an elderly man. She was in no hurry to come over.

When she did come, she did not look at Kate, but scribbled the order down hastily on a small pad, and went back to talk to the customer, before shouting the order through a hatch into the kitchen. It seemed a long time before the food came. Kate sat on, invisible, apparently, to the waitress and to the other customers: the place was filling now. She was shaking with impatient hunger, the need to cry. The feeling that no one could see her made her want to shout, "Look, I'm here, can't you see me?" She was not far off that state which in a small child is called a tantrum. It was checked by the arrival of a plate of liver and chips and watery cabbage, which was set in front of her by the waitress who still had not looked at her. Kate could not eat the food. She felt like a small child who has been told to sit in a corner to eat its food because it has been naughty, and then is forgotten. She was raging with emotions which stopped any sensible thought. Saying to herself that she had been ill, and was not to blame, she knocked over a glass of water. She expected the waitress to come over, even to be angry with her, but she did not notice. Kate got up herself, crossed the room to the waitress, who was now chatting with another customer, and said, "I'm sorry, but I've spilt my glass of water." Her voice was tremulous.

The waitress now looked at her—only long enough to see that here was a woman being difficult. She said, "I'll come in just a tick, love," and went off to lay a table. When she did come, she gave the sodden patch on the cloth an indifferent look, and said, "If you can manage, I'll change the cloth when you are finished."

And off she went.

What could be more sensible? thought the housewife in Kate—a wet patch on the cloth would not hurt her. But after a minute she called for the bill, and noted that as she left the restaurant, it was with a little flounce of her skirt that she could swear she had never used in her life before: it was like the sniff of a woman who means to convey: Well, I don't care! Why should you think that I care one way or the other?

Midday in the Edgware Road. The liveliest of scenes, particularly on a summer's day, particularly with everyone dropping in and out of cafés and sandwich bars where they were well known, for lunch, for a cup of tea, for a sit-down. Kate walked slowly across to the *Ristorante,* and looked through the thin muslin into the interior. If she had been inside there, with that attentive young man bent over her, she would not have wished to weep, to make pettish gestures—she would not have spilt her glass of water!

Well, being so long in that hotel, being looked after by Silvia, by Marie, had done her no good at all. She had been returned to childishness, she needed to have someone's flattering attention all the time.

She descended from the bright leafy day into the shade of the flat. On the floor of the hall, sprawled over cushions, lay a young man, face down, his arms spread. He was asleep. Maureen did not seem to be about.

Kate went to her room, saw there were no sheets on the bed, found a cupboard in the hall that had in it sheets and towels, took out what she needed without disturbing the youth, who hadn't slept for some time to judge by the depth of his sleep now, and put herself to bed. There she did something she usually did not allow herself to do. She wept, long and deliberately. A safety valve? That, too; but it was more an acknowledgement that there was something to cry about. She was being assailed on all sides, and from within, too, by loneliness. So a small child weeps on learning that he is to be sent away to boarding school, or that his parents are going off on a long voyage and leaving him with strangers.

But while her body heaved and manufactured tears, she was thinking, quite coolly, that coming here, coming to the hired room where no one knew her, was the first time in her life that she had been alone and outside a cocoon of comfort and protection, the support of other people's recognition of what she had chosen to present. But here no one expected anything, knew anything about her supports, her cocoon. Now she was looking back with pleasure at the little scene in the hall when Maureen came to the mirror: Maureen had been responding directly to Kate, to what Kate was, to what Maureen saw of Kate—which was a dry, wry, cautious smile.

She finished crying, went to sleep, woke in a strange room that was chilly but had in it a long ray of sunlight: since that morning the sun had moved from one side of the flat to the other.

She had to buy food. Now the cushions in the hall were empty; and she did not see the young man again.

In the kitchen Maureen was sitting by herself, eating baby food with a teaspoon. Apricot and prune pudding. There was a stack of baby food tins on a shelf, all desserts.

Maureen wore a scarlet frilled mother hubbard, and her hair was in a pony tail. She looked ten years old.

She said, "You'll find everything you want somewhere, I think," and jumped up, still licking the spoon. She flung the empty jar into the rubbish bin and the spoon into the sink, where it landed with a tinkle. She danced out.

Kate pulled towards her a shopping basket on wheels and a roomy grass basket, and was at the door before remembering she was not shopping for anything between six and sixteen people, but for herself. She went back up into the sunlight, with a plastic carrier bag. It was late afternoon, and the shops were about to close. There were a lot of shops which were the counterparts of the restaurant in which she had eaten, or rather, not eaten her lunch. They were all small, and crammed with tinned and frozen foods. There were no shops in this road like the ones she used in middle-class Blackheath. Block towers of flats were all about, and in between old houses whose inhabitants had lived there all their lives: these were the people who used the shops, which sold nothing which Kate would normally dream of buying. Inside one she bought a loaf of dead, white bread, half a pound of butter that had been dyed yellow, a packet of processed cheese, and a pot of strawberry jam of a kind which she would at home consider herself criminal for even considering. She noted that her emotions over buying these second-rate goods were very strong indeed. What she was feeling would be appropriate to hearing that she was about to be put into prison for a year: for all her married life a good part of her energies had gone into such classifications of excellence. She was thinking, too, that the people in the village in Spain had probably never seen such bad dead food, though they were poorer than anyone who ever came into this shop, which was full of what is known as ordinary people, that is to say, the British working people, who used the awful restaurants, these awful shops . . . *and so what*, what was wrong with her, what did it matter, she was on the point of bursting into tears, she could easily stamp her foot and rage and scream—why? Meanwhile millions of people were dying all over the poor parts of the world because they got nothing to eat, millions of children would never be normal because such food as she had put in her pretty plastic bag that had a design of orange and pink daisies on it did not come their way at all . . . At the cash desk, she was in a rage of childish resentment, and tears stood behind her eyes. Why? The man had not looked at her, had not smiled and said, Oh Mrs. Brown, oh Kate, oh Catherine, how nice to see you—that was all. His manner, she was feeling, was cold. She was insane, there was no doubt of it—so spoke her intelligence, while her emotions were those of a small child.

She walked in the direction of Marble Arch. There was a street market, ready to close. Then it must be Saturday?—there had never been a time in her life when Kate had not known the hour of the day, let alone the day of the week.

In front of her was a wooden platform on which rolled some tomatoes among flattening lettuce, the ravaged remains of that morning's display of fresh growth. In front of her descended a wooden flap. Like a door shutting—a panic of deprivation made her run around the side of the stall and almost shout—but she was smiling; she could feel the desperate grimace stretching her lips, "Can I have some tomatoes, a pound of tomatoes?"

The man said, showing dislike, "I'm shutting. It's past my time."

"Oh, please," she gasped, and heard her own voice making it a life-and-death matter.

The man now deliberately looked her up and down. Then he as deliberately turned and looked along a stretch of stalls open, still showing a scattering of fruit and vegetables. He then turned his back on her, and pulled down the side flap of the stall. To the air he delivered the verdict she deserved, as formalised as the rituals of a law court: "Some mothers do have 'em."

She went to a near stall, queued, and listened to the woman in front of her—a woman like the normal Kate, or rather, the normal Kate of the past, with a shopping basket on wheels and carriers and net bags, buying a large family's supply for the week.

She moved away, bowed down, weighed down, a slave, her shoulders saying how satisfying it was to bear burdens for others. Since Kate had her attention on this woman, she missed her place in the queue, and that complex of emotion was set going that is part of the queue rituals. The woman who had taken Kate's place was aggressive, and kept an adamant self-righteous cheek towards Kate, while she said to the woman on the other side, "I haven't got time to stand here all day if she has."

Kate bought, from a man who didn't look at her, two lemons and a green pepper, having suppressed the reflex to buy a dozen lemons and two pounds of green peppers.

She returned to the flat, knowing that she had not begun to understand what she had to face. She had not had an inkling of it before today. If she had not been low in vitality, if she had not been ill, she would not have had these excessively strong reactions—of course not. But how glad she ought to be that this was happening—otherwise, each one of these violent emotions would have been small impulses, minor spurts of pettiness. She might easily have not known what they were, might have been able to pretend she did not feel them.

But what was she going to do about this monster inside which she was trapped, a monstrous baby, who had to be soothed and smiled at and given attention on demand: the woman who for years has been saying, implicitly, of course, *Have you forgotten who I am, my position in this house?* Natalia Petrovna came straight out with it; the fact that Kate Brown would be ashamed to say it aloud showed there had been some progress?

Outside the flat, on a low wall, sat a languid young

lady with a large yellow chignon, eyes limned with blue paint, a bright pink doll's mouth. She was wearing an ancient black dinner dress in lace and satin.

The young lady's haughty face vanished in a wide smile, and Maureen said, "Why are you so thin?"

"Because I have lost a lot of weight."

"Makes sense."

"Not to me—yet," said Kate, and descended into the flat.

And now, like someone trying to deal with a faulty machine, an engine needing oil perhaps, she set about the business of making herself a meal she could eat. She had to eat. She needed the energy. She had to build up energy in order to defeat the monster which had swallowed her whole.

She made toast out of the awful bread, buttered and cheesed it, and sat herself down at the kitchen table to eat it. But each mouthful became an unswallowable mass. Maureen strode in, her lace dress flapping about naked ankles and feet.

"Have you been ill?" she demanded.

"A little."

Maureen pulled down off the stack a jar of baby food called Plum and Semolina and, hitching up her lace, sat on the end of the table and began to eat. Seeing Kate chewing, she waved her hand at the baby food and said, "Try that instead? I never eat anything else."

"You'll get a vitamin deficiency," said Kate, automatically, and sat fighting tears as Maureen rocked with derisive laughter.

Maureen handed her a jar of apple purée, and Kate was able to swallow the stuff.

"I like being ill," said Maureen. "It's better than hash."

"Hash didn't do anything for me when I tried it."

"You didn't persevere with it, did you?" stated Maureen.

There now entered a young man with a King Charles haircut, jeans, and a frilly silk shirt. He nodded at Kate, went past her to Maureen, lifted her off the table, and said, "We must move. It starts in five minutes."

Maureen pulled on a pair of white kid lace-up boots, and arranged a rather beautiful Spanish shawl, which was full of moth holes, over her bare shoulders.

The two left, nodding at Kate, who felt a wash of violent anguish appropriate to saying goodbye to loved ones departing for several years. She was full of loss because this delightful, ruthless inconsequence had been taken from her, even for an evening. Her children were much more solemn, not nearly so casual. It was her fault this was so? She ought to have . . .

She checked herself, as it were pleading with guilt, and with sorrow, to stay away till she had strength to withstand them.

Kate piled blankets on her bed and dived into them. She slept. She was searching for the dream of the seal but could not find it. Other dreams captured her, kept her prisoner, dreams smaller and less important; in her sleep she felt like someone a couple of yards from the centre of the maze, but no matter how she turned and tried, she could not reach it. The seal was there; it was being carried north by Kate whose business it was to do this, but this was going on in a part of Kate that was obscured from her by dreams like so many parcels that she had to balance and secure.

She woke. Air was flowing, carrying a multicoloured music. It was heavy air, damp, but reminiscent of irresponsibility, of gaiety, of people mixing and moving: this summer air, a summer Saturday night's current tingled across Kate's face in a thin dark that had leaf shadows printed on it from the window: there was a street light on the pavement outside. One of the patterns of music came from inside the flat.

Kate thought she was much better: the violences of the day seemed gone. It was because she had eaten something at last—she would go and eat again. It pleased her that she would probably run into Maureen. She put on a yellow beach robe, and went out into the hall. It was empty. She saw herself in the long mirror: there was nothing for it but to laugh at what she saw. It didn't matter, it would only be Maureen. The kitchen door was shut. She opened it with a smile, onto a scene that confused her, like an undeserved assault.

Five young people sat around the kitchen table, which had plates of food, and glasses of wine. A dark girl played a guitar. Kate realised that the smile that she wore was a habit of that other house, her own home: walking into a room there that had in it her children, their friends, it would be with this smile that expected a welcome, even if the welcome had to be inside the family convention of teasing, the "love talk."

"Ohhhh, look who has come in!"

"I suppose you are going to tell us to come and eat."

"That's my mother, that is! I told you, she's not too bad, I suppose."

That was from earlier, from the mid-teens, a raucous jeering that was quite friendly really, was full of need, which knew that she, mother, would be there, would come in always with that smile, would say not more than, "Thanks for the compliment. Yes, supper's ready."

Now it was adult politeness, much harder to take:

"Come in mother. This is my friend from Scotland/ Penzance/Spain/The States. Can he/she stay here a bit? I've bought a new sleeping bag. There's no need to bother about a lot of extra cooking, please."

It seemed to her now that the five faces, one of them Maureen's, were turning towards her in the same slow movement set to seem indifferent, which indifference was of course an affectation, but necessary to them, as protection against—what?

Five faces stared at a skeleton in a shocking-yellow robe, her hair in a dry mass around a worried face.

She fled from what seemed to her like a glare of hostility, muttering, "I'm so sorry. . . ."

In her room she knew that her feeling of total rejection was outside the range of anything rational; she could only observe it. She hurried herself into one of summer's beautiful dresses, bones inside a tent, tried to push her hair closer to her head, and gave up, then went out into the street. Under the street lamps, groups of young men hung about, hoping that something would happen: the pubs must just have closed.

She thought, *I can't, I can't go past them:* for each group of men, even a couple of young boys standing by themselves, seemed threatening. But she forced herself, a self-prescribed corrective to a need to dive back down into the flat, pull blankets over her head, and stay there. The street seemed wide, endless, each object in it embodied danger; she seemed to herself all vulnerable surfaces. She walked, with her eyes straight ahead, as she would in Italy or Spain, where women are made to feel overexposed, roped off like municipal grass: *Keep Off.*

No one took any notice. She received indifferent glances, which turned off her at once, in search of stimulus.

Again, she might have been invisible.

Her whole surface, the shields of her blank staring eyes, her body, even her trimly set feet, had been set to receive notice, like an adolescent girl who has spent three hours making up and who has staked everything on what will happen when she presents herself to batteries of search-lighting eyes. Kate felt light, floating, without ballast; her head was chaotic, her feelings numbed with confusion, she was suppressing impulses so far from anything she had ever had, or could have imagined as hers, that she was shocked by them as if reading about them in a newspaper: she knew that if she were not careful she would march up to one of these groups of lolling men and lift up her skirts to expose herself: *There*, look at that, I'm here, can't you see? Why don't you look at me?

A small café, serving exactly the same food as the one she had been into for lunch, was still open. But beside this menu was a slighter, almost apologetic card that indicated the Greek parentage of the place. They offered the skeleton of the Greek menu abroad: hummus, taramasalata, shish kebab. It was full of young people from the tall council flats, who did not want to go to bed now the pictures were finished, the pubs closed. No one took any notice of her, though she had stiffened herself to take criticism. She knew now, she had to know at last, that all her life she had been held upright by an invisible fluid, the notice of other people. But the fluid had been drained away. She swayed, had to sit down quickly at a table which had a young married couple and another girl—the sister, apparently, of the wife. The sister was sulking about something, but enjoyably: she was acting out being huffed and indifferent; the young wife was nagging to get back to her baby, because the neighbour who was looking after it would want to get to bed; the young man was looking around the restaurant and contrasting present bondage with past freedom.

The Greek who served the shish kebab was trying to make the sixteen-year-old look at him; and so Kate did not ask why they had not seasoned the food at all, did not say that not all English palates were bland; did not suggest that they might cook for her as they would for themselves. *Especially for me* were the words she found on her tongue.

She ate fast, and left the noisy friendly scene which seemed, as closing hour came near, to be swelling up like a boiling liquid which would overflow everywhere into the street.

Kate was congratulating herself that she had *not*, when she paid the bill, attracted attention by presenting an emphatic smile, sending out the signal: I am accustomed to being noticed.

In the flat, the door to the kitchen was now open, and Maureen stood against the wall near it, beside a young man Kate had not seen before. They held hands. Maureen saw Kate and said, "Why didn't you come into the kitchen before? You must, any time. You mustn't mind what we do." Before the girl had even finished, Kate's emotional self was weak with grateful emotion.

"This is Philip," said Maureen, and, removing her hand and giving the young man a small push towards Kate, "this is Kate. She's a friend."

Philip obeyed Maureen with a small smiling bow at Kate, and then went off down the hall to the door, remarking, "Right then, tomorrow." There was something admonishing about it, like an ultimatum. Maureen was reacting with a shrug, and a look of strain.

"All right," she said. "I promise. But I *do* think about it. But you come on so strong about everything."

"Of course I do. *I* know what I want," said Philip, and without looking around, went out into the night.

Maureen sighed noisily, wanting it to be seen that a weight had been taken off her, and went into the kitchen. In the half an hour since Kate had looked in on it, the scene had quite changed. The young people had vanished, the tables were cleared of plates, glasses, food. Only the guitar player was still there, her hair and her hands sweeping the strings. She took no notice of Kate.

Maureen was looking frankly and critically at Kate. She examined the mass of crinkling hair, with its wide grey band down the middle. She looked at Kate's dress, walking, or stepping, carefully around Kate to do so. Then she said, "Wait" and went off for a minute. She came back with some dresses, and held them up one by one, frowning, in front of Kate. The two women began to laugh: the laugh built up so that the guitar player glanced up to see what was so funny. At a skinny frilled dress stretched against Kate's bones, she smiled briefly, and retired back into her music.

One of the dresses was a straight dark-green shift, and Kate unwrapped herself from the one she wore and put it on.

It delighted Maureen that it fitted.

"You'd better keep that. No, use it till you get fatter again. No, really, you look such a sad sack of a thing in those awful couture-ish clothes of yours. You must be rich, I suppose."

Great waves of self-pity washed over Kate: never had she foreseen that she could be called a sad sack. But it was the girl's kindness that was forcing tears. To hide them, she made tea, her back turned, and when she returned to the table, with her cup, the guitar player wandered off, and could be heard from another room, and Maureen, spreading her black lace flounces, setting the heels of her white laced boots apart, had sat down and was frowning at Kate.

"You wear a wedding ring?"

"Yes."

"Are you divorced?"

"No."

Kate was afraid to use these monosyllables, in case the girl might withdraw her friendship, but after a while Maureen enquired, "Are you sorry you married?"

At this Kate first let out the small snort of laughter that announces it has been prompted by an indiscreet question; and then surprised herself by sitting down and laughing. Uncontrollably. She had to stop, for she was starting to cry. During this Maureen leaned her chin on her two forearms, that were on the back of a chair which she was using like a gate into a field on which she was leaning to watch horses, or at any rate, some kind of animal, and stared at Kate with a steady, stubborn blue gaze.

This she kept up when Kate had stopped laughing, so that Kate had to explain: "It is funny to be asked that, don't you see? I mean, after having been married ever since you were a girl."

"I don't see why it is funny," said Maureen.

"But I have children. Four. The youngest is nineteen."

Maureen changed neither her pose, nor her steady gaze for some moments after that. Then she got up, and dismissed what she obviously felt as a disappointment by shrugging, and then rolling herself a cigarette, in which were carefully shredded some strands of the acrid weed.

She went striding off after the music, not saying goodbye or good night.

Kate went to bed. It was midday when she woke. She lay looking through the window at the white wall that had plants in pots against it, and beyond the wall at trees, foliage, everything in heavy sunlight. There was not a sound in the flat. Without running into anyone she bathed, and went into the kitchen. No one had been in there since the night before. The telephone began ringing in the hall. Maureen answered it, and then came to stand in the doorway. Where Kate had stood last night, looking in at the five faces all turned to stare at her, now Maureen stood, looking at Kate. She wore white beach pyjamas, and her hair was in two pigtails over either shoulder, tied with white ribbons.

She came in, cut herself bread off Kate's loaf, spread jam over it, and sat down to eat.

"Are you going to dye your hair again?"

"I don't know yet. I've got nearly six weeks before I have to decide."

"What colour was it when you were young?"

"This colour." Kate saw an end of brassy red on her right shoulder, and said, "No, it was dark red."

"You must have been pretty," said Maureen.

"Thank you."

"If I went away and left you in the flat would you look after it? I mean, there wouldn't be all these people floating in and out, just you."

At this reversal to her life's condition, or life style, Kate could not help laughing.

"You wouldn't want to then?"

"No." With an effort, Kate stopped herself from saying, "But if you want me to, *of course* I will." She said,

"You see, it's not often that I get the chance to be absolutely free, and not to have to do things, look after things. I don't know when I shall have it again."

"How long?"

"What?"

"Since you had it, since you were free."

"This is the first time in my whole life that I've had it." Kate could hear the irritable despair in her voice, the statement: It's not possible, I can't believe it myself.

Maureen shot her a look that seemed unfriendly; then Kate saw it was because she was scared. Maureen got up, lit a cigarette—an ordinary one—and walked or stepped lightly around the room, on an invisible pattern that she was making as she went.

"Never?" she asked at last.

"Never."

"You married young?"

"Yes."

Another long, indrawn breath, of fright, of apprehension: the girl halted her stepping dance, that was like a bird's on a shore, and demanded, "But *are* you sorry? Are you? Are you?"

"How can I answer that? Don't you see that I can't?"

"No. Why can't you?"

"Are you thinking of marrying?"

"I might."

She went on with her dance—it was like the private dance-walk a little girl who has been brought up too strictly makes for herself: she was stepping over invisible bars, barriers, lines on the floor. Then she saw that her careful avoidance of these lines was making another pattern. She frowned, irritable, discouraged. At the other end of the room sunlight lay in a yellow square. She began walking around the square of sunlight, on tiptoe, like a soldier, one, two, one, two.

"If I left I'd go and meet Jerry in Turkey."

"To marry him?"

"No. He doesn't want to marry me. But Philip does."

"You mean, you want to run away to Jerry for fear of marrying Philip?"

At this Maureen laughed, but went on with her fast tiptoe walk around the square.

"And if I don't watch it, I'll start feeling guilty for refusing to be a housekeeper in the flat, thus forcing you into marrying Philip."

Maureen laughed again, and sat down suddenly at the table.

"Have you daughters?"

"One."

"Is she married?"

"No."

"Does she want to?"

"Sometimes yes and sometimes no."

"What do you want for her?"

"Can't you see that I can't answer that?"

"No." She shouted it. "No, no, no, no. I don't see why. Why can't you?" And she ran out of the kitchen her pigtails flying.

Mrs. Brown strolled in the park all afternoon. She had not at first realised she was again Mrs. Brown, but then she noted glances, attention: it was because she wore Maureen's properly fitting shift, in dark glossy green, because she had done her hair with the twist and the lift that went with "piquant" features—because she was, as they say, "on the mend," and the lines of her body and face had conformed?

A man came to sit near her on a bench and invited her to dinner.

She walked home through a summer Sunday dusk, among the possibilities offered by men's eyes.

Kate stood in front of the long mirror looking at the slim decorative woman—the haggardness of her face had as it were been absorbed by the over-all impression of an amenable attractiveness—and flung off the dress, put on one of those that folded and sagged, shook her hair out, and walked out into the evening. And again she might have been invisible.

Yet she needed only to put on the other dress, twist her hair so and so—and she would be drawing glances and needs after her with every step.

The maternal feelings of a woman are aroused, they say, by a certain poignant curve of the baby's head: cunning nature has arranged it thus. A goose just out of its egg follows a shape or a sound and is imprinted ever after by "Mother"—whatever that shape or sound chanced to be at a certain crucial moment of its chickhood.

A famous African hunter describes how, when hunting, he kept the shape of the duiker or deer somewhere behind his eyes, and this inner print fitted over the camouflaged beasts that were so hard to see among their patterns of light and shade: but in this way he did see them easily.

A woman walking in a sagging dress, with a heavy walk, and her hair—this above all—not conforming to the prints made by fashion, is not "set" to attract men's sex. The same woman in a dress cut in this or that way, walking with her inner thermostat set just so—and click, she's fitting the pattern.

Men's attention is stimulated by signals no more complicated than what leads the gosling; and for all her adult life, her sexual life, let's say from twelve onwards, she had been conforming, twitching like a puppet to those strings. . . .

Next day Maureen was not anywhere to be seen—she had perhaps gone to Turkey?—and Kate wore the dark-green dress and was Mrs. Michael Brown all day, for with the mask, the charade, the fitting of herself to the template, came the old manner, the loving lovely Mrs. Kate Brown, whom shopkeepers served with a smile, and waiters liked to hover over.

The well of tears in Kate that had been threatening to flood over at the slightest nuance of indifference subsided a little, the querulousness went out of her voice, and she did not knock over glasses of water.

On the day after that Kate was in a grocery shop when she saw at the cash desk in front of her a middle-aged woman with hair of dry brass—the dye had taken badly—high heels, a tight skirt. She stood squarely in front of the shopman smiling and chatting and emphasising her presence, while he said, "Yes?" and "Is that so?" and "Fancy that!"

On and on she went, the lonely woman, her eyes forced full of vivacity, her voice urged full of charm, until the shopman turned deliberately to Kate and put an end to her.

The other woman's face set into forlorn lines; she smiled pathetically while tears brimmed; she jutted out her chin and went out into the street with a little flouncing movement of disdain.

Kate followed her; Kate was following herself slowly, along the Edgware Road, watching how she looked long into every approaching face, male or female, to see how she was being noticed, *how she was fitting into expectation that had been set in that other person by the modes of the time,* she saw how she stood at shop windows that showed clothes, examining dresses that would be appropriate for Maureen, or her Eileen; how she kept sagging into tiredness, for her heels were punishing, then pulling herself up and throwing glances everywhere that were aggressive and appealing at the same time.

Kate came back into the flat to find Maureen lying on the cushions in the hall, looking at the ceiling. She wore a long smocklike garment in scarlet linen, with scarlet boots, and her hair was loose. She was like a doll.

"I thought you'd gone to get married," said Kate.

"Don't joke about *that!*"

Kate went to her room, took off her fitting dress, put back an ill-fitting one, pulled out her hair.

Maureen looked at her from where she lay and said, "Why?"

"I'm seeing something. I've got to understand something."

Blue smoke eddied—ordinary smoke, it lacked the dry nostalgic tang of the weed. Maureen lay beneath, as if she were drowning in smoke. Her silent question made Kate say, "*Who* has been married all this time?"

"I see."

"Ah no, you don't. Or I don't think you do."

"You patronise me," said Maureen.

"How can I help it? The questions you ask—there is no weight behind them. Not of experience, you see."

"And that's everything? Ripeness is all?"

"If it's *my* all . . . what else can I say? I haven't anything to offer. I've never done anything so that I could say—but I don't know what you value. I haven't travelled the golden trail to Katmandu or done social work among the aged or written a thesis. I've just brought up a family . . ." she stopped because of the bitterness in her voice. She sat abruptly down in a chair and said, "Oh my God—listen, did you hear that?"

But Maureen jerked to her feet, as blue smoke waves washed about the hall at waist level, and she was screaming, "You don't understand. Why don't you?"

"When I say what I feel, you say it's patronage."

"Oh fuck you all!" Maureen went off into the kitchen. Kate went to her room. In a few minutes Maureen came in without knocking and found Kate sitting on a straight chair staring at the window, along the top half of which people's legs were scissoring: a film had slipped out of true, and the top half of one frame—plants on a wall with sunlight—showed with the bottom half of another, legs without torsos.

"Philip is very hot on marrying me. He says: Please marry me. I love you. I will give you a home and a car and three children."

"Well?"

"I'm surprised you didn't say: Do you love him?"

"Is that what your mother says?"

"Oh my mother! But yes, she does. And I do too."

"What's wrong with your mother?"

"Nothing."

"Yes there is. What?"

"She's such a failure. She's such a . . ."

"A sad sack?"

"*Yes.* Who'd want to be like that? Why can't you—but *I'm* not getting into that, be what you like, I don't care. But what do *you* say?"

"Be what you like. I can't help you."

"Then what is the use of all that ripeness?"

"None, I think."

"He's coming to supper tonight. Would you like to meet him?"

"How formal."

"He is formal. On principle."

"Oh?" For there was more behind this.

"He's one of these new ones—the fascists, as they are called. Do you see?"

"I haven't met any yet. But my youngest went to a meeting and said he thought they were being maligned. He sounded tempted."

"Oh, it's tempting all right. Law and order. Values. And of course, one is made to feel absolutely like dirt—what could be more attractive?"

"All right, I'd like to meet him."

Maureen went out, saying, "Eight o'clock."

The table in the kitchen had a tablecloth over it. It had three places laid. There was a bottle of wine already opened.

Kate had made herself look respectable. Maureen on the other hand, asserting herself, was outrageous, in a dress that had every conceivable pattern and print, stripe and check, incorporated into it. It was a piece of skilled engineering, that dress, so that the eye kept returning and returning to it, to find out how it was done. And it was low in front, a screen of beige lace to the waist, showing breasts whose nipples had been painted like eyes. Maureen's own face was invisible behind a mask of paint.

Philip wore what was obviously the new uniform, a development of the old style; it was not so much the clothes that were different, as that they were worn differently. Jeans, but they were dark blue, unfaded, and crisp. His cotton shirt was dark blue and fitted him. His jacket was military, dark blue again, with buttons and tabs. He wore a narrow black tie. His hair was not short-back-and-sides, but getting close. It was the urchin cut again, the cap fitting over the skull without a parting, from a centre point. It had the effect of absolving him from responsibility: one wanted to run one's hand through it; it was boyish. One could assume that this style would soon be superseded by something sterner. But the general impression was of cleanness, alertness, a pleasant readiness to take responsibility. This, however, seemed not to be his attribute, but rather the result of an act of will—the collective act of will. Looking at the trim barbered man, suddenly his rather red, slightly overful, countryish cheeks, his eyes that overflowed with the need to impose, shouted that his real, his own nature, was other. But above all, and here was the point, he had the confidence which shouted that *he* was the new thing, on the rising wave; he knew that his presence was enough to make all the Jerries and the Toms and the Dicks and the Harrys look scuffy; suddenly all the long-haired ones, the fancifully dressed, the anarchists, the dissidents who so recently had stamped on them the approval of *the time*—all these were going to look wan, tatty, and as if transparent: ghostlike, they were going to have to fade away; Philip's presence would be enough to see to that.

Well, just as so many years ago an entire generation of young people (not her children, they had been too young, had had to fit themselves to the pattern as one after another they grew up) had come into existence, it had seemed overnight, with an identical vocabulary, manner, clothes, political and social ideas, millions of them, exactly the same as each other, now it was obviously time for a new metamorphosis. And Philip was it? No, he was likely to be an intermediate type; he would be superseded. Meanwhile his attraction was great: it was that of absolute self-assurance. He did not have to say in so many words that what he offered was a thousand times better than the anarchy and sloppiness of the other young men who—this was how one had to see them, compared with himself—slouched and slithered and slid through her life.

Maureen was serving paté and hot toast. All very correct. Because of Philip they were all three behaving like middle-class people at a dinner table.

But he wasn't middle-class. He was the son of a printer, and he had even "dropped out" of school; but had gone back again and taken examinations, was now in a job that looked, as far as anyone could see, secure. He was a municipal official, and his work was to do with deprived children. He had all the attractive experience of dissidence, of having refused what "the system" offered, behind him. He used the phrase "the system" as the generation before his had done, but he saw it as something that needed to be reformed, stiffened, made authoritarian, not rejected. He was, in short, the very newest model of authority figure, the welfare worker, the social worker, whose power derived not from: Do this because there is a law agreed to by all of us—we are a democracy, aren't we?—or, Do this because the Party says so—but Do this because you are poor, hungry, ill-educated and desperate: you have no alternative.

He also belonged to an organisation called The Young Front, which in turn was affiliated to something only recently formed, called The British League of Action.

And what did it all stand for? enquired Kate. Meanwhile Maureen was toying with fingers of toast, watching Kate engaged with Philip—she was trying to find out what her own reactions were, or ought to be? What her mother's reactions were likely to be? At any rate, Maureen was sitting back and letting Kate get on with it. Kate was back inside having to be responsible; she was accepting it: she had to.

"Well Mrs. Brown, I don't have to tell you—everyone can see the mess everything is in."

"Of course."

"We'll have to pull it together."

"Of course. But how?"

"We stand for responsibility. Not for all this carping and criticising and muck-raking and doing nothing. No, we do things. We will get things done. We don't mind getting our hands dirty." He was eating fast as he talked, he ate and talked, looking at Kate and at his love Maureen, who indolently bit into toast, while her painted eyes seemed far away from him, concerned only with herself. "Yes, I am not ashamed to say it, it is decency we want, we have had enough of muck for muck's sake, we need standards now."

"In aid of what?" asked Maureen suddenly. Her voice sounded tremulous. Beneath all the paint and lace and the flounces, she was in strong conflict—Kate could feel it. Well, Philip *was* attractive. In Maureen's place, offered Jerry and the rest as alternatives, she knew whom she would be responding to—and be feeling afraid of her response.

"Well look at you, Maureen," he said, in a bluff kindly way that sounded forced: the truth was he was trying to hold himself calm and steady inside the force field of her attraction. He could hardly look at her, because of the strength of his love, and his detestation. He kept giving wincing glances at her almost naked breasts, and then said angrily, "How much do you spend on yourself a week would you say? On your clothes, your face, your hair?"

"Not as much as you may think," said Maureen, getting up to lift away plates, butter, a fragment of paté. "I buy clothes off junk stalls mostly. And I make them. I am very clever. I don't spend much."

"But it's all you do, it's how you spend your time."

"And millions of people are starving? Millions of people are dying as we sit here?" She sounded troubled, while she tried to jeer—not at what the words meant, but at his claims for himself.

"Yes," he said gently, forcing himself to stand up to her, trying to make her face him. She did look at him, but sighed, and turned away with her laden tray to the sink.

"Yes," he insisted, "it's all you ever do, change your clothes all day and paint your face." He gave another anguished look at her bosom, and grabbed out for an apple. He remembered they were not at the fruit stage of the meal, and sat still, his hands in two fists on the tablecloth.

"No," she said, after quite a long pause. "That's not true. It's not what I do. It's not how I spend my time. That's what it looks like."

"You and all your lot," he insisted, gruffly and with difficulty, because she had been definite, had made a definite claim.

"My lot?" she said laughing.

"Yes," he said, dissociating himself from the past generation in that word.

Maureen lifted a pot of stew from the stove and drifted gorgeously to the table. "You are so fucking sure of yourself," she complained.

"Yes, in a way I am. I'm not saying we have all the answers."

"This we of yours," said Kate.

"We are getting a good deal of support."

"That isn't an argument in itself."

He did not take her point.

"What Kate is saying," said Maureen for herself, "is what you are saying isn't new. To put it mildly."

"To put it mildly," said Kate.

He looked from one to another, blinking a little. Just as, when the last generation had stepped as one man onto the scene, identical in voice and vision, they did not see themselves as a repetition of the one before—not in appearance or in belief, but in their conformity with each other—so, now, Philip: he saw himself as new, fresh-minted by history.

"They call us fascists," said Philip suddenly. He was hot, resentful—all aplomb gone for the moment. "Well, sticks and stones may break our bones but words won't."

"Yes, but what are you going to *do?*" said Kate. "You don't say."

"No, he never does," complained Maureen.

"The first thing is to get together, then to agree what should be done."

"You sound as if it will be easy. It won't be."

"Yes, perfectly easy," he said, using an arrogance that made Maureen sigh again. "First we have to agree about one simple thing—that everything is in a mess, it's getting out of hand. And then, put things right. There can't be much argument about what is the cause of the mess—there haven't been any standards for a long time. We need to get back to the old values. That's all. And eliminate what's gone rotten."

"Me," breathed Maureen, ladling stew into bowls. She propped her chin in one hand as she did this, her long eyelashes purple over bright pink cheeks. She was as it were sliding down and away out of her role as correct hostess, collapsing under the weight of everything.

"Yes," said Philip. "As you are now, yes."

"Then why do you want to marry me?"

He went scarlet, despite himself, looked in resentful fascination at Maureen, shot a glance of appeal at Kate: he saw her *in loco parentis*. He pulled himself up, with an effort, and said, courageously, for it was obviously hard for him to go on, "I don't want to marry what you are now. But I can see what you really are. I can. You aren't what you make yourself look. You aren't just a spoiled, silly . . ." He began hastily spooning in bean stew, not at all good-mannered now. The three of them had quite abandoned the good behaviour of the start of the meal. They were all disturbed.

"This business of getting rid of what's gone rotten," said Kate.

"Yes," said Maureen.

He said firmly, for the first time in history, "You can't make an omelette without breaking eggs."

They finished their stew in silence.

Maureen still had her chin on her one hand as she ate. She was irritating Kate as well as Philip. The girl was deliberately at a distance from the scene, as if none of it were her business. And Kate was feeling like a hostess: she ought to be making conversation, putting Philip at his ease, restoring a tone of formality for the sake of the occasion: she suppressed all this, and ate on in silence.

At last Philip cracked with: "It's just a question of organisation, of getting things organised the right way."

The women said nothing.

"Things have to be taken in hand—not allowed to go from bad to worse."

Maureen's sigh was not deliberate: it silenced Philip.

Kate was thinking that probably one or more of her own children would take to this Youth Front or something of the kind. Who, Tim? No, he was not organisation material. Why was she so sure? People changed, people became anything under pressure. Stephen? But surely someone who saw everything as rotten was likely to be saved from taking positions on this or that platform? Perhaps. James? Out of the question—he was too much of a socialist, a believer. Well, it had happened before. Eileen? She wanted to be married more than anything else: this was how one saw her future.

But it was undermining, thinking like this, diminishing. More and more the political attitudes seemed like the behaviour of marionettes, or little clockwork figures wound up and continuing to display their little gestures while they were being knocked about and around and blown in all directions in a typhoon.

Yet the Browns were political, like all the people like them; they were political as their parents had been religious. All their adult lives, ever since the war that had formed them, they had been setting their course, holding themselves steady in self-respect, with words like liberty, freedom, democracy. They were all varying degrees of socialist, or liberal. Whom did she know who was not? Yet the truth was she was thinking, and she knew that Michael did, more and more, that it was all nonsense. But they could not bear to think it.

Her violent reaction to Philip—that was fear. But probably all his little attitudes would turn out to be as much puppet-behaviour as everything else; his Fronts and his Leagues wouldn't be anything very much—words again!

Putting aside the words, what had Michael offered her when they married? This! No, of course he would never have used words like decency, responsibility, organisation —he would have been too self-conscious; such phrases smacked, then, of what the recently finished war had been fought to end for ever. They had not, then, the ring of fine new-minted truths, which she supposed they did have to young people after a decade or so of what this boy called "anarchy, licence, and self-indulgence"? But the life she had had with Michael was in fact that typical ordered middle-class "responsible" life anywhere, obedient to the necessities of work and the family. Just what this young man believed in and wanted Maureen to share with him. So what did the slogans matter? Except that neither she, nor her Michael—nor anyone they knew, if it came to that— would have spoken or thought of "getting rid of what's gone rotten." Well, here it was again, things had come round again, they always did. "Philip," she said, "when you say 'getting rid of what's gone rotten,' doesn't that strike a very old bell for you? You haven't heard it before somewhere?"

"Well everything's been said before," he said. Yet there was a look of guilt about him. It occurred to her that this evening might be the first time he had thought like this, had said it in words: but it had come out, he had heard what he had been thinking, perhaps unknown to himself. And it sounded all right, it sounded fine! Now it would be part of his new programme, the manifesto of The Young Front or whatever it was.

"Are you a leading light in this thing of yours?"

"I suppose you could say so. Among others. I didn't start it. But the people who started it were . . ." He stopped, remembering these were outsiders.

"They were a lot of wishywashy liberals but now you are putting some real guts into it," she said. He looked at her. "It can be taken for granted," said Kate, sweet, "that that is what has happened. And will happen." She nearly said, *Your turn next*. It occurred to her that her rage of opposition to him should be directed at history, not at a youth about the age of her second son. She tried to damp her anger; besides what was the point? What she was feeling was fear, of course.

"I think I am going to be one of the people you'll have to eliminate."

"Oh no," said he, shocked. "You got me wrong. It's not *people* who have to be eliminated. People's *thinking* must change. It must. It had to come. There are all sorts of things that are possible now. For one thing, new research says we can change behaviour—antisocial behaviour, of course, just what's dangerous to other people. With drugs. Of course that would be a bit tricky, but there *are* possibilities there haven't been before."

Maureen got up, removed the plates, brought back a platter of cheese in one hand, a loaf of bread in the other. She plonked down the cheese, and dropped the loaf onto the table from the height of a foot or two. Then she sat down, leaned back in her chair, spread her legs under her phantasmagoria of a gown, set her heels on the floor as if they were in boots—but they were in buckled high-heeled evening shoes—crossed her arms on her chest, and stared at the end of the room.

Philip coloured again, started to say something that sounded like the beginning of a speech or a statement, then glanced at Kate for aid. She would not give it, she looked down.

Philip stood up. He was visibly controlling something in himself.

In a moment he had succeeded. In the light humorous tone that probably had been his normal manner before his recent reincarnation as saviour of the nation, he said, "You don't give me a chance, Maureen, do you?" He went behind the girl, and put his hands on her shoulders. Kate could see how she shrank a little, then softened, then tensed: oh yes, Maureen was very attracted to him, very. Whether she liked it or not.

"I shall make a good husband," he announced, already confident again, laughing at her, at himself. "I love you. God knows why! You'd be mad not to marry me. You'll never get another like me."

"Never a dull moment," said Maureen, sounding both resentful and amused.

"No. And I'm not out of work. Nor am I likely to be. That's surely something?"

He was joking but he spoke with real pride, and was not ashamed of it: a revolution was complete!

"That's what I've been looking for all my life," said Maureen.

She laughed, though. He leaned over her, looking down at her sunset-coloured face, and past it, at her jewelled breasts.

She did not move.

"I'll go if you like," he said, huffy again. As she still did not respond he said, "Very well, then."

"No," said Maureen. "No."

Not looking at Kate, she got up, and the two went off to her room together, good night, good night, as they went.

It was midnight. Kate walked slowly to Marble Arch and back again, receiving looks, invitations, muttered compliments, the looks of grinding hate that poor sex gets from its prisoners. She was as prominent as a bitch in heat at that hour, in that street. And all the way there and back she thought that in her other guise no one would have seen her, literally, she would have been invisible, and yet inside, the way she felt, would have been no different, she was the same despite the masks. She would have walked past dozens of sober family men, respectable young men, good fathers and grandfathers and brothers and husbands, she would have walked for four miles along the pavements of London and never known that sex was a commodity much traded. After a certain age—or rather, after a certain age and presented in a certain way—a woman feels as if the streets have had a magic wand over them: where are all the hunters gone? Magicked into respectability, every one.

What a lot of rubbish, what a con it all was, *what a bloody waste of time.*

Everything was dark in the flat when she got back to it. In the room which in daytime was full of light, bringing birdsong and the scent of grass from the many back gardens of this rich street, Maureen was lying in the arms of Philip. She lay in a cocoon of sweet warmth. She lay safe and held. She lay inside arms that shut out all threat. Inside them, Maureen lay. Asleep? Of course, of course: remember the warm safe sweet sleep that is the dream of flying when you are young and lonely, which is all your fantasies come true at once?

Next day Kate woke late. There was a note from Maureen on the kitchen table: "We have gone to the seaside for two or three days. See you, Love. Maureen."

Kate noted that the conventional little word "love" triggered off in her a warm spurt of emotion. She tore up the note and said, *Shit to that!* using the word her children used, and Maureen used, but which she never had. She appropriated it, feeling it was her right: What a con! What a bloody great stupid game! What a load of shit.

To use the word was like entering forbidden territory —self-forbidden, self-censored, even a form of tact, like not going to America at the same time as her daughter, in case she might spoil things for her. Fuck had once been such a word. She could remember discussions with contemporaries about permissible language: bloody was then their word, but that had once been abrasive enough, so it was said. But fuck they would not use, they could not bring themselves to it: for one thing it was denigratory of sex and therefore deplorable. So, once, they had felt: but soon fuck was coming as smoothly off their tongues as bloody. But not shit, no, she had felt about that as once she had felt about fuck.

All her children shat, shitted, shit, in every sentence, like the workingman's fuck, fucking, fucked.

Now she had said shit without knowing she was going to.

So much for a word.

She went shopping in her old clothes, her hair falling, went up and down the street market, invisible, and as she did this, watched Mrs. Michael Brown walking—graciously was the only word for it—up and down the shops and streets of her own area, while everyone smiled, and acknowledged and recognised, and she smiled and basked and grew subtly fat and happy because of all the note taken of her, attractive Mrs. Brown, who had lived so long in Byron Park Road, and who had bought—and paid for—so many hundredweights of food and groceries from all these loving friendly shopkeepers, Mrs. Brown, the mother of so many consumers of food and travel and books and sports goods and . . .

She was quite alone in the flat. Young people came to ask after Maureen. One night a sullen girl slept on the

cushions in the hall, demanding to come in as her right—
she "always" slept there—and would not say Good Morning or Goodbye to Kate, but stared right through her, with
an indifference of total dislike. She disappeared again without a word.

Kate noted she did not mind about being disliked, yet
only a week ago she might easily have wept.

She was eating well again; her sag into sickness already
seemed in the past. She was getting restless. She started
doing things to the flat, scrubbing the sink, tidying a cupboard. Catching herself at it she finished what she had begun—her training was too strong to allow her to leave it
unfinished—and then stopped herself from vacuuming a
floor. If she was going to do all this, she might as well go
back home.

Who was going to go back home? But she didn't have
to make decisions yet. She still had a month before the end
of October.

A letter came from Maureen. Kate read it with a fatal-
istic contempt: *Oh well, what is the use? What can one
expect?* The letter was humorous and resigned and made
little jokes.

She said she had "more or less" decided to marry
Philip. "After all"—"what else"—"who'd have thought
that she, Maureen . . ." "Ah well, I suppose there's no
bucking it . . ."

Kate dropped the letter into the rubbish bin, went out
into the street without remembering to check in which of
her persons she temporarily was—she was respectable; got
onto a bus, went to Global Food, and found letters for
Mrs. Brown.

She returned to the flat before opening them.

Her husband was missing her very much, but was still

having a wonderful time. He was thinking of doing the same thing next year. She ought to come along too, what about it old girl? He would be back a week or so earlier than he thought. If the house was still let—he couldn't remember the exact date it became theirs again—he would find a bed in the hospital for a few days.

Kate knew to the minute when the house would be theirs again.

Stephen. Algeria was marvellous. The government was shit. He would be back as planned.

Eileen. The States was great. Everything was a mess but it was everywhere wasn't it.

James. The Sudan was fantastic. People in Britain had no idea of what went on in other parts of the world, insular didn't describe it, he would be back again soon.

Tim. He had caught some sort of a bug, he didn't know what. He had been quite ill, but had not written to say so before, because he didn't want to spoil people's holidays, but he was coming home three weeks early and as he had been told to take things easy he thought it would be best if . . .

Mrs. Brown stepped from her ashes, her hand stretched towards the telephone. She rang her own home and spoke to Mrs. Enders, who said what a funny thing Mrs. Brown had rung just then, she was thinking it would in fact suit them fine to go back to the States earlier.

Kate could take possession of her home in three days from now.

She stood near the telephone, her mind spinning in its grooves. She must send wires to various people, and then ring up the shop that delivered groceries—no, better first get in cleaners to undo the mess the Enderses would certainly have left, and then order the groceries in. It would be a sensible thing if . . . she knew she was smiling, that every movement she made had energy in it, conviction, decision. It would be best if Tim took over the spare bedroom on the second floor, which got sun all day, his letter sounded pretty depressed, and he would need cheerful surroundings.

She reached for the telephone. "Is that The All Purpose Cleaners?" she began, and saw that Maureen stood in the doorway, staring at her. Philip was behind her, his hands on either side of her waist, as if presenting her to Kate. Presenting something he had created? Maureen was different. The fantasy had gone out of her appearance. She wore a sensible suit, and her hair was wound in Gretchen braids around her head.

Kate flashed them an "I'm busy but later" smile, and went on telephoning. They came into the kitchen, and sat. Silently. They were watching her. Or rather, Maureen was; Philip was watching Maureen because of the intensity of her preoccupation with Kate.

Kate was soon too deep inside skilled organisation to remember Maureen and Philip were there. Making herself a cup of tea, in an interval, she turned to offer them the teapot, when she saw they were not there, but in the bedroom. They were quarrelling. While she rang Mary Finchley to ask her to tell the windowcleaner they both used that a special visit would be needed, she turned to see Maureen, eyes red, face swollen, seated at the table. She was again staring at her. "Don't cry!" she called cheerily; and saw the girl's face set in hate. "Don't talk to *me* like that," said Maureen, and Kate was almost checked. Not quite: she was still at the height of pleasure at her own capacities, unused, she was feeling, for decades, not weeks. But she was looking at Maureen, as she listened to the telephone ringing in Mary's house. Mary was out. Kate put the receiver down, and saw that Maureen's face had gone slack and pathetic with the force of whatever woe she suffered. It was a little girl's face, and she stared at Kate in fear.

"What's wrong?" said Kate, and as she heard her voice, understood that there was in it everything there had *not* been when she had said so mechanically, "Don't cry!"

Kate's limbs were beginning to understand that they had been in some kind of a fever, which was now subsiding: they had already lost their pleasure in decision. Kate was all at once tired, and understood that she had been, for the last minutes, a little crazy. She stared at Maureen. Maureen stared at her.

"But what *is* wrong, Maureen?"

"I've just told Philip I won't marry him," said Maureen. This was so much of an accusation, that Kate knew that everything she had organised in the way of returning to her own home was going to have to be undone again. She sat down at the kitchen table.

"Why?"

"I'd do anything, I'd live alone for *always* rather than turn into *that*."

Kate, in silence, now looked at *that*, her self of a few minutes before.

"It's my fault, is it?" she said, attempting a dry but humorous accusation, but she was not going to get away with it.

Maureen flashed back, "Awful. Dreadful. Awful. You've no idea—can't you see? If you could just see yourself." She put her head down on her forearms and cried.

Kate said, "That may be so, but you were miserable about marrying Philip, and something would have changed your mind for you, if I hadn't."

Maureen made a small gesture with her head that said,

That isn't the point. She brought out: "About marrying anyone." And went on crying. Noisily.

Kate sat down and kept silent. She was thinking that she had indeed made a long journey in the last months. Before it she could not have sat quiet, while a girl her daughter's age wept with misery because of her, Kate's, power to darken her future. Kate, at the other end of what she suddenly was feeling as a long interior journey, would have been "sensible," made balanced remarks of one kind or another, attempted consolation, because she had still believed that consolation could be given. Yes, that was where she had changed. She remarked, "Where I think you may be wrong is that you seem to be thinking that if you decide not to become one thing, the other thing you become has to be better."

Maureen nodded, without lifting her head. But she stopped crying, and after a time, straightened herself with: "All the same, when I was about *ten* I took one look at that and said I'd do anything, I'd rather *die* than be that. It's *awful.*"

"It's what I've become good at."

"All day long, busy busy busy—at what?"

Kate said, dry, "At bringing you up."

"Oh no you don't, don't put it on me," she shrieked—at her mother, obviously.

"You're saying this to me because you have never been able to say it to your mother." She laughed, and said, "Probably at this moment somewhere in America Eileen is screaming at some poor female because she never has at me. She's only . . ."

"What?"

"Sulked. Muttered. Broken plates. Slammed doors. Pretended to be pregnant so the whole of the house was in suspense for weeks—the lot. *You* know," said Kate, in a sudden flush of pure hate, retrospective and nothing to do with Maureen.

Maureen said, "You're wrong. I did say it all. *I* said it and said it. But they are impervious, that crowd. What they are is what they have to be. And what they are is right. I can't imagine my mother ever, not for a minute, stopping to wonder if she might be wrong. Her whole shitty life doing nothing, fuss fuss fuss about details, details."

"Bringing you up, and making not a bad job of it," insisted Kate.

"Oh no, I've said already. No, it's not good enough."

"Anyway"—Kate felt herself being carried on pleasurably on tides of reminiscent anger—"I'm not going to be saddled with the responsibility for your breaking with Philip."

"Who said you were responsible?" screamed Maureen. "Who? I didn't. Why does it have to be your responsibility? Why? Why does it have to be, always? I'm not going to be like you—it's my responsibility, saying no. I'm not going to be like my mother. You're maniacs. You're mad."

"Yes," said Kate. "I know it. And so you won't be. The best of luck to you. And what are you going to be instead?"

At which tears came back into the girl's voice; and she sat blinking them away.

She said, "What are we to do? What? The thing is, I think I love Philip." Kate must have been looking something she was not aware of, for Maureen insisted, "Yes. It's not the first time I've been in love. This is it. Love. It's why one gets married. I was in love before and I know. I wouldn't marry him either. I'm not going to be one of that crowd."

"Which?" said Kate, having a fair idea. For one thing, the flat: Maureen paid the rent, and Maureen did not earn money. And she had the careless, almost callous self-confidence that is the property of a class. On the other hand, an accent, and that same self-confidence can be put on, *is* put on, and quite successfully, by waifs and by adventurers.

"The aristocracy," said Maureen. "No, not my family. Mine is just a good family, you know, nothing special. But I was asked in marriage by a younger son. William. He is very nice. He is as nice as Philip is when he isn't being so *silly*—oh listen to me, I say *silly* because I don't want to know, but silly isn't the word for what Philip is going to be when he gets going, I know that. But what he's suddenly become, you know, omelettes-and-eggs, that's quite new. He was just like everyone else before, but reliable, not opting out. It's terrifying," she wailed, tears spattering, "what happens to them? But I would have been rich and everything with William, and I turned him down because of that crowd of his, you know, they never see anything that happens outside their little paddock, they're just nice and kind inside their paddock. So I'm not going to marry Philip after turning down William. But I love them, I do, I do, I do. When I fell in love with William I thought Hello, that's odd—so you want a strong man do you? But now I know it. First William and now Philip. I don't love Jerry. I don't love the others. I can't take them seriously. I mean, my mind can, but something in me doesn't. It's true, isn't it? Women can say what they like but . . . Jerry has been my chum for years and years. He's another like me, you see. He's a general's son, believe it or not. He's walked out of all *that*, like me. He's a bum and he meditates. You know. It's a full-time job with him. The perfect all-time alibi. Oh—he's very nice, very nice, why do I knock him? I'm not any better? I don't *do* anything, and I live on my father. But if I've got to choose between a Jerry and Philip it's Philip every time. But I don't have to choose. That's something."

"Anyway," said Kate. "I've got things to do." And she returned to the telephone, cancelling appointments, telling neighbours plans had changed, and causing groceries that had certainly already left their shelves—Mrs. Brown's custom was too valuable not to ensure the promptest efficiency—to be returned to them.

Maureen sat quiet, leaning a head that was obviously aching, against a wall. She watched.

Kate sent this telegram to the States: "Very sorry. Have already made plans returning end of October." She was adding, "Suggest Eileen take command" but saw Maureen smile. She ended, "All my love, Kate," believing that she would mean it probably, by the end of October.

To Tim she wired, "Very sorry unable nurse you house open from day after tomorrow."

To the Enderses she wired, "Leave keys Mary Finchley my plans changed."

The day went by. Sometimes one or the other made cups of tea, coffee. The door rang, or the telephone: they took no notice.

Once Kate said, "I've just remembered, I had a dream about you the other night. I dreamed you were a brilliant yellow bird dashing around this flat, but it was a sort of a cage, and you were darting in and out of dark spaces where shafts of blinding light were falling." Here the two women looked at the dusty spaces of dull sunlight that stood here and there in the subterranean air of this room, and laughed.

"And you kept saying No, no, no, no, oh no I won't."

They smiled, then they laughed. They began to be hysterical, rolling in their chairs while the tears fell.

"We've got to stop this," said Kate.

"Yes. In a minute."

"I've a dream going on—I don't know how to put it. It's a serial dream, you know?"

"Oh yes, I like those."

"Yes. Well. Shall I tell you? I think perhaps that is what I am doing—what I am really doing—at this time. You know, at this time of my life, since early summer." There was a long silence here, which Maureen waited through, watching. "*Yes*," said Kate at last. "Looking back —over this time, you know, since that afternoon, the after- noon everything changed—it was like a thunderclap or an announcement or something, at any rate, *out* I went, *out* of my life, since then, what I think has been really going on is my dream. It hasn't been all the other things at all. Or if so . . ." She waited again, waiting for the thought to finish itself. "If so, all the things that went on outside, the job I did, and the travelling, and the affair—I had a love affair, if you can call it that, it was silly really—well all that simply . . . fed the dream. Yes. It was the dream that was . . . feeding off my daytime life. Like a foetus. I've only just seen it."

"Go on then, tell me."

Kate told her about the seal, beginning like a fairy story or fable: "A woman was walking down a dark rocky hillside, in a northern country, and she saw something lying among the rocks. She thought it was a slug, a big ugly slug, then she saw it was a half-grown seal, and it was trying to hump its way across all those rocks. To the sea. It had to get to the sea, that was the point." She stopped.

There was a falseness. It was because she was evading something by putting in the third person. She was trying to protect herself from the force of the dream by *A woman who . . . she . . .* "And then I saw the poor seal's hide was all dry and rough, and its whiskers were broken and sticking out, and I splashed water . . ."

As she talked, she realised that night after night she was dreaming of her journey with the seal, and that she was waking often in every night, after stages of the dream, but was forgetting by morning. The dream had recently gone—she couldn't think of a better way of putting it—back into the dark, beyond her reach, except in flashes. Why? Because of the painfulness of this stage of the story? Or because her waking life at this time, in this flat, with Maureen was wrong, was not feeding the dream into a strength which would enable her to remember it? At any rate, what she did remember was the loneliness and difficulty of her struggle north into the cold dark. Night after night she lugged and hauled that poor animal with its patient eyes through a terrible cold that bit and ate them both. Storms of snow full of sharp cutting pieces of ices fell on them. All around her feet, and dragging at the tail and flippers of the seal which she was not tall enough to keep off the ground, sharp rocks jagged the snow, and the edges of cracked ice were like knives. It was now completely dark. She could see nothing. Sometimes she felt what seemed to be pressure or presences near her, and knew they were trees: several times she moved into the resistance of weighted branches: they swept about her, scratching her face, reaching for her eyes and the eyes of the seal, releasing their freezing showers of snow. She could not feel her feet. Her hands clutched the seal who slipped and slid in her grasp.

"I don't know how far ahead the sea is. If there is any sea. I'm full of fear that I am walking the wrong way after all. Perhaps I'll never find the open water the seal needs. Perhaps its all ice and snow and dark always, for ever, there is no end to it—perhaps I and the seal will fall into the snow and never get up again. But why then should I be dreaming at all? What would be the point of a dream that had to end in me and the seal dying, just dying, after all that effort?"

When Kate ended, and sat silent, Maureen who had been listening as if being told an old tale, jumped up saying, "Do you know what? I think we should have something to eat. And get ourselves fixed up. Look at us—we're both such a mess."

She cut bread and buttered it, put out a plate of fruit and another of cheese, fetched down a couple of tins of the baby food. They made their evening meal in silence.

Then Maureen said, "I think what you have to do is to finish your dream."

"Yes, but I can't make it happen."

"I meant, you must finish the dream before you go back to your family. You mustn't go back before it is finished."

Afterwards she bathed, did her hair, got dressed; and Kate did the same, finally tying her hopeless, intractable hair back with a ribbon: like a schoolgirl, but at least it was off her face. The grey band bisected her head from mid-scalp to forehead. And there it was going to stay. "Oh no," Kate heard herself muttering, as she looked at the grey, encouraging it to grow fast, to spread, to banish the dye with the truth, "oh no, not again, never again, I must have been mad."

In mid-afternoon the doorbell rang so long that Maureen answered it. There stood Philip. All quiet emphasis, but apparently non-accusing, he stood in the hall looking at Maureen, and, past Maureen, at Kate in the kitchen.

"I want you two to come with me. I want you to see something."

"What for?"

"Please. It's not much to ask." His manner had not at first seemed accusing because his being here was an accusation. That much was already clear. He was standing directly in front of Maureen, full of purpose, his hands down by his sides, his eyes pressuring hers. In his uniformlike outfit he looked a soldier.

Maureen was being drawn towards him, because of his deliberate dominance. At the same time, she was repelled: she stood indecisively there, pale, almost ill. At last she turned to look at Kate, who shook her head. But Philip at once commanded, "You too. Come on, Mrs. Brown. There's something I want you both to see."

Maureen shrugged and obeyed. Kate went after her. The open door showed leaves flying in a dusty wind. The women went up the steps to the car, which was a mini. It had stickers all over it: *Buy British. Support Your Country. Your Country Needs Your Support. Support Britain, not Chaos. Pull Your Weight. Be British.*

The car looked as if it had been decorated for a pageant, or perhaps a musical about the Thirties—but what had it been all about in those days, Japan, was it? Hong Kong?

Philip opened the front passenger door, but Maureen tried to get into the back seat. Philip held her back with a hand on her shoulder, and said to her, "No, I want you to sit beside me." His voice was gentle and authoritative; but it and his manner were making a caricature of an authoritative manner made gentle by self-belief. The scene, the car, everything, was becoming more and more like a charade or a "happening" and as Maureen got in beside him she said, "But this is so silly. What am I doing here? Why did we come, Kate?"

"Trust me," said Philip, in a voice radiant with sincerity. "Trust me, Maureen."

"Oh for God's sake," said Maureen, but after all the women were in the car, and Philip was driving down the Edgware Road. Ordinary traffic surrounded them until Hyde Park Corner, where a change became visible. Cars with stickers like Philip's were everywhere, and groups of people of all ages under large banners of The British League of Action held up placards and slogans of the same sort. People in cars made thumbs-up signs, and in one a woman shouted to a poster on the pavement which said: Back the Old Country! "Jolly good show, keep it up."

Down they drove past Buckingham Palace, where people hung about as usual to breathe its air, and then to the Embankment. There, all along the pavements, were long lines of people; hundreds of them, thousands. There were as many posters as people, but these were homemade, and amateur: the only professional banner of the kind specially designed to sum up a cause, or an occasion for the public said: *Feed the Hungry at Your Door. Feed Your Own People.* But on squares of cardboard, even on sheets of ordinary typing paper, were a thousand different individual appeals, scrawled in crayons and coloured inks— even typed: *You Want Us to Starve Silently? Out of Sight Out of Mind! . . . We Haven't Eaten Today. Have You? . . . Just Had a Good Meal? You're Lucky! . . . Have You Got a Job? I Haven't.*

Philip kept glancing at Maureen, and looked pleased with himself. He was driving them as slowly as he could.

At first sight the waiting people did not seem to be starving. For these were the poor who did not actually die of hunger, or not dramatically. They lived on the margins of hunger, kept alive on pensions and allowances and handouts that were never quite enough, and on visits from the Government Relief Vans. But, if one looked close, the listlessness, the apathy, of deprivation, became apparent; these were symptoms, of course, familiar from the television screens, but ones easily associated with other countries.

Men, women, children, stood about under the yellowing trees, as leaves whirled around them, and as one had to ask what was different about this demonstration, the answer came—not easily, for it was a long time since this phenomenon had been seen—that the difference was that the groups were families, mother and father and their children, not trade unions, or political parties, or pressure groups. Families had come out of thousands, out of many thousands of London homes, and now were standing in silent accusation along the streets, looking back at the fed and the—for the moment—secure, who looked at them. But the observers were not showing any confidence or superiority, far from it; since all knew how easy it was to make the step across into those hopeless queues. There were a great many people on the opposite pavement, staring. More were coming in every minute. The word had gone around the nearby streets, and people were coming to see their own fears embodied here.

Philip continued to drive as slowly as he could. He was becoming intoxicated with what he was showing them: he seemed to glitter. Maureen, for her part, was going pale and then red, and leaning forward to look at the hungry people, and then looking at him with incredulity, anger, hate—and, of course, attraction.

"Right," said she, "very well. Here we are. Fine. And

now what do you want me to do? Get out and distribute
my spare change? Perform the miracle of the loaves and
fishes. What?"

"I wanted you to see," said Philip. He was actually
trembling with exaltation, with purpose. The rather coun-
try-ish quality of him, the clumsy fresh cheeks and stocky
body and staring honest eyes, had gone, had been absorbed
into his transfiguration. What was becoming stronger every
minute, his need that Maureen should stand by him and
give him her support, could be felt encompassing her. She
was trembling too, but she got as far away from him as she
could in the corner of her seat. He saw this and said, "All
right, don't think I haven't got the message, you don't want
me, I'm not stupid, don't think I am, I just wanted you to
see."

These phrases, like the words of the woman in the
car shouting, "Jolly good show, keep it up!" sounded like
the phrases on the posters.

They had driven half a mile, past the long lines of
dying people, and past the pavements crammed with staring sightseers.

"What's the matter with you?" asked Maureen. "Well,
what is?" She too sounded as if she were manufacturing
words whose destiny was to be scrawled on a poster or
stuck on a car window. "Has it all just struck you or what?
Millions of people have been dying every year from hunger
for years. Millions and millions. Millions of children grow
up to be thick or stupid or mentally backwards because they
haven't had the right things to eat. Everybody knows that.
So why are you suddenly dragging us down here? You
can't turn the television on without seeing it going on
somewhere. We are solving our overpopulation problems
by letting people die . . . oh fuck it, what's the use," she

ended, in a rage of exasperation, her own words over-whelming her with their placardlike quality.

"It's here," said Philip, who had listened while his face worked with nobility and dedication. "It's here in our country. Not somewhere else. I don't care about the other places. But I care about my country. About Britain."

"Oh—shit," said Maureen, turning herself away from the interminable lines of people: but now she had nowhere to look but at the sightseers, so she turned herself away from them too and looked in front of her. They drove on and on, among cars that were all going slowly, full of watching people.

Police cars stood in groups at strategic places. But the police did not get out of their cars. They sat where they were, spectators with the rest of the population who were still in work, or who had private money. Or jewellery or pictures or land.

We don't want Charity, We Want Work. Give Us Work. Give Us Our Rights, Work and Food.

A man with a gaunt face walked out from the crowd of people and posters and began to make a speech to the sightseers. "As long as we starve quietly behind four walls, that's all right, isn't it? You don't mind that! But here we are, and here we are going to stay."

Two policemen jumped from a panda car, shutting the doors smartly behind them. They crossed to the orator and began shaking their heads and waving their fingers like nurses to a naughty child: it seemed that speeches were out of order.

But the man leaped onto the shoulders of two of his friends who raised their hands to support him as he strad-dled there: for a moment it looked as if this were the be-ginning of some circus act—a human pyramid. He shouted,

"Here we are. And we shall starve publicly, not out of sight. To the death, if need be. That is why we have come. We shall starve ourselves to death where you can see us doing it."

The policemen stood irresolutely side by side, looking up at the orator. Their personal sympathies were entirely with the demonstrators: they kept sending glances and smiles into the crowd to say this.

A television van stopped. Men were leaping out of it and running across the road amongst the traffic, holding their cameras in front of them. That evening's news was in the process of being manufactured.

"They surely aren't going to be allowed to stay there, are they?" demanded Maureen. She sounded furious, as if she wanted to sweep the demonstrators out of sight, or to have the police do it for her. Now her face had a sullen reddened look; she was crying; tears flooded over the swollen surfaces of her cheeks. Her tears pleased Philip. She knew this and struggled with herself. The more she fought what she felt—whatever that was, mostly rage from the look of it—the more she weltered in emotion. But now it seemed as if Philip had had enough, and he turned the car away from the Embankment and began driving them home.

Maureen turned her shoulder to him and stared out of a window where now there was not a vestige of hunger or similar problems. Philip was smiling. He seemed to feel himself that this was not an admirable reaction, but each time he glanced at Maureen he could not help himself: the victorious smile appeared again and he had to struggle to banish it.

"Very well," said Kate. "Now tell us what you propose to do about it all."

"Oh don't be so silly, Kate, you can see he has no idea, no more than anyone else."

"We shall put this country first, for a change."

"Oh how can you be so *feeble?*"

This word got to him, and he retorted shrilly, "We shall know how to act, you'll see."

"It's incredible," said Maureen, laughing, crying, banging her fist on the back of the seat—she looked demented: "The things he says, it's incredible. Unbelievable. But you do say them, Philip. All of you, it's not only you. You all say such bloody silly things. I really can't believe you are serious."

Said Kate the oil-pourer, the balancer, the all-purpose family comforter, "You never actually say anything concrete, Philip, that's what's upsetting Maureen."

"Well of course he doesn't," screamed Maureen. "You shitty idiot," she yelled at him. "Can't you see what is in front of your eyes? No you can't. Of course not."

"We must put our own house in order," said Philip promptly, and with decision.

It was clear that these two would continue, one hysterical, one woodenly confident, as long as they were together; able to talk only in windscreen sticker phrases or in incoherences.

But luckily they had reached the tree-lined avenue, the canal with its pleasure boats, Maureen's flat.

He stopped. "I'm not going to get out," he said. Maureen got out. Kate followed. Maureen stood looking helplessly at Philip, who was staring at her. Waves of attraction were washing back and forth. Then Maureen said, "Oh God *damn* it," and ran indoors, stumbling on high heels.

"Goodbye, Mrs. Brown," said Philip, stiff, correct, triumphant; and drove off.

Inside Maureen had switched on the television. Together they waited for the news. There was another earth-
quake in Turkey. A conference about the disposal of atomic
wastes. A report about the deliberations of a committee of
Global Food, in Chile. Then a brief item about the demonstration on the Embankment. The camera swept down the
lines, but rather fast, showing the banners and placards,
lingering on: *You Don't Mind If We Starve Out of Sight
Where You Can't See Us.* A van was serving soup and
bread to the demonstrators. An orator—the same man with
the gaunt angry face—was shouting, "Don't take it, don't
—it's to keep us quiet, that's all." But nuns were bending
over children who were pushed into orderly queues by
their parents, handing out plastic cups of soup, and bread.
Another van appeared on the scene: a Government Relief
Van. The groups of people were melting and re-forming,
making queues for the food. The orator was led away by
two policemen, a gentle arrest, the camera showed the com-
passionate faces of the police, who pinned the man's arms
back, while he shouted, "Starve—stick it out—it's better to
stick it out and starve here in the open, instead of like animals behind shut doors. . . ." The police helped him up the
steps into their van, the door closed and the van drove off.

"And now the weather report . . ."

As soon as the news was over Maureen bathed, and
changed into a severe dress in dark-brown denim—the female of Philip's outfit. She stood looking at herself in the
hall mirror, then said to Kate, "I want a uniform, don't I?
I'm probably longing for one. Well, I'm not going to!"
She whirled off to the bedroom, and came out in an assortment of clothes and jewellery, put on at random. She said
to Kate, "I'll cook you supper."

It was a couple of hours before she called Kate into

the kitchen, where she had prepared artichoke hearts and avocado as an hors d'oeuvre, then stuffed veal and spinach, then a salad, cheese, a pudding. She had gone to buy the ingredients, taking a taxi down to a shop that was open, had spent a lot of money. And there was some hock, which she had chilled.

This meal the two women ate at leisure, thinking of the people down on the Embankment, and the millions they represented.

Next day Maureen said she wanted to buy a dress: she had clothes in heaps all over her room. She went out behind heavy dark glasses, in search of a fresh identity, or mask. Or uniform? She could come back as anything at all; she might just as well be wearing a nun's habit as a belly dancer's . . . envy, oh yes, this was envy all right. Maureen could choose to dress as a gipsy or as a young boy or a matron in the course of a day: it was some kind of freedom. Would Maureen have sat for a year on a verandah playing the part of haltered Mediterranean woman with grandfather as a loving tyrant and an old woman as a duenna, even as a tactful submission to others, or as a half joke?—which had turned out to be no joke at all, for hadn't her life ever since—Kate's—proved that? No Maureen would not, she could not; she had gone beyond even the pretence of submission; her nature, what she was, would forbid it. That was true? Really? When she wore a 1930's black lace dinner dress off a barrow, split to the waist at the back, with red lips and curls, or a Jane Austen morning dress with high tight sleeves she could hardly move in, was that not out of nostalgia? If so, it was not for more than an evening, half a day. So if the girl was putting on the clothes of the circumscribed women of the past, out of need to be like them—because being herself was too much of a strain?—then it was never for long, and she indulged another change of mood. Why did she, Kate, use words like *indulged:* because for years her own fantasies had had to be muted to what the family could stand in her? There was nothing in the world to stop her going out now, and buying her fantasies, and wearing them here, in Maureen's flat. She decided that this was what she would do.

Down the street a corner block was being lifted to the sky in tall flats. The bottom part of this building was complete: it fitted exactly into its allotted area, with no space left over. For five or so floors it was as it would go on, save that the windows had scrawls of chalk on them. Then began disorder: it was as if the building at that point had been broken off. High in the air men walked on planks, dangled buckets, wielded trowels, manipulated cranes. Men were working, too, at ground level, preparing what was to be hoisted aloft. Kate realised that she was standing still, staring; had been for some minutes. The men took no notice of her.

The fact that they didn't suddenly made her angry. She walked away out of sight, and there, took off her jacket—Maureen's—showing her fitting dark dress. She tied her hair dramatically with a scarf. Then she strolled back in front of the workmen, hips conscious of themselves. A storm of whistles, calls, invitations. Out of sight the other way, she made her small transformation and walked back again: the men glanced at her, did not see her. She was trembling with rage: it was a rage, it seemed to her, that she had been suppressing for a lifetime. And it was a front for worse, a misery that she did not want to answer, for it was saying again and again: This is what you have been doing for years and years and years.

She made the transit again, as a sex object, and saw that a girl dressed like a Dutch doll stood on a corner opposite, watching. Full yellow skirts, a tight red jacket, hair in yellow curls, a bright pink patch on either cheek, wide blue eyes.

Kate arrived beside Maureen and said, "And that's what it is all worth."

Maureen deliberately batted her heavy black lashes up and down on her cheek and ran the gauntlet while the men howled and whistled. On the other side, out of sight of Kate, she waited. Kate made the journey as an invisible. She noted that as she did so, she was again filled with a need to pull up her skirts and show them her backside, as the Czech women had done to insult the Russian troops when they invaded; she would have liked to blow snot into their faces, or pee, publicly, like a cow, in front of them. All this had nothing to do with what she was thinking, which were her usual thoughts of carefully measured compassion for men who did that kind of work, and had to be so glad to get it; she was thinking, too, that an animal presenting its backside to another offered subservience, defeat, obeisance: which was probably what the Czech women were doing, not knowing that they did: they had been saying in effect, It is all too much for us?

Maureen, seeing her face, took her arm: it was trembling. Maureen said in a tentative, humorous rebuke, "Oh don't, don't take on like that, don't do that, it's not like you."

"Isn't it? That's what it is all worth. That's all. Years and years and years of it."

They went back to the flat. Maureen offered tea, but Kate shook her head, and hastened to her small cold room under the earth, got herself under many covers and lay huddled up in silence, facing the wall. She slept and dreamed, but did not reach the dream of the seal, the dream was all of Maureen, the bright yellow bird who was in a cage singing No, no, no, *no*.

It was dark when she woke. The lights were on all over the flat. Maureen sat in her kitchen, no longer a doll, but a little girl in an exquisite Victorian nightdress that had many tucks, flounces, lace, embroidery. She was eating cornflakes and cream. She mixed Kate a plate of this without talking.

Later they went to Maureen's room, and Maureen put on her record player, and dimmed the sound for Kate's sake. They sat on the cushions, and Maureen put bright pink paint on her toenails and fingernails. Kate drank a little wine; Maureen smoked a little marihuana, and they did nothing. It seemed as if they were waiting. For Kate to finish her dream?

The days began to pass much faster, one after another, all alike. Across London, Kate's home was open again, her family back in it, *her* life was going on: but she was not there. As they had done so often to her, she sent them brief notes: "Terribly sorry, very busy, will let you know before I arrive." And, once a telegram: "Having a marvellous time. See you soon." She felt childish and spiteful when she sent off these messages, but it was something she had to do.

The telephone had almost stopped ringing. The doorbell, however, rang a lot. Once a young man arrived on the doorstep just as Maureen was going out, and was told, "Sorry Stanley, come back another time, I just want to get on with something."

Maureen talked about Stanley. She classified him with Philip and William, rather than with Jerry: he worked in some organisation to do with the poor and ill-housed, he was left-wing in the old fashion, which now seemed so irrelevant, he would probably want to marry Maureen, if she gave him time to see the attractions of the idea. They had slept together, satisfactorily. But she was not in love.

"What is wrong with me? What is it? It's just that I feel all the time that it is so damned *irrelevant*. I mean all the welfare work, the rescuing of humanity—all that. I know I am heartless. I am wicked. I've been told often enough. But it's no good, I can't feel that it is important. William *still* feels obligated to the tenants—not that there are many, but what there are. He dishes out money to charities. And there's Philip—well, he'll be breaking eggs, if he hasn't started already, but how can he believe in it, how can he? *I* think he's mad, but perhaps I am. Stanley. He's the best of them, from the work point of view. He does good. All the time. But when I am with him I think: That isn't the point, it isn't the point, it *isn't*. So all right, you get three hundred people housed . . . and meanwhile? He can't see that at all, and probably he's right? What shall I do Kate? Why am I like this? Philip says it is because I am an upper-class bitch and I was brought up to think of no one but myself. But that isn't true. I spent a whole year working with Stanley—did you know that? Well, I did. I shared a filthy little flat with five other people and we worked day and night getting poor people under roofs. All the time I was thinking, But that isn't the point. What *is*?"

"I don't know, how do I know?"

Kate began telling things out of her past. She could not remember how they had begun on this, but soon it was how they were spending their days. Her memories were not the kind of thing that had struck her before as important or even as interesting: now she was assessing them by Maureen's reactions. It almost seemed as if the things she remembered were because of Maureen's interest—Maureen's need? It was Maureen who was doing the choosing?

For instance, once, long ago, when there had been only two children, Stephen and Eileen, two little things of about four and three, Michael had been away somewhere, and she had driven with them into the country. She couldn't remember where, but "it was the real country you know, I remember that much, I didn't see anyone all day. I was in a wood, and there was a stream."

She had sat on the bank with the two children and they had done small things all day: looked at leaves, watched butterflies, seen the water rippling in its patterns over pebbles. The children had shrieked with laughter as the sun sifted through thick green which moved in a breeze, making a shaking golden pattern on their bare bodies.

Maureen wanted to hear every small detail of that long-ago day, which had been all happiness, so that even now the charm of it was strong enough to light this dark flat. For autumn was closing in; a wet autumn, and it was rain, not sunshine, that fell outside Maureen's windows.

And Maureen asked for the memory again, so that Kate began further back in the day, saying how she had got up early, and dressed the children—Eileen had worn a yellow cotton dress with daisies embroidered on it—and how they had driven through the traffic, but soon had reached the wood, and there they had done this and that, so on, moment by moment, Kate remembering more as she told and retold it.

Or there was the time when Michael's mother came to stay with the children—how many by then? Three? They had all been born? But at any rate, she and Michael had gone for a weekend, the first alone since the children came. They were in a hotel on the Norfolk coast. It had been a rainy weekend, but the hotel was old-fashioned, with big fires. They had gone for long walks in the rain and sat in front of the fires and played darts in the pub with the local people, and made love.

Of this sort of reminiscence Maureen could not have enough, and she would say, as soon as the two of them had finished eating their nursery food, bread and butter, apple purée, or whatever it was, "Tell me a story, Kate, tell me a story." And she would fall on her cushions and listen smiling, while Kate remembered.

"Tell me about when you and Michael woke up that night and thought there was a burglar and then you found it was the cat, and you sat in the kitchen and had a feast and then Stephen woke up and joined you."

Maureen chanted this, like a song, with pauses in her chant, so that Kate could pick up her memory and go on from there. And Kate took it up: "And then we were all there except Tim, and we—that is, Michael and I—kept saying Shhh, because you see, he was so much younger than the others, but Stephen said, No, it's not fair—because he always looked after Tim, it was always Stephen who stood up for Tim—and he went up to Tim's bed and pulled him out and said, Quick, quick, our parents are having a party and they have asked us too. And Tim came down—Stephen carried him. Tim was about three, he was tiny, and he said, Quick, quick, we are having a party."

"And then you sat in the kitchen and ate cake and drank chocolate and then you suddenly looked up and the sun was going to come up. And you decided it was such a lovely morning it was silly to go to bed. And you all got into the car and drove to the coast. And the sea wasn't very cold, although it was April, and you all bathed and stayed by the sea all day."

"But the children had to have a rest after lunch, of

course, so they lay on the beach wrapped in towels in the shade of a breakwater and slept, and then we all had tea in a café. We ate eggs and ham and toast. Then when the rush hour was over we drove back home. The children still talk about that day. Or they did, until recently."

While their days were spent thus, searching Kate's memory for happiness, in her sleep Kate looked for the seal, for her dream. But while she knew she often entered that dream, it slipped away from her as she woke. She was afraid that she was not able to remember the dream because the seal had died. That area of her sleep was very sad, full of loss, of pain. She would wake thinking that her feet were cut, for she could feel they were cold and painful, but it was not so, they were quite warm. She woke feeling her arms ache with the weight of the seal. Surely it was heavier than it had been? Or was heavy because it had died? Far away behind her, far below the horizon, she knew that the sun still shone. But it never rose, it had not risen in her sleep now for days, for weeks. She was still travelling north, away from the sun. Ahead of her lay winter, ice, an interminable dark.

"Tell me a story, Kate. You and Michael went to a party, and you were bad-tempered and had been quarrelling for days, but then you discovered you liked each other better than anybody else there, and you fell in love for the second time."

"Or perhaps I could tell you about Mary Finchley. It took me a very long time to understand that Mary was really quite different from me. From every woman I've known. People say 'a savage woman'—you know, a man says, 'You're a savage woman,' and he is a little scared, but he admires you for it. And you are quite flattered, and you even play at being savage for a little. But it's not true.

No, Maureen, you're thinking, Yes, *I* am savage, I am not tamed! But you are. Mary isn't. Something's been left right out of her. She's like that dog that a man has spent months training, and then he says, He's useless, nothing takes. Nothing has taken on Mary. She hasn't any sense of guilt— *that's* the point. We are all in invisible chains, guilt, we should do this, we mustn't do that, it's bad for the children, it's unfair on the husband. Mary isn't, it's been left right out of her. But on the face of it she has had an ordinary upbringing. I've never been able to find out what was left out of it. Perhaps nothing was—it was left out of *her*. She married quite young. The first time I was struck by Mary was when she said, 'I chose Bill because he had a better job than the rest.' No, wait—a lot of women may think like that or act like that, but they'd say, Because I loved him the most or because I admired him or because he was sexy. Not Mary. That *was* why she chose him. Her parents didn't have much money. He adored her. He still does. They had a lot of sex. They still do. But she was unfaithful right from the start. I remember the shock I got. One day I was at the window sewing, and looking out and I saw the delivery man go into Mary's house. He was there a long time. I thought nothing of it. I thought he was having a cup of tea. Next day I mentioned it and Mary said, 'He's good value that one.' At first I thought she was joking. Then that she was boasting. No. That's how she is. If she goes shopping and she fancies a man and there's an opportunity, there you are. She never thinks about it again. All the time, when she was pregnant, when she was nursing. When I ask her about it she says, Oh I can't do with just one man! She looks rather embarrassed—but it's because *you* are a bit thick. I once fell in love with someone else— oh, it was very stupid, the whole thing, but it was then I really understood that Mary was quite different. She had never been in love in her life. She couldn't understand what I was talking about. At first I thought—as usual—she was joking. But *she* thought I was inventing it. Yes, really—she really believes that the way everyone goes on about love, being in love, is some sort of a conspiracy, the emperor has no clothes. It was about then I discovered she couldn't read anything, or look at a play on television or anything. She says, 'It's all about people torturing themselves about nothing.' She reads detective stories, and boys' adventure stories, and animal stories. I even thought for a while she was masculine. No. Love—all of it, romantic love, the whole bloody business of it—you know, centuries of our civilisation—its been left out of her. She thinks we are all crazy. You fancy a man, he fancies you, you screw until one or the other is tired, and then goodbye, no hard feelings. . . ."

"What about her husband?"

"There you are, you aren't savage, you *aren't* like her. You've been sitting there thinking, What about her husband, what about the children? Yes. Well. She had sex with other people almost from the first. But she was so casual about it it was some time before Bill believed it was really happening. He tackled her with it, and she said, 'Yes, but I'm like that.' Embarrassed for *him* because he wasn't. He made rows. When he did she got sad and uncomfortable. What was all the fuss about? That was what stymied him, you see, *her* attitude. She wasn't guilty. Then there were three children. Mary would say, Kids are all very well but they cramp your style. They weren't cramping hers much. One day Bill came home and found Mary in bed with some man whose name she didn't know. The baby was in the pram in the same room, and the little boy

—Cedric, he's sweet—was playing on the floor. Bill started a divorce. He was heartbroken. So was she. He got his divorce and custody. Mary didn't contest it, she couldn't anyway. About a year after the divorce they got together again. He wasn't in love with anyone else. He has said to all sorts of people that after Mary he can't really take to a woman, 'she's very immoral, but she's wonderful apart from that.' I suppose the point is that her being unfaithful doesn't attack him, isn't a criticism of him. And when he is unfaithful to her, she screams at him a little and then they make love. Well, sex. During the year they were divorced, they were both quite lost, they were operating from two different sets of laws. He had divorced his bad vicious wife who was corrupting the children, but she was the victim of a crazy man. 'Well what's the matter with you?' she kept saying. 'We get on all right.' When they married again he made all kinds of conditions, for the sake of his pride of course. He must have known she wouldn't fall in. And he wouldn't have married her again if she didn't suit him. And that's how they get on. The children are now in their teens and by all the rules they ought to be casualties. But they aren't any worse than most. It is true that Mary thinks it is all a bit much. She says that every time she has a bit on the side then it all gets discussed by everybody on its merits. She says no one can ever get the point—that there aren't any merits. She fancies a little bit and she has it. If the children have noticed—she does try a bit of discretion sometimes—then they discuss it, give their verdict, as it were. She says, Oh for God's sake, leave me alone, it makes me tired all your because's and why's. I like sex. Her children are in and out of my house all the time—they are younger than mine but they are a sort of family. My four have discussed Mary all their lives. They like her. Every-

one likes her. They got the point much earlier than I did.
It took me years. They understood that she wasn't like
other women. Really not. Once she seduced my husband.
If that's the word for it. No, she fancied him, and so she
had him. I was going through hell, and thinking of being
betrayed and God knows what. She said to me, next time
we were having a cup of coffee in her kitchen, 'He's all
right, Michael is. He gave me a really good time.' "

"And so?" said Maureen. She sounded defiant. "What
are you wanting me to conclude from all that?"

"I've never been able to conclude anything from it,
except that she's quite quite different from me. That's all.
Every time I do anything—or *don't* do anything, that's more
it, I like the look of a man and think, I wouldn't mind him
but of course I'd never do anything about it—then I think of
Mary. At one time thinking of Mary was a kind of comfort and support—I'd think I'm much better and finer-
feelinged and sensitive than that irresponsible creature. But
now I wonder. I really do. I sit in the theatre and see people tearing themselves to pieces about love, and suddenly
there's Mary, and she literally can't understand what all the
fuss is about. Or I sit in a cinema . . . sometimes I've been
with Mary, and its like . . . afterwards she says, 'What a
carry-on!' In the beginning, you know, when she said
things like that I thought it was a defence, the way we all
do it, but if you are with someone who really does think
it is a joke, but really, from the heart—if that's a word you
can associate with Mary—then it's odd, it changes your
perspective. There are times you know when there's a sort
of switch in the way I look at things—everything, my
whole life since I was a girl—and I seem to myself like a
raving lunatic. Love, and duty, and being in love and not
being in love, and loving, and behaving well and you

should and you shouldn't ask and you ought and oughtn't. It's a disease. Well, sometimes I think that's all it is."

"Once I believed my mother was in love with someone else. I still don't know how serious it was. It shattered me," said Maureen. "It really did. I thought she was going to leave Daddy and me. I've never looked at her in the same way since. I know it is silly. It was the worst thing in my childhood."

"Mary's children, and mine, discuss her goings-on as if they were the symptoms of a disease. To be tolerated."

When Kate told the girl about Mary she had not realised she was putting an end to *Tell me a story, please tell a story, Kate!*

But so it was.

Kate dreamed again about the seal, or rather, dreamed and remembered. The seal had made restless movements in her arms; it had wanted her to notice something. She stopped, while the snow fell silently, straight down, all about her. She could see the snow: the air was lighter than it had been? Immediately in front of her there was a glimmer, like candlelight, and there all by itself in the snow, was a silvery-pink cherry tree in full bloom. Kate pushed through deep snow to the tree and pulled off a flowering twig, and held it in her frozen fingers as she walked on past the tree into the dark ahead.

She told Maureen this new stage of the dream and Maureen said, "Well, I suppose it won't be long now."

This was, but unconsciously, forlorn. Kate saw that the girl was sad, listless. She had lost all her animation. Kate sat by her, put her arms around her, hugged her, as if she were her daughter. Maureen put her head on Kate's shoulder, and allowed herself to be hugged and petted. They fell asleep.

When Kate woke Maureen was sitting upright and cross-legged on a cushion in front of her. What Kate was looking at made her sit up, look again, shake herself into attention. Maureen's face was a new one, or at least, to Kate.

The girl said, "Do you know, when I woke up, I had my thumb in my mouth?"

Maureen had sat quiet there, on her cushion, waiting for Kate to wake so that she could shoot this accusation at her. Now, having said it, Maureen slid off her cushion and went off to the kitchen. Kate did not follow her. She was, of course, feeling guilty, in the wrong. She sat wondering where she had gone wrong, what she had done wrong.

An hour later, finding Maureen eating baby food, she sat down, wanting to know what the verdict was. Maureen said, "Do you realise? Your stories. We like different things. What you like is to tell about your children when they were very young. That's what you remember best. That's what you wanted to tell me, and when I wanted you to talk about being happy with Michael, you had to tell me about Mary."

"Was that why?"

"Yes. And it was a destructive thing to do. That's what I think. Yes, I think so. What use is Mary to me or to you? She's no help at all."

Maureen finished her food, washed up, made the kitchen tidy, while Kate sat and watched. Then the girl slung a satchel bag over her shoulder and went out.

She came back in the evening, and at once looked for Kate so that she could say, "I've been at the zoo." She was exploding with emotions. She was very angry. With Kate? Was she the cause? Why had the girl come at once into this dismal little room in search of her? "Yes, I've been there all day."

"It's not my fault," said Kate, attempting humour. Maureen said, "Who cares whose fault? That isn't the point, is it?" She was on her way out of the door when she turned with, "Why did you say that anyway? Why does it have to be your fault? It's just megalomania. That's all you are, a megalomaniac." Kate could not say anything. Then Maureen said, "Oh I'm sorry, I'm sorry. But it's all very well for you, isn't it?" And she ran out of the room, crying in her unashamed noisy way like a child who has been slapped but who knows that tears are part of the thing, to be taken no notice of.

What she was saying was: You're already through it, you've done it, for better or worse, but I have to decide whether to do it or not.

Her concern over Maureen told her the girl's accusations were just. Maureen had become one of her children; she felt for her as she did for them. More so, she told herself, with the stubbornness that means one is defending something, holding fast to something one had no right to— *that one hasn't earned*—the last weeks had held the delight in companionship with a young creature that she had not enjoyed with her own children for . . . she had been going to think *years,* and the exaggeration checked her. The family always had times of enjoyment in being together (remembering these, Kate was longing to go home this moment), and this was true even when there was antagonism between the young ones and the parents—for Michael had his difficulties too, she had not been remembering that; she had not chosen for some time to think that Michael and his sons fought, or sulked or competed and that Michael worried over it. What it all amounted to was that because family life was difficult at times (as of course every authority let alone experience said it had to be), because Kate played the role she had to, a mother who had to be resisted, fought, reacted against, because she wasn't always loved and appreciated, then she had to damn it all, see it all as black, as ugly . . . her reactions of the last few months had been nothing more than that? She had not been loved enough, noticed enough, licked and stroked enough? Was that all it was?

She was on the point of feeling so; and this was as much of a reversal of her view of herself as the one before —a gradual reversal, that had been—when she had come to see herself, and the family, and her husband, as a web of nasty self-deceptions.

What she thought about it was probably not important at all.

The mood she was in when she walked in at her front door again would be irrelevant: now *that* was the point, it was the truth. We spend our lives assessing, balancing, weighing what we think, we feel . . . it's all nonsense. Long after an experience which has been experienced as this or that kind of thought, emotion, and judged at the time accordingly—well, it is seen quite differently. *That's* what was happening, you think; and what you thought or felt about it at the time seems laughable, jejune.

How was her summer out of the family going to seem to her in a year or so's time? She could be quite certain that it would not seem anything like it did now. So why bother to assess and weigh, saying, This is what I am thinking, and therefore I should do this or that, this or that is happening . . . at which point in Kate's deliberations (for she was, of course, doing what she was deciding was pointless) Maureen came in, and said, "Kate, you know what it is? It doesn't matter, that's what it is. I can't feel that it matters. Whatever I decide to do." She went quickly out again.

Next morning she asked Kate to go to the shops with her. On the way there they saw coming towards them a young woman about Maureen's age, who was pushing a fragile push-chair in which a small child was tightly strapped. She was pulling another along by the hand. The infant in the chair was tear-stained and uncomfortable, for his mother had piled a package on the foot rest in such a way that the small legs were sticking straight up over it. At a casual glance, it was just a baby in a chair; then its bewilderment, its distress seemed to shout to the street, yelling for aid against the tightness of the straps, and the awkward parcel, and the noise of the traffic that was roaring past, and the sun dazzling into its face. The mother, half mad because of the irritation of the two small children, was pushing the chair in sharp hard jerks, and then was pulled sideways by the other child who was lagging, tugging at her hand. This child was sullen with rage, because he had been slapped. One side of his face was scarlet.

"Come on," said the girl, "get a move on or you'll get it again, I'm warning you."

The child still hung back; because his rage was claiming all his energy, not because he had decided to.

The girl let go his hand, and hit him back and forth across the face with her palm, then with the back of her hand, then with her palm again. The child stood still, and stared at her. Slowly the tears filled his eyes, and poured over his reddening cheeks.

"Come on," shouted the girl, frantic. She snatched his hand again, and dragged at him: he swung off his feet, fell against her, caught at her dress to save himself, and was on all fours on the pavement. He held his scarlet face in front of him, as his lips blubbered and snot ran from his nose.

"And now look at my dress," said the girl. He had left smudges over it of grease, sweat, tears, and sugar from the lollipop which he held in his other hand and which was now splintering on the pavement.

"If you don't get up and walk home I'll strap you till you can't sit down," said the girl, bending down to whisper this message to him, her eyes full of hate.

He slowly got up. She grabbed at his hand again. The baby started to cry. It was out of misery, not rage, or sullenness. This set the little boy off, who began to cry in the same hopeless way. He trotted desperately after his mother who was flying in great strides up the street, pushing one child in front of her, pulling the other. Her face, as she came level with Kate and Maureen, was as miserable as her children's. She saw the two women looking at her, and flashed them looks of defiance and mind-your-own-business.

She took in Maureen, this morning in an embroidered smock—white, with flower patterns in blue—over which her yellow hair fell in pigtails. The girl's look at Maureen said everything about what she had lost when she became the mother of two small children. Water filled her eyes and the three creatures went on up the street, more slowly now, all three in tears.

"You never remember anything like that," said Maureen. "Why don't you?"

Kate was going to say: Because nothing like that happened. But she walked on in silence, trying to remember if it had.

Then Maureen said, "If I married William, then I needn't bother, need I? Nannies and nurses all the way. Well, perhaps that is what I'll decide after all. I'd be running true to form, wouldn't I? A few years in the wide world and then back to the home paddock."

Maureen looked white; she seemed ill. She was very far from the girl who should be inhabiting the bright effrontery of the smock. As soon as they reached the flat Maureen ran off, tugging the smock over her head. She came back in a dark sober dress. She sat down, leaned her head against the kitchen wall, and shut her eyes. Tears flooded her cheeks. Soon she wiped her face dry in a businesslike way with tissues, splashed water on her eyes, and went out.

Kate tidied herself and left the flat—the cave rather, for it was a space dug out of earth and lined with brick. It was a cave, whatever it was called. This thought took her to the bus stop where she could catch a bus to the zoo.

As soon as she got inside the place she saw Maureen ahead of her. Or rather, she saw two dazzling plaits on dark muslin.

It was a weekday, the place not very full. The sun was at midday position, and unobscured. The zoo was full of a thick damp sunlight. Kate had not come to watch Maureen, so she set off by herself. She saw a sign: To the Sea Lions, and stood by their pool where, conscientiously, she put a coin in a machine that dispenses information. While she watched the sea lions, larger and more cumbersome than the half-grown animal whose weight in her arms she could feel all the time now, even in the day, she heard that these animals were not real seals, because they had small ears and could move easily over rocks and earth. No, her seal had no such mobility. She wandered on to the round pool where the real seals were, and there she leaned, watching the two of them, swimming around like goldfish in a bowl. To vary the tedium of their captivity they had made up little games. They turned on their backs for part of the circuit, then flipped back again; they played in and out of the jet of water that came up from the base of the pool in rays of bubbles; they swam across each other, under each other, around and around.

Kate felt that Maureen was beside her: she turned and saw her. Together they watched the seals, and then, without speaking, drifted on.

Ahead was a girl who might have been Maureen's sister. She was about thirteen. Her yellow hair was done like Alice's and she wore jeans and a bright blouse. She was rather plump: was in that stage where a girl's body and her clothes are at odds. The jeans were too tight; the blouse looked as if it had come from her mother's cupboard. She was in herself beautiful, a Renoir girl, all plumpness and sunshine, but her face was desperate. She trailed after a boy of fifteen or so. He was a tall, lithe boy, and his face was very attractive; everything about him was appealing and the two women understood why the girl had to follow him. But he, too, was desperate about something, in a turmoil of some kind. Maureen followed the couple. Kate went with her: the four people went on through the thin crowd.

Outside a monkey's cage the boy stopped and stood frowning in. The girl was just behind him.

Food had recently been pushed through a hatch, and a young monkey lay on a shelf on its back, lolling there in the most attractive relaxation, eating a hunk of fresh cabbage. The monkey was the picture of indolent enjoyment, and the boy smiled. It was not a self-conscious smile, he did not know he was being charmed by the monkey. The three females were watching him and the monkey, and an anxiety which he made them all feel was relieved, as if they had been able to put their arms around him. As the monkey lolled there, eating, another on a shelf across the cage sat up and saw it: the enjoyment of his fellow inflamed the watching beast, and it sprang into the air to reach the other shelf. Apparently the lolling monkey had seen nothing, but while the one which had jumped was still in the air, it was off its back and in the air on its way to a third shelf. The monkey who had ousted the other now picked among bits of cabbage and carrot and orange, but it was not hungry: it had envied the other's enjoyment, not its food. This one, the envious one, had an erection: a long spike of red stuck out. The one who had had to jump away from its enjoyment watched the usurper, and, as it watched, its own penis lengthened, and it began to masturbate. Now the boy frowned and went white. He had not seemed conscious of the little girl, but he turned and abruptly led her away, disapproving of her seeing the masturbating monkey. The little girl turned her head once, to stare at what she was being forbidden; then, obedient, she shot the boy lovely glances under her golden brows. But the boy was already forgetting her, his arm had fallen away, and in a moment he had gone on ahead. The little girl came behind, then the two women.

Next he stopped at an enclosure in which there were three gnus. The boy had peanuts in his pockets, and ignoring the notice forbidding feeding, he held out nuts to an animal smaller than the other two. At once one of the larger ones knocked it aside and took the food from the boy's fingers. The boy waited, patient and long-suffering, until the big ones had moved off. Again he held out some nuts to the smaller gnu. But the same thing happened: again and again the boy scooped nuts from his pockets and tried to give them to the smallest of the animals; again and again, the strong ones knocked it aside and took the food. The boy was in a rage of misery, but he persisted. The two big animals had had all the nuts, the smallest one nothing.

He was crouching against the wire of the cage now, looking in a passion of protectiveness at the little gnu. The women knew that if there had been no wire, he would have embraced the gnu, might even have put his face on the animal's rough hide and wept. By now Maureen and Kate loved him too, as much as the little girl, who was in an anguish of love. She could not look away from him, and she hovered just behind him, longing for him to notice her, and to give her credit for her wanting to help him in his hopeless task of letting the smaller animal get the food.

The boy took no notice of her. He broke away from the pain of his frustration and strode off. The girl went after him. He was running—to shake her off? She ran too. He turned off into a bird house. When the women arrived there he was looking at a cage not larger than a small packing case which had a bright bird in it, and was reading a notice which said the bird had been donated to the zoo in 1925. His face was now all red and swollen: like the slapped face of the little boy on the pavement. He went from cage to cage reading the notices which said how long the birds had been in them. A keeper or attendant came into the room, and the boy went up to him and said, "That parrot, do you ever let him out?"

"We couldn't have them flying away now, could we?" said the man.

"But never? They never get out?"

The man reacted to his emotion and walked away, saying, "No, they stay where they are."

"But do you realise that bird has been in that cage for half a century? Fifty years?" he said, forgetting himself, tugging at the man's uniformed sleeve.

"That's their lives, isn't it?" said the man. He took a brush broom from the wall, and swept the floor, his back to the boy.

Who was in a transport of suffering. The little girl stood near him, but not daring to touch him, and offered him smiles that said they could bathe away all the pain in the world. But the boy was ill with what he felt, his face was peaked; it was lined and shadowed; all the substance had gone out of it.

"Do you realise, Jane? Some of these birds have been here for *years? Decades?* Longer than our parents have been alive?"

Her face offered him nothing but consolation: he brushed her aside and walked out.

On the side of the walk stood a machine of some kind: perhaps for cutting grass.

It was deserted, was just standing there. The boy stood looking at it. Behind him was Jane, who loved him. Behind her stood Maureen. Kate was to one side. She was looking at the three—she saw them like that, a unit of three, and herself excluded. The handsome miserable boy, who could not stand the world, the pretty little girl who knew he was excessive in everything but would get over it, the beautiful young woman who was examining her future.

The boy pulled some peanuts in a transparent bag from his other pocket and held them out, as they were, inside the bag, to the machine. As—in his imagination—the machine reached out for them, he pulled back the nuts, with a clowning grin.

This self-consciousness made Kate wonder if he had seen Maureen, knew that more than one female trailed him.

But it did not seem to be so.

Again he held out the little packet, through which could be seen the tempting nuts: again, as the machine responded, he snatched them back.

He was laughing now, and theatrical, so Kate knew he must be aware at least of Maureen: and so it was, for he whirled around and held out the closed packet to Maureen, as he had to the machine, laughing aggressively at her. Maureen did not shrink back, or smile, or frown. She stood looking into his face. He quieted. Now he saw her, a beautiful young woman with her bright pigtails over the dark thin dress. She dazzled in the low thick light. His face, which had been contorted with the pain of having to be his age, began to soften. He ripped off the top of his packet, and held it out. Maureen put her open hand, at the end of an outstretched arm, close to him. He had to pull back the packet to shake the nuts into her palm: it looked as if he were shaking the nuts against his own chest. He laughed. She smiled, and threw the nuts into her mouth, showing a dazzle of teeth. The two walked off side by side. Behind them went a woebegone little girl. Behind the girl, the middle-aged woman.

The two who followed could not see the faces of the couple. They seemed to be animated. They seemed to laugh. They walked past the snake house and into the aquarium.

Behind them went Jane, then Kate.

In the half dark of the aquarium the four moved along the brightly lit walls crammed with fishes. The two who led did not talk. They moved sedately on, giving, it seemed, equal attention to each tank. But outside a wall of water into which a gush of bubbling water came from a pipe they stopped a long time. In this aerated water was a skate. It was playing. It held itself in the fresh stream and it waved and rippled and seemed to dance: it was intoxicated with the air coming in from the world outside the tank.

Maureen, laughing, kissed the boy.

Fiercely, he kissed her.

Hand in hand, they moved on.

Behind them went Jane, watching them, only them, seeing nothing else, not seeing the fishes, not seeing the skate playing in the bubbles.

Kate left the aquarium meaning to go away, but, like Jane, she had to see, to be in at the death, to be nailed on her cross. She waited. Then she saw Maureen come out still hand in hand with the boy. Behind them was Jane.

Maureen, laughing again, kissed the boy, in a hard fierce triumph, a challenge to everything, a slap in the world's face. She saw Kate and did it again. But now the boy had withdrawn from her; he felt used. He stood watching Maureen move away. Then, although it seemed that he had not noticed Jane, he went to the girl, put his arm around her, and said, irritable but patient, "Oh don't, Jane, don't, why do you have to make such a fuss all the time?"

"I can't help it!" She burst into tears, and put her face on his shoulder. He put his arms around her, and sunk his cheek on her head. But he was watching Maureen walk away.

Kate joined her, and Maureen said, "Very well then, I shall marry Philip."

"Why not?"

"Why not? Stanley? They care, don't they. About beasts and birds and fishes. Not to mention people."

"Oh don't be so bloody . . ." Kate was furious. She was in a blaze of anger. She walked fast away from Maureen, who came after her and said, "I'm sorry, Kate."

After some moments Kate cooled and said, "Not at all, *I* am sorry." She sounded pompous.

When they reached the flat Maureen said, "We keep apologising to each other."

"Yes, like families."

"Yes."

"Well, it won't be long now."

That night Kate dreamed as soon as she fell asleep. It was still a thick cold dark. The seal was so heavy now she was not able to do more than drag it over the snow. She was no longer anxious about the seal, that it might be dead or dying: she knew that it was full of life, and, like her, of hope.

A strong breath of salt air came to her; she was breathing in salty sea air. The snow had stopped falling. The light touches she felt on her face were not snow, but a fresh warm breeze.

She saw that the snow had gone from underfoot: she was walking over spring grass, a bright thin green with soil showing dark and wet between. The grass was full of spring flowers. Ahead the ground rose sharply. She climbed it, and stood, the seal in her arms, on a small promontory, looking down into a sea that reflected a sunlight sky, blue deepening on blue. On the rocks seals lay basking.

Using the last of her strength, she lifted the seal well off the earth, so that its tail would not be made sore by dragging it, and she staggered down a little path that led to the sea's edge. There, on a flat rock, she let the seal slide into the water. It sank out of sight, then came up, and rested its head for the last time on the edge of the rock: its dark soft eyes looked at her, then it closed its nostrils and dived. The sea was full of seals swimming beside each other, turning over to swim on their backs, swerving and diving, playing. A seal swam past that had scars on its flanks and its back, and Kate thought that this must be her seal, whom she had carried through so many perils. But it did not look at her now.

Her journey was over.

She saw that the sun was in front of her, not behind, not far far behind, under the curve of the earth, which was where it had been for so long. She looked at it, a large, light, brilliant, buoyant, tumultuous sun that seemed to sing.

She turned, knowing that she had finished the dream. She woke.

She told Maureen, who said, "That's all right then, isn't it."

"I suppose so."

"I mean, it's all right for you."

Maureen was sitting at the kitchen table, and she sounded critical.

"Do you think dreams are just for the person who dreams them? Perhaps they aren't?"

"*I* didn't dream it," said Maureen. "Did I?"

"I suppose not."

"That's not the sort of thing *I* dream. Cages and being shut in are much more my style, you were quite right."

She would not say any more, so Kate went to the telephone and rang her home to say that she would return next day. It was Eileen she spoke to. Eileen had been running the house all this time. "Oh it's all right mother, we have been managing perfectly well."

Kate went back into the kitchen and said, "Do you know what? I'm unemployed! There's nothing for me to do. What do you advise? Social work? Soup kitchens? Global Food—that's soup kitchens, I suppose."

Maureen made an irritable movement, and Kate left her again.

Later she came into Kate's room to say, "I'm going to have a party."

"Why sound like that?"

"It's frivolous to have a party, wouldn't you say so, Kate? Heartless? Mean?"

"When?"

"Tonight. Please come. No, I'd like you to, I really would."

She spent the rest of the afternoon on the telephone, while delivery men arrived one after the other with drink and food.

She came into Kate's room, where Kate was lying on her bed, like a traveller ready to depart, her suitcase filled, her possessions neatly stacked, and she said, "It doesn't matter a damn what you do. Or what I do. That is the whole point of everything. It's what no one can face up to."

"I don't believe it," said Kate.

"I don't care whether you believe it or not." She went out and came back. "Your seal is safe, isn't he? He's been rescued and he's safe."

"I don't see it as *my* seal."

"Yes. So if you dropped dead tomorrow it wouldn't matter, would it?"

She was hysterical. Kate stopped herself in the middle of the thought that she should *do* something about it— what? Offer aspirin? Good advice? A cup of tea? The telephone started again and Maureen went out saying, "Whatever it is that is important, if it is, if anything is, then no one has told *me* about it."

Kate hovered, waiting for the telephone call to end. Various arrangements of words suggested themselves, probably from newspaper leaders, or the religious hour on television. For instance, "The world has often been in a bad state before, and people have despaired." "It doesn't help to get morbid."

Then there was what she was thinking herself: "Millions of people are dying, will die, perhaps you and me among them, but there's got to be some around with cool heads to carry on." "But the history of this planet has never been anything but catastrophe, war, misery; it's a bit worse this time." "What you are really looking for is a man who knows all the answers and can say, Do this, Do that. There's no such animal."

She heard Maureen saying, "Yes, a party. It's short notice. I only thought of it today. Yes, do, good." She was emphasising the voice of her upbringing.

Kate could not do anything for Maureen. But she had children: it would be nice to take them home presents: she had quite a lot of the Global Food money left. She shopped. She saw herself in windows; her body was back in recognisable shape. Her face had aged. Noticeably. *They* could hardly fail to notice it. What would they say? Pretend it hadn't happened: you look *marvellous* mother! The light that is the desire to please had gone out. And about time too . . . Her hair—well, no one could overlook that!

Her experiences of the last months, her discoveries, her self-definition; what she hoped were now strengths, were concentrated here—that she would walk into her home with her hair undressed, with her hair tied straight back for utility; rough and streaky, and the widening grey band showing like a statement of intent. It was as if the rest of her—body, feet, even face, which was aging but amenable—belonged to everyone else. But her hair—no! No one was going to lay hands on that. All her adult life, or, to be precise, since she had left her grandfather's house in Lourenço Marques, she had been in an atmosphere where everything was said: thoughts, feelings, impulses, were things which had to be recognised quickly, both by herself and by others—delay or ambiguity here being possibly dangerous—and then classified, catalogued, allotted their places on shelves. Or, if you like, in a computer. She had lived among words, and people bred to use and be used by words. But now that it was important to her, a matter of self-preservation, that she should be able to make a statement, that she should be understood, then she would, and would not, do certain things to her hair: substance squeezed slowly out through holes in her scalp like spaghetti out of a machine, the only part of her that felt nothing if it was stroked, pinched, or handled. The clothes, hair style, manners, posture, voice of Mrs. Brown (or of Jolie Madame, as the trade put it) had been a reproduction the slightest deviation from which had caused her as much discomfort as the scientist's rat feels when the appropriate levers are pushed. But now she was saying *no:* no, no, no, NO: a statement which would be concentrated into her hair.

She found Maureen sitting on her, Kate's, bed, doing nothing. It was now seven. Arrangements for the party had been made, but Maureen had not changed. Maureen did not get off the bed. She was reclaiming it for herself, her friends? Kate said, "I've made a discovery. Going back home, the way I'm going to make statements—though I'm not sure what about; but my area of choice—do you know what I mean?—well, it's narrowed down to how I do my hair. Isn't that extraordinary?"

Maureen shrugged.

"I was thinking. I've said absolutely anything I've felt to you. About everything. But for years I've been doling out what I've thought and felt in small rations. I say to myself, I shouldn't say this to so and so, I can say this to Eileen, but I can't to Tim. Mary won't understand this: for instance, I couldn't ever tell Mary about the seal. But I could tell Tim. Of course I tell things to Michael, but it's as if he listens to something such a long way off it has nothing to do with him. I wonder if he feels that that is how I listen to what he tells me. Of course he doesn't dream, he says. What happens to him is always from the outside. It's impossible that I should be such a distance from him? When we've lived together for so long? It's not that he would be shocked or surprised by anything I ever said, but quite obviously he's always listening to news from another continent. And he's never visited it nor intends to. But it seems to me as if little bits of me are distributed among my family, Tim's bit, Michael's bit, Eileen's piece— and so on. Or rather, were distributed. Were. That's over. But to you I can say anything."

"Ships that pass," said Maureen. "Like people meeting on journeys. We'll probably never see each other again."

She went out, shutting the door.

An hour later, there was a still absolute silence through the flat, Kate looked for her. She had put on a 1930's evening dress, of the kind that is cut on the bias and fits closely. It had a low back crisscrossed with narrow straps. It was of black satin. She had cut off her hair. She had cut it straight around at the level of her lobes. It was fastened down with slides and clips, but if she was conventionalised as a syren to her neck, her head looked like a woman who has just come out of prison or boarding school.

She sat on a cushion in the hall making something out of the cut-off hair. She held this object up. Her eyes did not choose to meet Kate's. She had looped the hair into a figure like a harvest doll, a corn doll.

Kate was shocked: as of course she was meant to be. "It's going to be some party," she said.

"That's right."

The bell rang. Guests stood in the door.

"Hi!" "Hi." "Hello." "Hi." Kisses. "What's that you've got, Maureen?"

"It's my hair. Can't you see? It's my baby." Maureen began dancing in front of them, not looking at them at all, but holding up the doll that dangled from her wrist: a bright fragile puppet.

Soon the rooms were full. The many people, the numerous young men who followed Maureen's black satin body with their eyes—among them Stanley, Philip, and a man rather older than the others, solid, authoritative, who could be no other than William, the passport back to her own people if she wanted to use it—all the multifaced crowd, seemed like a map or like a statement of Maureen's rich life, full of possibilities. But her guests had been greeted by the hair doll, not by her. She did not seem able to look at them, to stay with any one long enough to talk; she moved fast from group to group, or danced a step or two with some man before sliding away from him; or absented herself by fussing over the drinks and the food.

Kate wondered why she should not go back to her home now; this minute, tonight; there was no need to wait until tomorrow.

She left a note for Maureen with, since she could not think of anything better, anything that would be right, a bottle of scent.

She stood in the hall with her suitcase and looked for Maureen.

Maureen was in William's embrace. He leaned with his back to the wall, on solid feet, supporting Maureen by holding her around her waist with his two large hands.

She drooped in his grasp, one hand fiddling with the twist of hair that dangled from her wrist, frowning, not looking at him.

"You know quite well that you'll marry me in the end, so why not now?"

"Do I know that? I don't think I do," said Maureen, spinning the doll around and around.

"Give me that thing, I don't like it." But rushing the defences was not the right thing at all, for she guarded her puppet and said, "You aren't supposed to like it."

She sounded petulant; a good augury for his chances?

One could easily imagine them together, in their large house in Wiltshire or somewhere, deep in plentiful horses, children, and dogs, everything according to the pattern, including their humorous comments on it.

Beyond William in the kitchen door appeared Philip, uniformed as usual, accompanied by a neatly pretty English girl, her femininity well battened down by responsibility, duty, service—the lot. At first glance an omelette-maker, a willing bearer of unpleasant burdens and choices, she wore a dress that seemed as military as Philip's gear, a dark-blue crêpe with a little white collar, and a brooch like a medal on the upper slope of her firmly confined left breast. Perfectly mated these two, and she had her hand in his elbow; but Philip was unable to prevent himself glaring and yearning after Maureen languishing gracelessly there in her William's arms.

"I simply will not have you being so silly," said William, attempting the elder brother and trying to jerk the twist of yellow hair off the girl's wrist.

"No, no," she shrieked, "no, stop it." But she stayed where she was.

And there stood Philip watching them both; and the girl jealously watching Philip.

No one noticed Kate with her suitcase. So she picked it up, let herself unobserved out of the flat, and made her way to the bus stop and so home.

A Note on the Type

This book was set on the Linotype in Janson, a recutting made direct from type cast from matrices long thought to have been made by the Dutchman Anton Janson, who was a practicing type founder in Leipzig during the years 1668–87. However, it has been conclusively demonstrated that these types are actually the work of Nicholas Kis (1650–1702), a Hungarian, who most probably learned his trade from the master Dutch type founder Dirk Voskens. The type is an excellent example of the influential and sturdy Dutch types that prevailed in England up to the time William Caslon developed his own incomparable designs from them.

Typography and binding design by The Etheredges.